ON ONE CONDITION

"... I'm going to give you seven days to raise the money."

"What?" Kendra whispered, almost unable to believe her ears.

"On one condition."

"What's that?" she said, panicked.

"You kiss me."

An involuntary tremor passed through Kendra as he stared down at her. To her surprise, she felt her heart give an erratic thud as his eyes held hers and deepened with an intensity that held her captive. She wanted to shake him for his arrogance and for the financial hold he had over her, but as his warm breath fanned against her cheek she was conscious only of a new kind of awareness which caused the discordant thudding of her pulse. "You can't have me," she said, "and I'm not going to give you any leeway to humiliate me. I'll find a way to pay you back your money, with interest."

"Until then," Shay said, his voice deep, velvety, and unmistakably American, "I'll take my first installment now."

BOOK YOUR PLACE ON OUR WEBSITE AND MAKE THE ARABESQUE ROMANCE CONNECTION!

We've created a customized website just for our very special Arabesque readers, where you can get the inside scoop on everything that's going on with Arabesque romance novels.

When you come online, you'll have the exciting opportunity to:

- View covers of upcoming books
- Read sample chapters
- Learn about our future publishing schedule (listed by publication month *and author*)
- Find out when your favorite authors will be visiting a city near you
- Search for and order backlist books from our online catalog
- Check out author bios and background information
- Send e-mail to your favorite authors
- Meet the Kensington staff online
- Join us in weekly chats with authors, readers and other guests
- Get writing guidelines
- AND MUCH MORE!

Visit our website at
http://www.arabesquebooks.com

Roses Are Red

Sonia Seerani

Pinnacle Books
Kensington Publishing Corp.
http://www.arabesquebooks.com

PINNACLE BOOKS are published by

Kensington Publishing Corp.
850 Third Avenue
New York, NY 10022

Copyright © 1998 by Sonia Seerani

All rights reserved. No part of this book may be reproduced in any form or by any means without the prior written consent of the Publisher, excepting brief quotes used in reviews.

If you purchased this book without a cover, you should be aware that this book is stolen property. It was reported as "unsold and destroyed" to the Publisher and neither the Author nor the Publisher has received any payment for this "stripped book."

Pinnacle and the P logo Reg. U.S. Pat. & TM Off.

First Printing: May, 1998
10 9 8 7 6 5 4 3 2 1

Printed in the United States of America

For my mother Minor, and in memory of my father, Stephen

One

"Girl," the old man raged furiously, his brown eyes blazing his displeasure at seeing the young woman standing before him. "Get your pretty legs out of me house."

The chandeliers in the mansion hallway glittered mercilessly above his head, and Kendra Davenport felt their diamond glares of yellow light bathe her stunned oval face. She stared in disbelief at the man's cold, mahogany profile, aware that the jazz music and laughter she could hear from within the house had stopped abruptly, replaced by the sound of footsteps approaching. The people who materialized, dressed in patterned African clothes and more contemporary styles, sporting elaborate hairstyles and expensive gemstones, began to form themselves in a circle of comradery, eyes intent on lending support to their host.

"I'm not here to cause any trouble," Kendra pleaded shakily, allowing her mouth to form a faint smile in an attempt to appease him.

Benjamin Brentwood, obviously enraged to see her, was a man grazing sixty-three of majestic frame whose giant, Jamaican-American baritone was enough to dim sounds of the thunder outside his Wimbledon estate in London and cause his twelve, speculating guests to congregate in the hallway and look on with curiosity.

Everything about his expression registered a measure of alarm inside Kendra and she wondered why on earth she'd made the impulsive decision to come there.

But she knew why: one of his two sons had trumped up false embezzlement charges against her innocent sister, and she'd thought that by confronting the Brentwoods head on she could persuade them to leave her family alone. But Benjamin Brentwood seemed content to remind himself of the deep-seated hatred he had for her father, and particularly for the newspaper her father had singlehandedly molded into the largest African-Caribbean press in England. She now realized, with some foreboding, that she was not going to make any headway. Perhaps the best recourse for her would be to leave.

"I'm sorry I bothered you," she declared helplessly, retreating a step back out on to the porch. "I only wanted—"

"Always wanting something," Benjamin pointedly interrupted, ignoring Kendra's plea to be heard as he transferred a smoldering Cuban cigar from one hand to the other. "Well, take this message to your papa. Tell him that I'll never forget what he stole from me and I intend to make him pay."

Kendra looked at him, a little puzzled. Surely he couldn't mean the newspaper her father had presided over for more than thirty years, of which she was now editor-in-chief. That had been dutifully paid for, despite Benjamin Brentwood feeling outdone, and Kendra quickly took it upon herself to remind her enemy of that point. "My father worked hard and paid dear for the *Nubian Chronicle*," she told him heatedly. "He would never cheat anyone."

"Your papa is a thief," Benjamin admonished loudly, the icy blast in his voice made more horrific as it eclipsed a bolt of lightning which chose to strike at that precise moment. "Now get off my land before—"

"Pops?" A soft, mellow, American voice halted Benjamin and instantly prompted everyone's attention toward the direction from which it came. The figure which slowly emerged from the shadowy interior of a room adjacent to the hallway was that of a man in his midthirties whose face showed that he was particularly concerned with the commotion that had evidently disturbed him. "What's going on?" he demanded with impatience.

"Son, we have been honored with the presence of a Davenport," Benjamin announced with sardonic irony. "What do you think of her bringing her bony behind all the way over to my yard?"

The newcomer stepped forward into the lighted doorway and took a good look at what had interrupted his father's traditional domino party. With persistent slowness his gaze moved across Kendra, taking in her slightly wet, auburn, relaxed hair, her damp, pale blue, linen suit, and her startling, ebony complexion which was an asset to her wide, mink-colored, almond shaped eyes.

Never in her twenty-eight years had Kendra felt subjected to such flagrant masculine appraisal. For several seemingly interminable seconds, no one moved as the coolly brooding glance from his startlingly dusky brown eyes raked her slender figure and delicate features. She was immediately conscious of every line of his taut, muscular body, from his shoulders beneath his open-necked, white shirt to a slim waist and lean, athletic build beneath the dark trousers he was wearing.

Yet, as his gaze intensified Kendra did not feel unnerved by the newcomer, for his was a kindly face. He offered her a casual smile when he spoke. "I think she has amazing courage for a sista so skinny," he uttered finally, advancing yet another step so that Kendra was made instantly aware of his towering frame, which suddenly seemed to diminish her five-foot-eight inches. "I'm Shay Brentwood," he introduced with a lazy grin. "You must be Arlisa's sister. Kendra, right?"

Kendra clutched her car key as she looked into his warm, embracing face and felt at last that there was hope she might actually be heard. "Yes I am," she answered coolly, surprised that he knew her by name.

"I guess your sister's holed up somewhere?" he asked. "Not in the British state penitentiary, I hope."

Kendra's brow furrowed. Benjamin's son was not going to be of any help to her. His exclamation about her younger sister signified his involvement in trying to get her falsely convicted. Shay Brentwood was the culprit she was looking for. He was the cause of her family's recent anxieties and anguished ordeal in keeping Arlisa protected against the accusations leveled against her. And he was the one who almost got Arlisa fired. It could hardly be true of someone with such a nice face, she thought treacherously, of someone with such friendly eyes that he looked as though he could be trusted.

"My sister is not in prison, where you'd obviously intended to put her." She bristled knowingly. "Arlisa's safe at home with my father."

"Is she?" Shay asked dismissively, his casual tone causing Kendra instant alarm. The arrogant mouth twisted. "Are you both all right?"

"No, we are not," Kendra declared angrily. "That's why I'm here. Life may be fun and games to you and your lying, conniving, deceiving family, but for me, my sister, and my father, it's important. It's about honesty, decency, and respect." She drew in a steadying breath before surveying all the enraged faces set upon her. "There's enough famine and disease in the world without people like you making things worse."

"But see ya," a jowly, West Indian female screamed

from the small crowd who were all making sounds of discontent and showing general uneasiness. "What an unruly child."

"Your momma never teach you manners?" another woman said, bristling.

"Ben, no bother with the girl," a St. Lucian man derided smoothly. "I want to play my domino hand. Come, let's finish the game."

Benjamin Brentwood's heavy eyebrows knitted furiously. "You better go now, Girl," he ordered sternly.

"Don't worry, I'm leaving," Kendra snapped, stepping off the porch and out into the rain. The torrid downpour washed over her hair and soaked her skin and clothes as she rushed over to her white convertible. Throwing herself into the driver's seat with the sound of rain drumming on the roof of the car, Kendra wondered through the unholy torrent what on earth could motivate such people to be so truly disreputable. On igniting the engine, she couldn't resist glancing backward in her rearview mirror to look at the audience, who had seemed like alien beings from another planet. She was surprised to see only Shay Brentwood left standing at the lighted doorway.

He had a guarded look in his eyes which gave Kendra a shiver that seemed to reach every nerve in her body. He was watching her, his caramel face aimed intently in her direction as if he'd become suddenly intrigued. To her chagrin, she found herself recalling his compelling features; a hardhitting square face with no softening features, his nose broad but straight as a blade, his mouth harsh and yet sensually formed, and his short hair, sleek and black like a raven's with tiny curls that seemed as silky and soft as those of a baby.

Power seemed to emanate from him as he stood there, magnified by an illumination of lightning which suddenly flashed above his granite image. His demeanor revealed him to be a man who'd taken charge of his own destiny, whose finger was on the pulse of self-empowerment and achievement. What a shame that the feud between their families had shaped his destiny into an endless chase down the same narrow alleyway of deceit and revenge it had his father, she thought angrily, determinedly flooring the accelerator.

The screech of rubber tires pierced the night air like a giant scream as the Golf Cabriolet reversed to the spot where Shay Brentwood stood. Flicking the switch that lowered the windows, Kendra kept the engine purring as she bent her head forward and yelled, "If I had a shred of evidence, you'd be the one heading for the high jump. As it happens, I only have my well-founded suspicions and a few tips on good authority."

"From the eligible Selwyn Owens, M.P. no doubt," Shay answered with a curling twist of his lips. "Well, you'd better tell that Minister of Parliament to back off before he gets more than his feelings hurt."

"He told me that you'd threatened him," Kendra said with a level of disgust. "Afraid that he might pull a number of skeletons from your family's closet? My, I await with baited breath."

"Then I hope the worthy Selwyn Owens lives up to your expectations," Shay roared above a crack of thunder, his dark eyebrows raised in mock sincerity, though he told himself that he was up against a remarkable woman. "It would be terrible if your hopes were to be crushed."

"I'm sure he will expertly manage to disturb your comfortable little life," Kendra retorted.

"You disturb me," Shay answered. His gaze made no secret of it as it roamed across her delicate features with an intensity that almost took Kendra's breath away. The brief scrutiny made her feel ridiculously shaky, for even in her heightened state of anger Kendra found herself having to admit that Shay Brentwood was irresistibly attractive. Without another word, she automatically switched the window shut and pressed her foot down on the accelerator, keeping it there until the car sped down the estate's long driveway toward the main road. She did not look back. She dared not look back, for in truth Kendra realized to her self-loathing that she had enjoyed the way Shay Brentwood looked at her.

Kendra slammed the door of her bedroom and rushed over to her wardrobe. Selecting a grey suit, she quickly went over to where her fresh underwear was neatly folded in a drawer and took her pick before slipping out of her wet clothes and seating herself at the dressing table. For a few seconds, as she began to tissue the rain from her wet face, a feeling of panic hit her. She should never have gone to see Benjamin Brentwood. His temper had been frayed just by the mere sight of her, and though she had matched his temperament measure for measure, if her instincts were correct she might just have lit a long fuse leading to a terrible explosion.

Shay Brentwood would most likely detonate it, she thought, consciously forcing herself to take a steadying breath as she reached for her pink towel. That arrogant man would have to be stopped before he caused her family further harm, she decided sternly. She was about to contemplate a strategy for how she could best proceed when her bedroom door shot open and her younger sister of three years hurried in.

Kendra straightened in her chair and wrapped the pink towel around her damp hair, thick, dark lashes disguising her recent ordeal as Arlisa suspiciously closed the door. "Sissy," she remarked, calling her younger sister by her childhood name. "I haven't time to talk to you right now." Swiftly removing her shoes before deftly unlatching her watch and onyx necklace, she added, "I'm meeting Selwyn and I'm already late."

She frowned, unsure now whether she actually wanted to attend the dinner they'd been invited to at Lord Conrad Finsbury's London home in Belgravia. Kendra knew she felt out of character mincing words with political types, most of whom had received old-school-tie educations and did nothing but talk shop, mainly party politics and election promises, omitting the finer details of serving their constituencies. She was aware that Selwyn—whose father, a Guyana-born war veteran, had been determined his son should be a public-school boy—was raised to believe that such socializing was a means to advancing himself and so she sighed. "I forgot to ask Selwyn whether the dinner party tonight is formal or informal. There's nothing worse than being over or underdressed, and you know Selwyn, such a stickler for protocol."

"Kendra, you have to help me." Arlisa was panicked, the tremors of anxiety and frustration etched in her voice. "I need to talk to you. I've been waiting for ages for you to get back."

Kendra quickly scrutinized her sister. She'd never seen Arlisa look so shell-shocked. Her sister's usual glowing, tawny complexion was cane pale with anxiety, and her chiseled, rounded cheekbones were wet with tears that had spilled over from her huge, fawn brown eyes. Kendra wondered what was wrong, and knowing her sister's colorful lifestyle, she quickly hazarded a guess. "Don't tell me you're pregnant?"

"No, it's nothing like that," Arlisa cried, her tall, slim body slumping onto Kendra's bed. "You're going to hate me for this," she began miserably, "but I didn't know what else to do."

Something slimy and snake-like seemed to twist through Kendra's innards as she rose out of her chair and joined her sister on the bed. Facing Arlisa, expecting to hear something disturbing, she queried, "What is it?"

"The money." Arlisa chewed at her lower lip. "I took it."

Kendra's eyes widened. "What?"

"I had some debts to pay," Arlisa explained with regret. "The easiest way was to take money from the Black Press Charity Fund."

"Oh God," Kendra muttered, reminding herself of the terrible confrontation she'd just had with the Brentwoods, and more precisely what she'd accused them of. "But—but I thought you said the BPCF committee had cleared you of embezzlement?" she said weakly, unsure of whether she could bear to hear the answer.

"They did. I replaced the money with funds I borrowed from the Association of Black Journalists," Arlisa confessed tearfully, the relief of disclosing her secret evident in her face. "As treasurer I have access to both accounts, but if I don't replace that money by Friday, then I'm in deep, deep trouble."

"I don't believe this." Kendra sighed heavily, her voice pathetically weak, her mind wheeling on how her father could've misused his influence and placed Arlisa in a position of such importance. Not only was she taken aback by her sister's deceit, but she was shaken with the awful realization that she owed Shay Brentwood and his father an apology. Slowly removing the towel from her hair in disbelief, she faced her sister, anger beginning to mount in her gut. "Why didn't you tell me this before?"

"I thought I could replace the money," Arlisa stammered, nervously fingering her long mane of braided hair and not daring to look at Kendra. "How was I to know that Joel Brentwood and his wife saw me at the bank and overheard the clerk tell me that I had exhausted the funds?"

"So Joel Brentwood saw you," Kendra concluded, tight-lipped, mindful of the fact that she might've accused the wrong brother but consoling herself with the thought that she was still correct in her assumption that it was a Brentwood that was guilty all the same. "And let me guess. It was he who went to the BPCF committee and tipped them off. How clumsy can you get, Arlisa?"

"That's not the worst of it," Arlisa continued, now panicked and thoroughly shaken. "His brother, Shay Brentwood, is one of the members of the Association of Black Journalists. Remember? I told you he'd joined? Anyway, Cedric Carter is in hospital mending his broken leg, so Shay Brentwood was asked if he would be responsible for countersigning all checks for withdrawals at the bank. He agreed, and now he's due to examine and balance the books on Friday." Arlisa's eyes were stone grey with remorse. "If he ever finds out that I forged his signature and put a hole in the Association's account, then—"

"We could be in a scandal," Kendra concluded, in shock. "My God, Arlisa. The *Nubian Chronicle* would be linked, on the strength of you being the proprietor's daughter." Kendra felt mortified, numbed, and terribly sick. She closed her eyes for a fleeting moment, unable to digest everything because it seemed so horribly untrue and unreal. Rubbing her forehead with agitation, she eyed her sister coldly with a quick solution. "I'll give you the money to credit the account. How much is it?"

"One hundred and fifty thousand dollars. U.S. dollars."

Kendra rose abruptly from the bed, her eyes bulging wide, her voice a whisper hardly audible. "What?"

"I know how it looks," Arlisa began shamefully by way of an answer, "but you see—"

"That's how much you took?" Kendra thundered, her

face murderous like that of a raging bull having just seen the color red. "This is going to kill Daddy," she breathed, shaking her head in denial. "Why did you do it? What on earth were you thinking of? Have you any idea where I've just been?" She heaved a sickly breath in recollection. "The Brentwoods were not happy to see me, Sissy, but I risked going there to protect you. And guess what? I accused *them* of conspiring to commit your now obvious indiscretions. Heaven knows what I have just done."

"Kendra, I'm sorry," Arlisa cried with renewed tears, ejecting a hiccup for good measure in the hope of abating her sister's anger. She knew how ruthless Kendra could be. Many of the *Chronicle*'s executives often had slight panic attacks as soon as she buzzed them on the intercom, and after every morning conference journalists left sharing glances of relief and clutching vital editorial statistics to their chests as if their lives depended on them. Secretaries sidled out of Kendra's way when they saw her coming, to avoid confrontation.

If Kendra was anything it was adept at solving problems, for getting the task done, however difficult. She'd seen Kendra in action, witnessed firsthand her sister's demonic working pace, so naturally she felt Kendra would have a solution to their problem. "What are we going to do?"

"We?" Kendra yelled, shaking a stern finger. *"We* are not going to do anything." Adopting a deadly tone she said, "Whatever it is that *you* have bought that *you* cannot pay for can go right back to the point of purchase first thing tomorrow, if I have to drag you there wi myself."

"It's not a purchase . . ." Arlisa cried, " please don't shout. Daddy might hear us."

"Right now, I don't care if our father

sins of his youngest daughter at full volume," Kendra raged in return.

"I paid off a gambling debt," Arlisa screeched.

Kendra's voice instantly dropped by two octaves. "What do you mean, a gambling debt?"

"I owed money to the Rolling Dice Casino in Monte Carlo."

"Wait a minute," Kendra said incredulously, "Are you telling me that all those trips to the south of France were to gamble away a hundred and fifty thousand dollars?" When Arlisa remained mute, Kendra yelled, "You're mad. That's what you are. Mad. I could ring your bloody. . . ." Kendra took her seat on the bed and attempted a supreme effort to calm herself.

Rationally, she knew the situation was grave. Memories came flooding back into her mind of a man who stood beneath a torrent of lightning, determination to destroy her and her family set in his sparkling, dusky eyes. The thought made Kendra conscious of a sudden tension in her limbs, a feeling of irrational panic threatening to choke her. She had to think. Think fast.

Swallowing hard on the tightness of her throat, she faced Arlisa's tear-washed face, intent on exploring all their options. "Can any of your sugar daddies bail you out?"

"I've split up with Jarvis," Arlisa admitted sheepishly, "and Brad's in the Bahamas shooting a video. His camp just won't put me through."

Kendra's brows furrowed briefly. "What about Todd?"

"Dear Todd." Arlisa bit her lip in response. "He's still contesting the family will for his inheritance of that Jamaican estate in Montego Bay."

"And to think you dropped Jerome, that fine, rich, ing Nigerian barrister, for Todd." Kendra couldn't resist aiming the jibe. "One of these days, your past is going to catch up with you."

"I can get him back," Arlisa declared, executing another hiccup.

"You may need to, at that," Kendra added in truth. "He'll probably waive the standard retainer when he represents you in a court of law."

Arlisa winced just as there was a knock at the bedroom door. "Girls, are you in there?" their father beckoned.

"Yes, Daddy. What is it?" Kendra asked, breathing shakily as an involuntary shiver ran through her.

"Selwyn is here for you."

"For me?" Kendra echoed, recalling that she and Selwyn were to meet in the lobby at the Grosvenor Hotel on Buckingham Palace Road before taking the short ride to Lord Finsbury's house. "I'll be right down, Daddy."

"Well, don't keep him waiting," her father answered. "He's in the den."

"He's here with the police." Arlisa was panicked, twisting her hands in frustrated anxiety.

"Don't be silly," Kendra whispered, curious as to why Selwyn had come there. "He must have changed our plans for tonight. I haven't time to change into anything. Hand me my bed coat. And for heaven's sake, Sissy, calm down."

Donning the flimsy, pink chiffon garment over her damp underwear and casting a warning glance at her sister, Kendra re-wrapped her hair with the pink towel and made her way downstairs.

Taking a deep breath on reaching the pair of whitewashed doors which sealed the sun den, she stoically repressed a shiver before making her entrance. Surveying the room and its interior filled with abundant plant life, she couldn't see Selwyn's lithe, tall body anywhere.

Feeling confused, she was about to decide whether to call her father when a rush of heat and cold all at the same time traveled quickly along her veins.

Shay Brentwood stood next to the room's wide glass windows, studying her with penetrating intensity as she stood facing him; the glittering sweep of his dusky eyes charting the translucence of her ebony brown limbs beneath the thin chiffon lace.

"You!" She swallowed convulsively on a high note.

"You might as least look pleased to see me," Shay returned evenly. "I'm the answer to your prayers."

Two

"What are you doing here?" Kendra barked, unable to believe that Shay Brentwood, her enemy, stood within the confines of her father's house.

Unnerved, she wondered whether she had imagined the note of satisfaction in his voice and found herself curious about whether that same satisfaction was etched across his face, for at that moment she couldn't quite tell.

Shay had taken a step toward her, and in so doing was momentarily lost against the nebulous dim of the houseplants around him. But as his face came into focus, Kendra couldn't prevent her tiny indrawn breath. She had thought Shay attractive before, and he was devastatingly so now, having changed into blue Karl Kani jeans, overshirt, black designer boots and a Koschino jacket.

Feeling underdressed, she hastily pulled the pink-colored ties of her pink bed coat closer together, a movement quickly detected by Shay which instantly brought a grin to her enemy's craggy face. "I think it's time we talked," he told her with a smirk that left Kendra feeling ridiculously uncomfortable.

"How did you get past my father?" she countered crisply. "I can only imagine that you lied and told him you were Selwyn."

"I told your pop I wanted to see you," Shay answered coolly, his heavy feet slowly obliterating the distance between them until his very closeness made Kendra intensely aware of him and the musky tang of his expensive aftershave. "Ain't my business who he thought I was."

Kendra made a grimace to disguise the sudden, delicious rush of turbulence she was feeling and swore an oath that she would, as soon as it was feasible, introduce her father to Selwyn Owens, if only to prevent Shay from ever coming there again. "What do you want?"

Shay allowed his mouth to quirk faintly. "I thought since you came to my house, accusing my family and insulting my father's guests, that I'd come over here to get your personal apology."

"What?"

"And talk about my proposition for the *Nubian Chronicle,*" Shay concluded evenly.

Kendra tapped one bare foot. "So you're here to pledge a personal offer for my father's newspaper," she surmised, annoyed. "Your father isn't wasting any time, is he?"

"This is a matter between you and me," Shay told her firmly, slipping out of his Koschino jacket. "And I prefer to concentrate on the matter in hand rather than . . . let's say . . . more alluring prospects." His gaze lazily traveled the length of her body before making a rapport with hers.

Kendra almost stumbled a step backward in surprise when he began to drape his jacket around her shoulders, a motion she instantly blocked by shedding the warmth and comfort of it. "Tell your father we're not interested," she snapped, obstinately. "And since I have a dinner engagement, I'd like you to—"

"Good business practice should permit you to listen to what I have to say," Shay interrupted bluntly. "So before you go for drinks with Mr. M.P., I think you ought to know that I'm also here about your sister."

Kendra glared at him, profound shock rendering her immobile.

"She's still hiding?" Shay chortled knowingly. "I can't say I blame her. A one hundred and fifty thousand dollar problem is a hard rap to take."

Kendra felt her entire body quiver with an overwhelming adrenaline rush. She hardly knew how to react. The realization swiftly sprang to mind that this man had come there to win his father's war. "What do you really want?" The question was out in a strangled whisper before she could stop herself.

"So you know?" Shay sounded a little puzzled. "The way you were acting, I assumed—"

"I just found out," Kendra admitted forlornly. "I should not have held you responsible, but your brother Joel has a lot to answer for."

"What does *he* have to do with your sister's problem?" Shay's eyebrows rose in annoyance.

"He didn't have to report her to the BPCF committee," Kendra snapped. "Arlisa did replace the money."

"It's not my brother's fault that your sister is unfit for treasurer status," Shay answered in return. "She could have financially crippled the BPCF, and was stupid enough to risk the entire solvency of the ABJ to try to rectify one set of depleted funds. And forging my signature, not to mention that of Mrs. Adina, the company secretary, is a criminal offense."

Kendra's body quaked at the evidence. Her stomach tightened with nervous tension, even panic, as she was mindful of the fact that she had no choice but to listen to what Shay Brentwood had to say. It made her tremble. His family wanted the *Nubian Chronicle,* and her sister's indiscretion was just what the Brentwoods needed to get the paper back.

Memories of how hard her father had worked to build the foundations of such a great newspaper suddenly wheeled through her head. She remembered him sweating over the books on bright summer weekends, rearranging the house furniture to hide the threadbare carpet. And when she had first started working officially for the paper at twenty-two, after graduating in journalism six years before, her father was still getting slammed door rejections following weeks of preparation to bring in huge budget advertising, the source of income for any newspaper.

It was all for a dream; not only of wealth or leisure, not even of security, but of something to acquire and bequeath to his family, to his race. That was all her father ever wanted. And he'd achieved it, too, through sacrifice, dedication, and the will to survive. He'd also done it without Benjamin Brentwood.

She'd heard the puzzling story. Benjamin Brentwood and her father were once partners. The *Nubian Chronicle* was founded in Jamaica by the two. But Benjamin moved to New York and got married, leaving her father with a bank loan tied to the newspaper. Her father was forced to pay off the loan and then he emigrated to London, where he and her mother were married before he revamped the paper into what was now Europe's leading and most influential Afro-Caribbean broadsheet.

Then Benjamin Brentwood, like a seafaring buccaneer, decided he wanted his share of the *Chronicle* back, tirelessly reminding her father through a barrage of lawyers that he had never legally signed over his rights. The shock at receiving the stipulations in legal typeface had simply added to her father's grief, coming days after her mother's death. Having already built an African-American cable empire in New York, Benjamin Brentwood was to Kendra a person interested only in extending his power to gratify an insatiable ego.

He had only one objective—to be the biggest. To be the best.

She'd never talked to her father about him, but the family rumors were enough to put her on guard. That night Benjamin Brentwood had made it clear to her that he wanted the *Chronicle* back. She couldn't understand why he had waited so long to launch his bid for it. She'd inadvertently given him the privilege of telling her about it personally, and now one of his sons was right there in her home, purporting to know of her sister's grave shortcomings.

Passing her tongue over her dry lips she blinked hard, trying to force her whirling mind into focus. "Let's get this over with," she conceded harshly. "Exactly why are you here?"

"I thought I'd come over and offer my help."

Kendra's eyes narrowed with suspicion. "In return for what?"

"Well, that's up to you," Shay's voice deepened as his eyes roamed across Kendra's thinly concealed body. She was not to know that her damp underwear had caused her pink bed coat to cling seductively to her trembling limbs, allowing her feminine curves to display her womanhood. Nor would Kendra have cared. For, at that precise moment her mind had settled on something far beyond how she was dressed or the desirous emotions Shay Brentwood was already evoking in her. She knew exactly why he had come there, and she also knew that she had to keep a level head if her father was to retain ownership of his newspaper.

"What did you have in mind?" she queried, undaunted yet nervous at the very prospect of their ensuing conversation.

One of Shay's heavy eyebrows shot up. "I thought maybe something that would appeal to your sense of fair play," he answered easily.

Kendra tipped her chin in silent rebellion, disguising her internal instability with a glacial smile. "I need a drink," she said.

"Then I'll join you," Shay responded.

She marched on her bare feet toward a split-level archway which led directly into a lounge with co-ordinated pastel colors where a large, blazing, open fire welcomed them into a warm interior. Heading straight for the wine cabinet, her mind filled with un-palatable thoughts of how she could protect her father's newspaper even as her ferocious enemy followed in hot pursuit, she asked, "What would you like?"

"Actually, nothing for me. I'm driving," Shay answered. "But you go right ahead."

Kendra fabricated a smile and turned to find her fingers trembling as she clasped a bottle of liquer. She willed herself to suppress the motion long enough to pour a small measure into a glass, but as she brought the glass to her lips she was suddenly struck by a spastic shaking, and the glass jittered against her teeth as she emptied it.

Placing it back on the cabinet, she braced her hands against its wooden frame to steady her nerves and then returned her gaze to Shay, who had seated himself in one of the soft, floral chairs by the fire. "This is a nice room," he said with a warmth underlying his tone which Kendra hadn't detected before. It didn't make her feel any better, only more suspicious.

"Let's get to the point," she jabbed.

"Is your temper always so combustible?" Shay inquired in a relaxed voice.

"Only when there's an adversary within the confines of my sanctum sanctorum intent on blowing smoke in my direction," Kendra snapped rudely.

Shay chuckled. It was a warm, soft chuckle, almost tranquil in sound, so that for a fleeting moment Kendra was reminded of a pair of startling, dusky brown eyes that reflected a sweet gaze of genuine warmth she so seldom saw in the countenance of a man. Only fate could play such a cruel hand by allowing that same devastatingly handsome man to be a foe at her heel.

"You can relax," Shay declared openly. "This morning I replaced the money your sister took out of the Association of Black Journalists's account. She can now avoid the stain of another investigation."

Kendra's brows rose fractionally in disbelief. She swallowed hard on the tightness of her throat, the fear vanishing, only to be replaced by a far more tangible awareness of the man sitting opposite her, whose motive she had yet to hear. "Why?" she asked finally, anxiousness causing her to lean against the cabinet for blessed support.

Her skin felt almost ice cold even though the room was warm. She was unnaturally cold not because she had on little clothing, but because the *Nubian Chronicle* was most definitely at stake. Her fears were confirmed. "I thought I'd take your pop's newspaper as payback," came Shay's crude reply. "I think he'll hear it better coming from you."

"No!" Kendra screamed before placing her hand against her mouth. Lowering her voice, she pleaded, "Please, don't." Panicked, she walked over to him and stared into those same dusky brown eyes she'd found so attractive. "You can't do this to my father, not so soon after what. . . ." Tears sprang to her eyes as she heaved an unsteady breath. "I know you must've heard about my mother—you seem to know everything else. She died last year. Everyone knows how withdrawn my father became afterward. That's why I was forced to take over the newspaper. I now suspect that Arlisa's gambling is just part of the instability she's suffering."

"Yeah, your sister is sure mixing with some . . . interesting people." Shay nodded unsympathetically. "Sista sure knows how to party."

"She's just a little outgoing," Kendra said sternly.

"Especially with the opposite sex?" Shay chuckled derisively.

"You're not paying any attention to what I'm saying, are you?" Kendra bristled coldly. "You've come here like a burglar in the night to steal something that isn't even yours."

"Steal!" Shay exclaimed, his eyes suddenly losing their familiar warmth. "My father worked his tail off for that paper. All hell would've frozen over before he sold out his rights. Your father—"

"My father was left with the debt that your father ran away from," Kendra screamed. "What is Benjamin Brentwood anyway? A man or a mouse?"

"Are you insulting my father?" Shay stormed, raising himself out of his seat to his full six-foot-three-inches. "He believed in what he was doing."

"Really?" Kendra goaded. "He's waited all this time for an opportunity to roll all over my father and you're here, right now, waiting to run home to Daddy to tell him how my sister's stupidity has given you the key to the *Chronicle's* lock. Well, not while I'm still in the house. You're sadly mistaken if you think some big time media deal is going down here. So if this is your idea of appealing to my sense of fair play, then there's the door. Put yourself on the other side of it."

Shay frowned as he glared at Kendra, alerted to how deeply wounded she was. His mind was stamped with the impression of intense feminine sexuality, a powerhouse of a woman who was larger than life, voluptuously curved and ultra all-female, yet highly accomplished with polished acumen and a mind as sharp as a saboteur's knife. She didn't seem the sort who would miss a trick, but he could challenge her. He'd heard that she thrived on risks, not unlike Arlisa.

"You know," he began, unsure as to why he wanted to win over this woman's trust, "when I was a kid and I saw something I wanted I always doubled my efforts to get it, but I never cheated and I never played dirty. So I'm going to give you seven days to raise the money."

"What?" Kendra whispered, almost unable to believe her ears.

"On one condition."

"What's that?" she asked, panicked.

"You kiss me."

Kendra laughed. "I've met enough frogs in my time," she bit through clenched teeth, "but never one so bloated with self-importance, and particularly one who attempted to humiliate me." She paused long enough to analyze her antagonism, for Kendra knew she was jolted by the sheer magnetism Shay's words had projected. It had almost seemed that the earth had shaken under her feet at the thought that she could so easily seize the opportunity and kiss him. The thought of what it would be like had certainly crossed her mind. On leaving his mansion, all she could recall was a mouth that flagrantly invited ravishment and sensual indulgence, a vision she stoically repressed out of a sense of loyalty to Selwyn.

Fueled with that same faithful indignation, she said, "As Arlisa is the one who owes you the money, I suggest you take your proposition to her."

"I don't want Arlisa." Shay's voice was husky and deep. "I want you."

An involuntary tremor passed through Kendra as he stared down at her. To her surprise, she felt her heart give an erratic thud as his gaze held hers and deepened with an intensity that held her captive. She wanted to shake him for his arrogance and for the financial hold he had over her, but as his warm breath fanned against her cheek she was only conscious of a new kind of awareness which caused the discordant thudding of her pulse. "You can't have me," she said, determined. "And I'm not going to give you any leeway to humiliate me. I'll find a way to pay you back your money, with interest."

"Until then," Shay said, his voice deep, velvety, and unmistakably American, "I'll take my first installment now." Before Kendra could even begin to comprehend his meaning, Shay reached out and jerked her into his arms, his lips capturing hers within seconds of locating them. Kendra instantly tried to push him away but her body felt weak, as though it had become possessed by some great sensual influence.

The sensation was exquisite. The kiss was deeply persuasive, making Kendra's head swim with the realization that it would take no effort at all to become a serious collaborator in this man's proposition. He was terribly good at what he was doing; his lips pulsing in tantalizing little caresses over the tissues of her mouth in slow, coaxing, tempting motions. In the turmoil of her mind she sensed that Shay was fully aware of her, for his hands had begun to mold themselves around her waist, slowly familiarizing their way across her back as though they would delve at any moment beyond what the thin, pink fabric of her bed coat allowed.

She felt the warmth of his body reach out to her like an invisible bond, its hold so frighteningly intense that she felt almost powerless to break free. To her chagrin, her own response was as needful as his possessive invasion. Any space between them was crushed out of existence as their bodies instinctively made their own exploratory discoveries, making small shifts and adjustments to push their addictive revelations further.

And it wasn't just one kiss, although where one ended

and the other began was not easy to define. Rather, it was one long, sweet, raw, lazy, insatiable manifestation of heady nuances of sensation which began to intensify the moment Kendra felt the soft, testing tip of Shay's tongue delve briefly into her parted lips. It was a sobering shock to feel such a fiery emotion so quickly, and in her desperation she pulled her mouth away, reminding herself sternly how dangerous it would be to try to reciprocate any of this man's feelings.

"Don't get stuck on the idea that I'm some wide-eyed young bait," she gasped, her limbs still quaking with emotion from what they'd just shared but acutely guilty and embarrassed by the experience. "Your money will be back to you within seven days."

Shay's voice was rough-edged as he reached to the chair where he'd been seated for his jacket. "I hope I don't have to count on that," he answered raggedly, his hand brushing against her shoulder. Brief as it was, the contact was sufficient to trigger a whole wealth of signals Kendra was working desperately hard to suppress.

When Shay left, she went over to the wine cabinet and poured herself an extra large liquer, applying that to her eager lips with the same motion she had earlier. Her anxiety had returned and she was suddenly struck with depressing worries about how she could find one hundred and fifty thousand dollars.

She paced the floor, taking the bottle with her only to place it on the coffee table in her progress. She was afraid to sit down, afraid that if she relaxed too quickly she would scream. But, as the alcohol began its sedating effect she realized that what she was suffering from wasn't so much the pressure of keeping hold of her father's newspaper, but the fact that she wanted to experience again the way Shay Brentwood had kissed her.

Three

"I hope you're satisfied," Kendra rattled as she slammed the door of her bedroom and glared murderously at Arlisa, who sat crouched on the bed.

It had taken her all of ten minutes to gather her bearings before she'd decided she could face Arlisa with the terrible news. It was an unrelished task she wasn't quite prepared to face. "That was Shay Brentwood downstairs," she began jerkily, making her way across the room. "You're damned lucky he didn't come with the police."

"Shay Brentwood was here?" Arlisa rasped in disbelief.

"In the flesh," Kendra admitted forlornly as she shakily removed the pink towel from her hair and absently dropped it to the floor in disregard. Taking her seat at the dressing table, she stared dazedly at her anxious reflection before adding gravely, "He's replaced the money you took, on the provision, of course, that he gets Daddy's newspaper in return."

"Oh my God," Arlisa murmured, her tears returning in a sudden flurry of remorseful sobs and snorted gestures. "What . . . what did you say to him?"

Kendra's mouth quirked bitterly as she recollected exactly what had happened. Fighting the emotions that were still causing freakish havoc within her, she said,

"Short of telling him to go to hell, I made him leave with the impression that he's getting a little more than what he came here for."

"The paper!" Arlisa surmised, stammering at the imminent thought.

"More the idea that my personage is tangible collateral," Kendra responded numbly, mentally girding herself to fight the stifling oddness she was feeling about the whole situation.

"No!" Arlisa said in awe, immediately composing herself in a manner which bordered on miraculous. "Don't you think that's a little rash?"

"Agreeing to pay for your trips to Monte Carlo was rash," Kendra clipped solemnly. "I was forced to kiss that man for the mercy of seven days to find the money or lose the paper."

"You kissed Shay Brentwood?" Arlisa breathed, skirting entirely over the leniency they had been given. Drawing herself up to an alert position on the bed, she ejected a stupendous, "Wow."

"Believe me, it was under sufferance," Kendra lied profusely, taking a deep breath to settle the fluttery weakness in her stomach. "But if I can save Daddy's newspaper, then I'm going to try."

Arlisa suddenly confronted her sister, confusion marked across her tawny face. "What are you going to tell Selwyn?"

Kendra instantly had the sense that she was treading a thin and dangerous line. She was somewhat unusually at a loss for thought. She knew Selwyn wouldn't understand. Only last week he'd been thumping the podium at a Labour conference, proclaiming in full view of the TV cameras that his party should take a firmer stand against moral deprivation within government.

This had become a public issue of late, and was more commonly termed "sleaze." There was the spectacle of Conservative M.P. Colonel Roger Gray, the man who betrayed his wife back in England and shacked up with a United Nations helper while commanding a British force in Bosnia. And more recently there was Sir Peter Kelsey, a former cabinet minister and veteran of the Conservative Party who was alleged to have made a £4,000 payment to a call girl at King's Cross Station to buy her silence after their affair ended amidst alcohol and substance abuse rumors, sordid details which had led him to resign from office and build his career as a forthright House of Commons backbencher.

The media, never missing the correct tip-offs, gave both stories the kind of sensational coverage that was damaging to any party's national support. As a politician, Selwyn led a life quite open to public scrutiny, particularly as he was the first black candidate to be elected as Minister of Parliament to the Brent-South constituency.

Since becoming a widower—his wife having died suddenly, he'd told her—Selwyn had conducted their relationship with such exemplary standards that there were times she'd felt in awe of his principles. And so, raising a shaky hand to her forehead, she willed herself to think, but nothing sprang to mind except the brooding image of Shay Brentwood's enigmatic profile. His very image annoyed her. It seemed this man had the power to invade her private space even in his absence, making her feel off balance.

Frowning inwardly, and aware that her instincts were warning her that behind those brilliant, dusky brown eyes was a coiled cobra poised ready to strike, she challenged, "I'll take my chances."

Arlisa became alarmed. "I don't want you to sacrifice yourself on my account," she blubbered shamefully, her criminal actions exposed across her face in contorted lines of culpability. Then Kendra did not miss the vivid twinkle in her sister's eyes as she said, *"I'm more than willing to pay the penalty."*

"You would too, wouldn't you?" she retorted, now recalling that it was only a few days ago that Arlisa had told her about a recent feature in *Ebony Man* which had placed Shay Brentwood among the ten most eligible African-American bachelors. "Unfortunately, he specifically asked for me."

Arlisa shrugged off the daunting prospect with her own assurance. "I'll get you out of this," she promised. "I'll try to reach Jerome about a loan, first thing tomorrow morning."

"I hope for your sake you do," Kendra advised sardonically, noting the desperation in Arlisa's eyes, which she knew mirrored her own. "Because Daddy will curse the day he loses the *Nubian Chronicle* to Benjamin Brentwood."

"Good morning, Miss Davenport." The green-eyed Barbadian smiled as she observed Kendra striding out of twin elevator doors at 8:30 A.M. promptly and into the usual hustle and bustle that was familiar on the *Nubian Chronicle*'s editorial floor.

"What's good about it, Leola?" Kendra asked drily, rudely sweeping past her secretary and straight through a set of rosewood doors which led directly to her office.

Tossing her briefcase in one direction and shedding her red cashmere jacket only to toss it in another, she arrogantly jabbed at the intercom button on her desk and waited for it to connect her to the paper's research department before she snapped herself into action.

"Trevor," she ordered over the loudspeaker, a sense of power zinging through her veins at the very idea that there might be a way out of this situation yet. "I want you to find everything we have on the Brentwoods, and I want it five minutes ago."

"Are you referring to the Brentwood Communications Group, Inc., in New York, and the family that goes with it?" Trevor curiously inquired.

"Know of any other Brentwood?" Kendra snapped.

"Am I looking for anything in particular?" came Trevor's unperturbed but astute response.

"I'll know it when I see it," Kendra proclaimed firmly. Flicking off the intercom, she pivoted on her heels and immediately marched back into Leola's workspace. "What's in my mail today?" she inquired irritably. "Anything important?"

"That information you wanted on school board members in Oakland, California has arrived," Leola answered instantly. "It outlines their position on Eubonics being taught in the classroom, but we're still waiting to hear from the National Association for Bilingual Education."

"Oh . . . that language issue which emerged from the ghettos?" Kendra mused, recalling that she had intended to run a feature on it on the International News page, debating whether Eubonics should become part of the linguistic repertoire of young children. "That can wait. Anything else?"

"Selwyn had a note sent over. A courier brought it fifteen minutes ago."

"Thank you," Kendra said, grimacing as she took the small, unsealed envelope Leola handed her. Selwyn was always sending notes over. It was a perverse habit he had of clarifying their appointed schedule—whether they were going out to dinner, the cinema, a West End theater, or simply planning lunch.

"Would you like any coffee, Miss Davenport?" Leola ventured quickly.

"No," Kendra breathed, walking back into her office.

She flopped down into her black leather swivel chair and turned to stare lethargically with glazed eyes at the misty, late September weather which projected through the double floor-to-ceiling windows situated behind her wooden desk. "Damn you, Shay Brentwood," she whispered under her breath, her mind spinning a carousel of their detailed conversation the night before.

His words had offered her no solace. Until the dawn, her mind twisted and turned in all directions as ugly thoughts of how her father would react on hearing about Arlisa's misdeeds paraded endlessly through her troubled mind. Amidst it all, Kendra was disturbed as to why every avenue of thought led her back to Shay Brentwood and the memory of the volcanic excitement he'd evoked in her.

Why was he affecting her like this? she questioned now, absently turning the small envelope around in her hand. At times she'd tried to block the image of him out, but he was too firmly implanted, like the African prince of her teenage dreams, all too clearly visible, so that she felt almost able to trace her fingers along his masculine, shaven jawline.

She'd thought she'd gotten over those idle, wistful, adolescent dreams of unattainable idols. As a young girl she'd felt shattering disillusionment to learn that her dream lover was only a figment of her imagination, an impossible perfect image of a man grafted in her head.

Yet, amazingly, Shay Brentwood fit that image. His was the face she could imagine bending over her in the rapturous moment of which she had so often dreamed. And yet, she was realistic enough to know how dangerous her thoughts were—to attribute to him all the qualities of her ideal man—especially when it was not so long ago she had decided that Selwyn was all that she needed.

It was Shay's long, lingering kiss which had changed that resolve. Even now, Kendra felt her body quake in evidence of how much he had affected her. She shifted uneasily in her chair, her nerve ends screeching in frustration and amazement. There was no point in denying the awful truth. Shay Brentwood fascinated her. Yet she had to admit that his very name frightened her more than a whole series of earthquakes.

Only less than six months ago she'd been briefly introduced to his brother, Joel Brentwood, a well-built, mustached snob of a man who had been invited to preside over a business networking function. That was when the Brentwoods had arrived in England and were first making themselves known to the business and media circuit. Arlisa had initially been taken with him, delving with her usual charm to beckon Joel's attention in her direction, even though good authority declared him a married man.

She had no idea then what their true purpose was for coming to England, nor that Joel had such a devastatingly attractive younger brother. The first she'd learned of Shay's existence was when Arlisa had one day rushed home with gossip about a handsome male specimen who'd recently become a member of the Association of Black Journalists, a move Kendra now recognized to be part of their scheme.

At the time she hadn't paid any attention to her sister because Arlisa was always talking about men, a topic which had intensified over the years. The only part of the conversation she recalled was Arlisa's affectionate description of him: *"If Mr. Cool Lover's attributes were listed according to preeminence,"* she'd intoned, *"handsome comes first, rich a close second."*

On reflection, Kendra detested her own stupidity. It should've been obvious to her—having heard the family rumors over the years, and more recently Selwyn's commentary on how Shay Brentwood had threatened him over a nightclub license investigation—precisely what the Brentwood's presence in England meant. Theirs was a well-planned, intricately woven strategy which she was only now beginning to piece together. Moreover, it preyed upon her conscience terribly to discover how deeply attracted she was to her enemy, a matter she found difficult to reconcile with her supposed commitment to Selwyn.

With that thought, she opened the note Selwyn had sent over. It was brief, inquiring why she had not met him at the Grosvenor Hotel the night before, explaining in the long curling strokes of his handwriting why he had not called her, yet firmly insistent that she give him an explanation. Kendra grimaced again, knowing she owed him one.

She felt consumed with guilt, because she also knew that the kiss she'd shared with Shay was, to him, just a brief aberration which he had quickly dismissed, while Selwyn had always cherished every kiss she'd given him in the ten months they'd been together. Her only consolation was in the knowledge that she at least had the power not to allow it to happen again. She was, after all, a woman of willpower, wasn't she?

Having bolstered that resolve in her mind, Kendra was about to embark on her tasks for the day when the intercom suddenly buzzed on her desk, abruptly breaking into her musings with a jolt. "Miss Davenport," came Leola's soft, mellow voice. "I have Selwyn Owens, M.P., on line one."

Kendra's body stirred in blind apprehension as she quickly put the envelope down, switched on the loudspeaker, and heard Selwyn's smooth but concerned baritone instantly fill the room. "Kendra, Honey. Are you all right?" he demanded curtly. "I phoned your house just now, thinking you might've caught a cold or something, but I got Arlisa. She told me everything. Ignore my note. I didn't know."

Kendra's eyes glazed over in painful awareness of what must've transpired. "I couldn't see you last night, Selwyn," she began to explain, bringing to mind her agonizing decision to not meet him for dinner. She hadn't been looking forward to it, anyway, and she knew the political debates would simply have left her nauseated. "I would've made your evening miserable and—"

"I understand," Selwyn interrupted sympathetically. "It's all a bit of a mess, isn't it?"

The stupefied moment of silence which followed as that question hovered indecisively amongst the telecommunication static caused a lump to form in Kendra's throat, and prickly tears to tug at her eyelids. She could just picture Selwyn's face as he awaited her response: his hazel eyes full of pity and gracious understanding, his bearded, chicory jawline tilted with forbearance and commiseration, his tall, slim, lanky body—lean, tapered and unmuscled—braced with condolence and benevolent compassion. The very image made her feel absurdly tearful and ridiculously childlike, as though she were a baby in desperate need of comfort and support.

With her voice on a hoarse, high note, she whimpered, "Selwyn, I—"

"Listen, Honey," Selwyn intruded, oblivious to and not heeding Kendra's predicament, "I'm on my way to Parliament. Sir William Hendon wants to see me about something before he goes into the House of Commons. By the way, we've been invited to spend the morning with the Beaufort Hunt."

"Foxhunting?" Kendra quivered, alarmed. "When?"

"A couple of weeks. Look, why don't I call you later? We'll talk then."

"You will call?" Kendra sniveled in anticipation of

Selwyn's warm assurance. She knew he didn't like to use the telephone now that there was a general sense of paranoia about leaks and wire tapping, but she wanted to feel emotionally secure.

But even as she heard him answer she was aware that he was really unmindful of what was going on. It wasn't a purposeful, immoderate reaction, just Selwyn's usual basic apathetic indifference to all the pieces which made up her life. It still annoyed her that he had chosen to not meet her father, a poignant issue she had yet to discuss with him, for she considered her father to be one of the main pieces he should've now stumbled upon. But for the moment she concentrated on snapping out of her unpleasant depression and on bringing her mind into focus while Selwyn talked.

"I'll call," he concluded, sounding out a series of muffled kisses which traveled the telecommunication line. Kendra was about to say good-bye when her office door shot open and two intruders rushed in.

"I'm sorry, Miss Davenport," Leola apologized weakly as a tall figure boldly preceded her. "I couldn't stop him. He insisted on seeing you right away and—"

"Selwyn, I have to go." Kendra hastily reacted by flicking off the loudspeaker. Rising abruptly out of her chair, she faced her intruder indignantly.

"Hello, Kendra," Shay Brentwood greeted shamelessly. He returned Kendra's gaze, his frankly appraising eyes roving over her black ski pants, white ruffled shirt, and the studded black belt which encircled her enviable slim waistline.

He seemed struck by something, Kendra realized, as he stopped dead in his tracks and subjected her to the same masculine assessment he'd given her the night before. This time she felt troubled by it. She had not forgotten how formidable Shay could be in the flesh. He looked suave and elegant in the dark navy suit he wore, and his whole being projected a magnetic dominance that he seemed to achieve without any exertion at all.

To her horror, her body shook at the sight of him. It wasn't only because her mind had been propelled back to the ultimatum he'd given her, she told herself bluntly, but more because the determined look on Shay's face stirred her to a restlessness she didn't feel comfortable with. Yet as she slowly moved from behind her desk in an attempt to stop her knees from shaking, Kendra reminded herself that he was in *her* office, and that warranted her supremacy. The inner exultation she derived from the thought spurred her to inquire pertly, "Is there something you want, Mr. Brentwood?"

"World peace, end of famine." Shay's voice was calm and spirited even as Kendra detected that he seemed to give himself a little shake back into reality. "But for now, I'll settle for you."

Kendra dismally realized as she caught up with Shay at the door that her constructed look of lofty disdain was being wasted on her intruder. She'd thought her scornful expression would distract him, but Shay was evidently in a mood that served only to cause his eyes to harden like black pearls. Turning to her secretary, she said, "That will be all, Leola."

As she watched Leola leave Kendra's mind quickly latched on to the possibility that Shay had come there to tell her that he'd planned to put the wheels in motion to immediately take over, that he'd changed his mind about the seven days he'd given her. Her hands began to feel warm and clammy at the very prospect, for she felt sure she was about to hear the words spring triumphantly from his lips.

Instead, Shay echoed another sentiment. "Mr. M.P. seems to like you a lot." He grinned cheekily. "But I think he needs a major tip."

"And what would that be?" Kendra rebutted, aware that Shay was majestically moving his way around her furniture in general curious scrutiny of her things.

"He's got to learn to kiss the girl, not the damn phone." His eyes glittered with some suppressed emotion Kendra considered to be insolence.

She felt embarrassed that he should have witnessed Selwyn's private intimacy with her, but she was more enraged that this impertinent man should stand in her office and behave as though Selwyn had barely discovered the female sex. It was obvious to her that he thought himself to be a better man, and that fueled her anger further. It also annoyed her beyond belief that her heart should agree with that assessment, because it had begun to cavort in a most intemperate fashion, and the rest of her was beginning to react treacherously to the pull of him.

She had to put a stop to this control he had over her, she decided as she gave a peeved response by repeating Arlisa's potent reference to him. "What would you know about it, Mr. Cool Lover?"

Shay halted his movement and straightened to his full height, his gaze holding Kendra's with a kind of menacing intensity. "I know that when a red-blooded woman needs to be kissed, she wants full physical contact," he retorted.

"And do you think a kiss should be forced upon a woman?" Kendra asked quickly, calling up the reserves of all her innate stubbornness to return a look of equally steadfast determination. "Especially when the man delivering it is an odious, loathsome, abominable, insolent rat?"

Shay glared at her for several seconds, then shook his head in denial and began to make his way around the room again, laughing softly—even pleasantly—to himself. "I didn't force you," he said finally.

"How perceptive you are, Mr. Brentwood," Kendra drawled icily. "I'm glad you know what you are, but I wasn't aware that *you* were the topic of this conversation."

Shay's mouth quirked, comprehension of Kendra's speedy treatment of him exposed in his hardened profile. It gave Kendra a secret sense of triumph, though it was a short-lived one. Within seconds of her deriding him, Shay took up their conversation again, his face wiped clean of any expression betraying his thoughts on that subject.

Deliberately pointing at a glass display cabinet which housed her collection of Egyptian statuettes, he proclaimed firmly, "I think my team's basketball trophies will look nice in there."

Kendra followed his gaze to the cabinet and instantly felt her chest expand as she drew in a deep breath. "I thought we agreed on a week," she said, her reminder arresting Shay to the point that she saw his face tighten. Embellished with renewed confidence, yet impatient to know why he had come there, she continued. "I was expecting you to arrive for your money next Wednesday, and I've decided to pay you ten percent interest, three percent above market value."

"*Twenty* percent?" Shay amended, his eyebrows raised in mock disbelief as though she'd offered it. "How generous of you."

Kendra gritted her teeth, but only in a moment of disquiet to display minimal lack of reaction. "Plus an undertaking to leave the *Chronicle* alone," she added.

She watched as he turned aside and walked around her wooden desk to gaze through the windows of her office. For a moment he stood there in silence and seemed to appreciate the view of Fleet Street, the heart of British journalism. Then, just as Kendra was wondering whether she should demand his assurance he would stay away from her father's newspaper, Shay wheeled round and contemplated her diligently.

"Tell me," he probed, curiously inquisitive. "What's the story with you and Mr. M.P.?"

Kendra's eyes widened. "What?"

"Does he satisfy you?"

Kendra glared at him. Every instinct she possessed told her that Shay was fully aware of the quivering she was experiencing inside at his presence, and that he was probably goading her into admitting it to him. Her answer would need careful phrasing, for his mind was undoubtedly braced at full level to dissect her answer.

If she told him it was none of his business, he would instantly surmise that she was unhappy, and if she told him that she was more than content with her relationship, he would assume that she was lying. And he had every reason to.

Shay and she had shared a kiss that was neither casual, friendly, or sociably genial. It had been more like a movie kiss; lips moist and parted, tongue tip penetrating, breath warm and slightly frantic. She had been astonished by it, but only for the few seconds it took to become an eager collaborator, and that surprised her even more. Perhaps because she'd adjusted to the sudden, splendid upheaval he'd evoked in her with such ease and serenity.

In truth, there wasn't an appropriate answer she could give him except maybe what he wanted to hear, and Kendra was not going to give him that. "I'm a very busy woman, Mr. Brentwood," she evaded sharply, erecting for strength her usual professional facial exterior. "You're wasting my time asking silly questions."

"It's a simple question," Shay challenged in reply.

"It's a barefaced question," Kendra said, wondering why on earth she was even bothering to stay on the topic, let alone take up the challenge. "You must have too many women at your beck and call to even ask it."

"Some."

"And what are they normally like?" she pressed disapprovingly.

"Like all the rest." Shay shrugged.

Like all the rest, Kendra mused, realizing that he'd pronounced that rather wearily. "You're not choosy, then?" she jabbed. "I suppose you go for the scatterbrained, dumb, little-on-the-ball type?"

Shay flashed a devilish grin. "They're usually ambitious, intelligent, and successful, like yourself, actually."

"Oh," Kendra gasped, backing down slightly. "I find myself at times mirroring my mother's judgment when it comes to people, or . . . shall we say, her middle-class values."

For the first time since she'd met Shay Brentwood his face was neither smiling or teasing. It reflected only deep thought. "That's admirable, having values," he replied simply.

"There's nothing admirable about it," Kendra stated tersely. "I'm hardworking, a little tough, because I've had to be, and I grew up knowing that there are principles to live by. Not many people are so . . . clear-headed."

She met his eyes and discovered to her surprise that she suddenly hated to recall that there was a Selwyn Owens. Guilt immediately caught up with her, and she added without thinking, "Perhaps that's why I prefer someone honest, who is bound to give me an absolutely secure life."

Shay Brentwood studied the determined woman with mink-color eyes, whose first appearance had captured him thoroughly. She *was* remarkable—shapely, bold, honorable to her man, and honest about herself. But dammit, she belonged to Selwyn Owens. "So," he probed diligently, "are you going to answer my question?"

Kendra fumed. This man wasn't going to let go until he had an answer. Tilting her chin in defiance, she stated convincingly, "My relationship with Selwyn is more than substantial."

"But less than serious," Shay said immediately.

Kendra hesitated. "You'd like it to be that, wouldn't you?"

Shay's gaze intensified. "I want to know what you'd like."

"I'd like your assurance that you'll leave my father's newspaper alone," Kendra said, deliberately regarding Shay with a fixed expression.

A line between Shay's heavy eyebrows deepened in irritation. "No can do," he remarked simply, though his eyes reflected his dislike of the shift in conversation. "It's a tough world. Survival of the fittest, kill or be killed. Regardless of Arlisa's actions, I'll still be after your father's newspaper."

"Is that what you've come to tell me?" Kendra demanded flatly.

A shadow seemed to cross Shay's face. "No," he admitted, moving around her leather chair to deposit himself in it. Propping his long legs up on top of her desk and then crossing them at the ankles for comfort, he said, "It's time Arlisa resigned."

"Arlisa resign!" Kendra shouted, before she marched herself across the room to her desk, heels thudding quietly on the beige carpeting. *How dare he,* she thought furiously, her features marred with such determination that Shay instantly brought to mind the Queen of Sheba, Queen Hatshepsut, and all the female giants of ancient Africa who had commanded great kingdoms without male dominance.

He was aware that she resented his suggestion, but he didn't know that Kendra's mind had already divulged to her that he was probably right. She knew Arlisa could not be expected to hold another public position after what she'd done. It just wouldn't be ethical, or fair to the donors who had entrusted her to look after the fund's money. But she wasn't about to admit that to this handsome man whom she hated, and whose audacity in the way he sat in her chair created a sight she couldn't bear to witness for another minute.

"Nerve—unabashed nerve," she ranted scornfully, knocking Shay's feet from her desktop in angry contempt. "You'll just not be satisfied until you have us both out of a job, will you?"

"Okay, you want it your way," Shay jabbed, readjusting his position by flicking his right ankle over his left knee, remaining rooted in the chair, "then let's wait for Mrs. Adina to discover what Arlisa has been doing." He stared at Kendra gravely, studying the subsiding fury in her mink-almond eyes. "I can quiet Mrs. Adina as long as she knows the money has been returned, which it has, and that Arlisa is out."

When Kendra remained silent, Shay raised himself out of her chair and walked the short distance it took to reach her. "If I could dodge this thing, like an oncoming train, I would," he consoled. "But I can't."

"You must be feeling quite pleased with yourself." Kendra swallowed, defeated, her body aware that Shay had situated himself within inches of her, his body braced in an almost sympathetic manner.

"No," he said quietly, resting his hand briefly on her shoulder and then removing it.

Kendra's body quivered at the contact. She didn't think that Shay was meaning to kiss her again, and of course she didn't want him to. But his nearness evoked memories that clouded her mind, making the passage of any thought a difficult business. "Why . . . why are you going to so much trouble to protect my sister?" she uttered weakly. "Especially after what your brother did?"

Shay's gaze moved down to Kendra's mouth. "J B wasn't thinking, but he is now," he admitted. "And we've decided that there's an interest at stake in protecting the reputation of the newspaper."

Kendra's lips started to tremble. She compressed them sensibly and ejected a smothered cough, but it did not remove the constriction in her throat. "I don't understand," she choked out.

Shay lifted his hand and softly stroked a finger down her nose. "So young, and yet so disillusioned," he whispered.

The finger dropped to her upper lip, and to Kendra's complete and utter chagrin she instinctively stuck out her tongue and licked its soft human flesh. It was as if she were obliging some secret fantasy, and she sensed the tremor in Shay's body in response before he removed his finger and put it into his mouth to taste her. Their gazes clashed, a mutuality of purpose blazing between them, and Kendra realized that she desperately wanted Shay to kiss her, even as she knew a part of her was still nursing an aversion toward him.

Her mind felt muddled and chaotic, but the dictates of her body were methodically and systematically clear, for the moment Shay brought his lips tantalizingly closer to her eager lips her entire body propelled itself forward, yearning to be reawakened with the devastating spirit of his kiss.

But his tangible voice bounced against the softness of her warm mouth, quickly transporting her back to reality with a bump. "My father wants the newspaper clean," he told her hoarsely, his New York accent restrained and controlled. "No indiscretions. No scandals."

It wasn't until the words had sunk in that Kendra comprehended his meaning. By exposing Arlisa, the Brentwoods would find themselves damaging the reputation of the very newspaper they so desperately wanted to acquire. Media coverage alone could kill sales in one fell swoop. But protecting her, media focus could concentrate solely on the Brentwood's status as the *Nubian Chronicle*'s newest proprietors. It was a marketing tactic which had obviously been given full and meaningful consideration.

Kendra fumed. "Get out!" she shouted, ascending quickly from the euphoric spell she was under to the full light of day. Staring at him, she wanted to raise her hand and strike out at him, but remembered that her mother had put everything good into raising her. "Let's get one thing clear," she stormed. "Don't have any illusions about walking in here to steal this paper from under me. I may've been stupid, but not anymore."

Shay offered her a wry grin, acknowledging her declaration with a simple raised eyebrow. He had the feeling of growing a little older, a little weaker, and a lot less sure of himself, but he made an effort to disguise all that as he placed a hand under Kendra's chin and tipped her head so that he could look into her menacing, dark eyes. "There's a low-level war going on here," he remarked softly, his suggestion implying that there was something deeper than what could be seen at face value. "I'm beginning to wonder who's going to win."

Kendra knocked his hand away and marched toward the door, bracing her own hand on the knob before pulling the door open in a bold gesture to show her enemy his exit. "I'll see you next Wednesday for your damned money," she said, bristling nastily, using every vestige of venom she could muster in her voice.

Shay switched his gaze to the door, then back to Kendra. "Until then," he acknowledged with a wry smile, making his way there. Stalling at the entrance, he dug his hands deeply into his pockets and allowed his dusky eyes to sweep over her auburn tresses. "I like your hair like that," he added in approval, studying the way Kendra had swept it up loose into a bobtail with short tendrils falling about her forehead and earlobes. "Wear it like that next Wednesday. I'll be here around eleven-thirty."

Refusing to be swallowed into the compliment though she felt maddened by the way her body trembled at hearing it, Kendra offered sternly, "There's just one more thing." Capturing his attention, she went on. "When you arrive, make sure you bring a deposition from God. You're going to need it if you want to sit in my chair again."

Four

Two days later Kendra found herself sitting quietly over the remains of an enormous sweet potato pie, noting Selwyn's animated, self-absorbed political conversation with touches of ambivalence and indifference. As he looked at her from across the table in the luxurious West End restaurant, his left hand nervously fidgeting against a clean napkin, she felt dejected that his thoughts were so work-oriented. It was quite an effort to be cheerful, particularly as Arlisa had tactfully decided to avoid her since they'd talked about her resigning her position, and Trevor's painstaking excavation into the Brentwood's preeminent past had dug up nothing of any real value to anyone.

Even as unscrupulous ideas began to form in her head about desperate measures she could take to curtail any threat of Shay Brentwood ever taking over her father's newspaper, Kendra knew she couldn't share them with Selwyn, because he seemed to measure tactics by some stupid yardstick of morals. His invitation to dinner and going to a new nightclub opening that Saturday night simply served as another reminder of how detached he was.

In fact, it alarmed her that he appeared more interested in her accepting defeat than fighting. Her dinner had been spent toying with her food, rubbing at her sapphire and diamond earrings, fingering her hair, which she'd simply left hung loosely around her face, and listening to Selwyn voice his disapproval of what she was wearing before pontificating on the many other challenging things that the future would hold for her. Though he had displayed his typical animosity for Shay Brentwood during a brief conversation about her problem, his timid solution that she should sit back and allow the situation to run its course was an outcome that did not sit well with her, and she felt annoyed enough to tell him so.

Reclining in the dralon-covered chair and eyeing Selwyn carefully as the waiter cleared the table and served coffee, she protested against his topic on the Labour Party's stand on public privatization by saying, "I'm really surprised that you think what has happened, because of Arlisa, is for the best."

Selwyn eyed her, startled that she should interrupt him so. "Kendra, Honey," he said reasonably, adjusting the cufflinks Kendra had presented him with on his thirty-seventh birthday. "Shay Brentwood will only let you go so far. He has connections all over. Take that nightclub license his friend got. You can bet strings were pulled there. When I tried to find out, as a favor to Colin Parker, Tower Hamlet's M.P., look what happened. I got threatened."

"You can't go around accusing people of corruption," Kendra argued. "Didn't it occur to you that Colin Parker was using you to get information because you're black?"

"Stop turning this around, Kendra. This isn't about me. You've only just met Shay Brentwood, so you've no idea. I've been told that when Benjamin Brentwood sneezes, the whole of New York catches a cold. He's so sharp people have wondered how he hasn't cut himself. So if Shay Brentwood is anything like what I've heard about his father, you can kiss the *Nubian Chronicle* good-bye." He paused. "Now, as I was saying . . ."

Kendra dissolved into silence. What was the point of explaining? Selwyn's typical attitude was just what she should've expected. Didn't he care that she could be out of work the following week? Didn't he believe that she should have a life, too? It seemed all he cared about was politics and the devious play for favors, and that in itself was a subject she detested. Just listening, as his conversation took a decisive tactical turn, made her blood begin to boil.

". . . inventing policy on the hoof and trying to cover up their U-turns," Selwyn said passionately. "I'm sick of it, and the recent vociferous factions in this party. Now Sir William Hendon is saying I need to ease up on my schedule, that I'm overworked . . . the gall of the man. Do I look stressed and overworked to you? Am I falling apart at the seams? Kendra?"

Kendra glared at him, her mind trained elsewhere. "So you're saying that I should let status remain quo?" she jibed, taking him back to her immediate denial of potentially losing her father's newspaper.

"No!" Selwyn heaved a weary breath and massaged his receding hairline before he itched at his full-bearded jawline arrogantly. "Kendra, look. I'm saying that this is a time for you to reflect, to put your life into perspective. It was understood that you wouldn't be working on your father's newspaper forever."

Kendra's eyebrows rose in confusion "Understood! Understood by whom?"

"Well, your father, for one," Selwyn assumed. "Surely he—"

"You've never met my father," Kendra reminded him tersely. "So I really don't know what you mean."

"I meant that I understood it wouldn't be forever," Selwyn retorted angrily.

There was an uncomfortable silence, heightened by a sudden feeling of embarrassment when Lord Harry Creswell, former director of the Equal Opportunities Commission, singled out their table as he was making ready to leave.

"Miss Davenport," he began sardonically, placing himself within inches of her chair. "I read your . . . interesting piece in the *Nubian Chronicle* today." His eyes narrowed coolly, as though he was reminding the entire room that as a black Conservative peer in the House of Lords, he was within his rights to comment on it. "There's been much discussion of the usage of the term Afro-Saxon as opposed to Afropean. However, I don't think the . . . *Editor's Column* is the right place to voice arguments without the relevant facts on the matter."

Kendra eyed his expensive pinstripe suit, noted his manner of authority, and reminded herself that it was times like these which had made her into a tough, uncompromising editor. She knew Lord Creswell was in favor of inventing a better term to denote someone ethnically African and European in attitude, but she was also aware that many of the *Nubian Chronicle's* readers originated from the Caribbean, and so felt it important that they deserved some recognition in the debate, too. The matter should hardly have called for his snobbish objection, so she responded just as coolly. "We have a *Letters to the Editor* column, Lord Creswell. Why don't you . . . air your views there? I'll be more than happy to publish whatever you have to say."

She noticed him wince a little at her retaliatory remark, but he disciplined his mature expression as well as a sixty-nine year old man could, with well practiced reflexes. "My views are kept firmly within the confines of the House of Lords," he declared diplomatically. "Heritage is well appreciated there, which is why we are all more than aware that the London black community has grown so from its humble twenty thousand in seventeen eighty-five." He looked at Selwyn and slightly inclined his head in apology for his intrusion and as a bold indication that he was going to end the conversation there. "Good evening, Sir."

Kendra reeled inwardly at the chauvinist gesture. "Lord Creswell?" He turned and looked back at her. "We're planning the Black History Supplement for next month. You would do well to read it. That year? It was seventeen eighty-seven." His face froze, and Kendra triumphed as he left without another utterance.

Selwyn spoke first. "Kendra, you had no right to do that."

"Yes, I did," she boomed. "He's gone over ground well trodden and scuffed, so if he and his . . . dinosaur chums can't make a decision, then we, the media, can." She suddenly caught herself up short. "That's if I have a newspaper by the end of next week."

Selwyn's eyes softened at the prospect. "What I was saying before . . . about you not having the newspaper forever? I was simply implying that there would come a time in your life when other things would matter." He looked at her deeply, seriously intent on making her understand. "I never wanted to rush you, Kendra. I've always felt that there's an appropriate time for everything, and that's why I didn't rush head on into meeting your father. I wanted to be sure about you first, and naturally, since coming to terms with my wife Katherine having gone I gave myself the time to do that."

"Naturally." Kendra was peeved, aware that her earlier outburst had served to elevate Selwyn from supplicant bystander to man in charge. Now she felt ineffectual and trapped into listening without protest to what he had to say.

"What has occurred has given us the opportunity to decide what we want," he continued, peering into his coffee before taking a swallow of the milky stuff. Kendra could tell he was measuring his thoughts carefully as he did so. "I want to experience again what I had with Katherine, and I think we both want the same things out of life, Kendra." His eyes shifted from his coffee cup to her face. "Happiness."

Kendra shakily brought her own coffee cup to her lips, but instead of sipping from it, she stared into the brown liquid, fancying it as a pool designed for drowning. It all seemed clear now. Selwyn had prepared this dinner in advance, rehearsed his role, and was now bracing himself to deliver a punch line following his prefix of happiness. Yet that one simple word spoken from his lips in that contrived, empty context was almost obscene to Kendra. How could she ever expect to be happy when this man was silently conspiring that she should allow her father's newspaper to be stolen from her?

"Selwyn," she intoned sternly. "I think—"

"Let's get married, Kendra," Selwyn interrupted crudely.

Kendra glared at him. "What did you say?"

"I said, let's get married."

Kendra blinked for several seconds, her mind blank, her head spinning. Confused, in turmoil, she realized that Selwyn was making an heroic effort to control himself, giving her space and time to come to grips with his proposition. Her instincts had warned her that something was coming, but not this. Never this. She felt torn between giving him immediate assurance and prolonging his agony. In truth, she had no idea what to say.

Selwyn spoke for them both, it seemed. "The traditional thing is for you to say, 'Yes'," he cajoled, his tone implying some deep significance. "What's wrong? You can't say the traditional thing?"

"It's not as simple as that," Kendra blurted awkwardly, brushing a strand of her auburn hair from her perspiring forehead. "You see, I . . . I have to figure out where I am and . . . well, Shay Brentwood—"

"Shay Brentwood!" Selwyn snapped. "What's he got to do with us?"

Kendra shook her head, as though forcing herself out of a daze. She hadn't realized she'd said Shay's name until Selwyn repeated it. It wasn't something she'd intended to say. She imagined it to be some involuntary quirk of subconscious phenomena that was reminding her of the terrible plight she was in, causing her to blurt out the root core of her problem. "I can't give you an answer while that man is hanging a rope around my neck," she told Selwyn apologetically. "Please understand."

Selwyn rose abruptly out of his chair and tossed down his napkin. Kendra was astonished. She'd never seen him so violently angry. "When you do know what to tell me," he exploded, "call me."

Kendra was shocked. Selwyn didn't even glance back at her. He just pivoted on his heels and stormed out of the restaurant, not caring how she got home though he'd driven her there, leaving her to the preoccupation of curious diners who all looked at her with accusing speculation. Embarrassed by the unwanted attention, she waved a bartender over and ordered a drink. He arrived dutifully with a martini. Kendra instantly swallowed a mouthful, then coughed uncontrollably for several seconds from the sheer strength of it.

Her pulse was racing as if she'd been running for her life, and in a way she had. First there had been the hurdle she was forced to leap over to get past the trauma and loss of her mother. Then her elevation to editor-in-chief of her father's newspaper had begun to add to the pressure.

The responsibility was like a soaring rock face she was expected to climb, and in her own determined way she'd scrambled her way up it, slipping a couple of times when she'd dealt with employees who seemed unable to accept her new status but at the top nonetheless, a powerhouse editor feared by all who came within a foot of her.

Outwardly, she was the epitome of confidence and control, but inwardly, she'd realized that there were many facets of her emotions she had not yet dealt with. The long distance track of life was a runway that was concrete, hard and cold, she decided. She wanted to escape, but where could she run?

Arlisa's impropriety and the prospect of watching that very rock face she'd climbed crumble about her was now adding pressure again. Shay Brentwood's threatening presence and having to find a hundred and fifty thousand dollars added more unbearable pressure. Now Selwyn's proposal was sending her into overdrive. She had to calm herself.

I've got to get through this, Kendra told her mind forcefully, again and again, the words resonating in her brain. *I've got to get through this.*

"You drink a lot?" The sudden sound of an African-American accent behind her jolted her body and caused her heart to stop as she turned and watched Shay Brentwood walk boldly around the small table and lower his bulk into what had been Selwyn's chair.

Kendra compressed her lips as if clenching her teeth at the same time, then forced enough relaxation to push out words in a slow, precise delivery that bespoke grimly held rage. "Only when stressed," she hissed icily. "I'd say the last few days came under that category."

Hard self-mockery answered her: "And I'm the cause, right?"

"That's my reigning sentiment." Kendra grimaced tersely, dispelling the undesired pleasure she felt at seeing him. He was immaculately dressed in grey designer trousers, a sporty white jersey, and a blue cashmere jacket. His short, dark, raven hair was salon groomed and slightly wet, indicating that he'd just come in from out of the grim rainy weather. His caramel, square jawline was shaven and tinged with a pleasant aftershave aroma, and he was looking at her with a thoughtful, almost watchful expression that was impossible to decipher.

"It'll all be over next week," he remarked, examining Kendra closely.

Kendra wondered if it was the low cleavage of her tight royal blue velour dress which had attracted his attention or whether he couldn't resist seeking her out to bother her again about his imminent takeover of her father's newspaper.

She decided that he didn't find her in the least attractive and that the lure of his approaching victory was what had brought him over to her table. Tossing out an equally combative remark, she fired off, "It should've been over the day your father crawled away like a baby, or is it that he's still looking for a toy to play with?" She stared at her enemy. "I could say I'm now the resident expert on Benjamin Brentwood now that I've done my homework." Kendra adopted a challenging position in her chair. "Let me see. He had teething problems back in nineteen seventy-two when he tried to publish the *Harlem News*, right? Poor Pops. Fell on his bottom with that one."

"He was learning the ropes," Shay informed her in defense of his father. "Sure, he made mistakes."

"And what about Pops's first steps in nineteen

eighty-one?" Kendra continued repressively. "He stacked up all his little bricks to put out America's first premier magazine for young teens, but he tried to run before he could walk. Stumbled big time."

"He miscalculated the market," Shay admitted drily. "America just wasn't ready for a revolutionary publication. But our new magazine is selling beyond our expectations coast to coast."

"And now Pops has crawled his way into cable TV," Kendra concluded, ignoring Shay's explanations. "I hear he's still shuffling around on his bottom, though, and hasn't quite learned how to stand up on his own yet."

Shay's eyes narrowed sardonically. "Hold it right there," he warned scathingly, his dusky brown eyes freezing over like iced cocoa. "My father's been leapfrogging ever since I was a kid."

"Yeah, right over the backs of smaller media publications," Kendra quipped knowingly. "How does it feel to know that you've deliberately put other Afro-American publications out of business?"

Shay straightened in his chair. "You're going to give me a lecture about enterprise and morality?" he raged.

"Someone has to," Kendra answered bluntly. "From what I've read in the news cuttings my research department have dug up, your father has intentionally used his influence to monopolize and control. He's tied distributors to exclusive contracts to circulate only his newspapers and magazines. Your cable TV syndicate doesn't accept advertising from any other media. And he's renowned for copycat tactics, deliberately publishing spoilers of someone else's ideas. Your family is presiding over a forty-seven million dollar industry because of unscrupulous and deceptive business practices."

Shay snatched at Kendra's wrist and caught it in a grip that locked her hand to the table. "Keep going and I'll have a team of lawyers all over you so fast for libel it'll feel like a rash." His eyes blazed furiously. "My father's earned a reputation as a hardworking, no-nonsense media player who knew exactly how to deliver news and advertising to the community. Because of him I'm no natty dreadlock, island mango picker doing a shuffle steppers rhythm on the seafront. And in spite of what you think," he interjected coldly, "we give back plenty to the community we serve."

"Which is why you're taking the *Nubian Chronicle*, right?" Kendra snapped, abruptly releasing her hand. "Black Britain's number one community paper should make a nice addition to the Brentwood's playroom."

"Let me remind you that your sister brought that situation about," came Shay's crude reply. "But don't worry, Kendra. We'll be doing things with it that your father never dreamed of."

"There's nothing wrong with the *Chronicle*," Kendra quickly defended. "It's everything my father ever dreamed it to be, and it makes an important media contribution."

"It's supposed to be a broadsheet, but it reads like tabloid trash," Shay stormed murderously. "And you know it. It doesn't analyze, it doesn't campaign. It just reacts. And when was the last time you guys broke a story that you didn't pick up from other media?"

"We run exclusives every now and then," Kendra wavered lamely, her brain desperately trying to recollect the last time they'd done one. "Our readership is always happy."

"Your circulation audits show that you have a seventeen percent fall in readership," Shay said knowingly. "That tells me the *Nubian Chronicle* is no longer reflecting the aspirations and concerns of its target audience."

His knowledge forced Kendra back into her chair. "Those figures—"

"And wasn't it just under a year ago that the *Chronicle* was branded as 'out of touch' by a group of college journalists at a publishing awards dinner?" Shay interrupted thoughtfully. "They also accused your father of being oblivious to the ethnic mix of your readership."

"They were letting off steam," Kendra bellowed, recalling the incident well and wondering how Shay came by his information. Three students had inquired of her father why he had not yet set up a scholarship fund to break wide-eyed hopefuls into the newspaper profession. Her father had thought himself competent after the recent loss of her mother to attend the British Publishers' Awards, but he'd handled the situation badly. The three students directed an avalanche of criticism against him, propelling him into further depression until he'd finally entrusted her as the family custodian of his life's work. It was an incident Kendra would rather forget.

"At least we're not into your deal crazy, dog-eat-dog world of checkbook journalism and unregistered handouts which my research assistant, Trevor has informed me much about," Kendra hit back. "I imagine that's the direction you'll be taking the *Chronicle*."

"To get a scoop and make that front page headline," Shay stormed shamelessly, "you have to know when to make a shrewd bid. That's newspaper politics. As for the direction we'll be taking the *Chronicle*, we'll immediately add an educational supplement, increase the regional and European coverage, and a finance and money section wouldn't go amiss, either."

Kendra raised an eyebrow in surprise, a reaction which somewhat abated her anger. "These plans," she nosily pried, probing for further revelations, "whose ideas are they?" She could hardly believe the arrogant

Benjamin Brentwood had anything to do with them. She was right.

"As executive vice-president of Brentwood Communications, I told my father what I felt were the *Chronicle*'s weaknesses and where I felt we could improve on your and your father's work," Shay admitted evenly. "I believe the *Nubian Chronicle* has great potential, and I also think its stature could be such that mainstream papers would follow its lead and seeks its opinions about our community. Interested observers from all over the world should even consider the *Chronicle* indispensable and a media tool from which they can learn."

"And you think you can take it there?" Kendra countered, a part of her reluctantly swept away by Shay's fresh vision and hope, and the uncompromising pace he wished to travel in order to revamp the *Nubian Chronicle*.

Shay nodded.

Kendra folded her arms across her breasts and contemplated him wryly. She detected honesty in his face, sincerity in his eyes, and an invisible pride of thought which seemed to emanate from him and encircle her entire being. If he'd been her brother she would've felt truly blessed.

There were times she'd often wondered whether her father had wished she'd been a son so she could continue the Davenport name as proprietor of the *Nubian Chronicle*. Instead, here she was listening to his enemy's son who was planning to steal that legacy from her. It was almost odd listening to it all, knowing that she was involved only to a point before she would be silently discarded because a master plan deemed that a cruel necessity.

To Shay Brentwood she was of refugee status, a foreign, external problem that needed to be eradicated.

And added to the strangeness which encased her was the knowledge that all this was coming from the man who also seemed to possess the power to sweep her into the bosom of passion and release her into the arms of expectations and dreams.

Unsure how to react, yet certain that she should not believe that all had been lost, she cautioned, "You're getting ahead of yourself, aren't you?"

"Not really," Shay responded wistfully. "But I guess your date did. What happened?"

"Sorry?" Kendra breathed, startled.

"What'd you tell him?" Shay taunted boldly. "The way he shot out of here like a bat out of hell, I'd say it was something disappointing."

Kendra gasped. Shay Brentwood was far too perceptive for comfort. Until that point, she'd forgotten all about Selwyn's proposal. Surely he couldn't know about that, too, she mused, wondering whether the words were engraved across her forehead. Absurdly, she placed her hand against it, and naturally there was nothing there. His foresight, however, annoyed her immensely, and she scoffed, "That's none of your business."

"Well, a lot of guys don't have the ego . . . strength to deal with a successful woman," he said tersely. "I suppose you intimidate them."

"Do I intimidate you?" Kendra bristled, deciding to behave exactly as the powerhouse editor Shay obviously knew her to be.

He laughed. "Why should you? I have powers that in modern circles are awesome."

"And you always get what you want, right?" Kendra seethed, nodding away her disbelief at Shay's egocentric behavior. "That's why you've considered me fair game. Well, take a good look, Mr. Brentwood, because you're never going to have me."

Shay's smile deepened wickedly. "You're allowed sex after success, Kendra," he advised. "Or hasn't the Right Honorable Minister of Parliament discovered that yet?"

"You're deplorable."

"Am I deplorable now?" Shay teased. "Maybe I should kiss you again."

"Don't bank on it." Kendra reeled, suppressing the delicious rush of pleasure she felt on hearing the suggestion. "On the Kendra scale, Kendra being ten of course, I'd give you a six."

"So," Shay pressed in his lazy voice, "did you tell Mr. M.P. he got a three, or a two?"

Kendra shook her head, refusing to answer.

Shay raised his eyebrows. "A zero? Zilch?"

This man was unbelievable. "I don't want to talk with someone who's more interested in my love life," Kendra diverted, downing the last of her martini to still her nerves. "I'm going home. I'm sure your date is waiting." Reaching for her handbag and then her coat, she raised herself from the table and started to make her way toward the cashier.

"Wait a minute," Shay said, following Kendra to the cashier where she had produced a credit card in settlement of her meal with Selwyn.

"I don't have a date."

"No?" Kendra took a brief look around the room. "Why don't I believe you?"

"Believe what you like," Shay answered wryly.

Kendra raised a brow curiously. "Why are you here? Not following me, I hope?"

"Look," Shay coaxed, his dusky brown eyes registering pleasure at seeing her long, shapely legs below the short, deadly provocative dress she was wearing, which ended four inches above her knees. "I have two tickets for a party tonight. Would you like to come?"

"What kind of party?" Kendra enquired absently.

"A friend of mine is launching his new nightclub."

"Millennium Two thousand," Kendra acknowledged, realizing this was the place Selwyn had planned to take her after their meal. "I know about it, but I don't want to go with you," she lied.

"Okay," Shay suggested, undaunted by her refusal of him, "let's call a truce."

Kendra's eyebrows rose in speculation. "A truce?"

"Yeah," Shay prompted, his voice etched in encouraging tones of gentle persuasion. "You shut down your battle stations for tonight and I shut down mine."

Kendra couldn't resist a grin. "Do we throw away all our ammunition, too?" she teased.

"We bury it, and all our differences, with a shovel," Shay cajoled, noting her curled-lip smile. "Then we bury the shovel."

Kendra laughed, unconvinced, as she retrieved her credit card and receipt. "I think I'll still go home."

"Well, it's your call," Shay enticed, his gaze traveling down to the three-inch blue suede shoes which embraced Kendra's delicate, brown ankles. "I guess I made the mistake of thinking you knew how to get down, with your bad self an' all."

Kendra's face froze. Was this man suggesting that she didn't know how to dance? Pointing a finger sternly into his chest, she admonished scathingly, "I know how to get a groove on."

"Yeah?" Shay countered, his firm hand snapping over hers, his dusky eyes baiting her, challenging her to prove it to him.

By the time Kendra returned his hard, rebellious stare, her sharp, positive answer was out before she could stop herself. Clear, concise, and suffused with excitement.

Five

Booyakka-ba-da. Boom-da-bombastic. Boom-dum-bum.

"Great music," Shay shouted above the noise as he helped Kendra remove her wet overcoat, handed over the two private door entry passes in his possession, and surveyed the specially handpicked party troopers who were dancing in the flash of colored lights, spinning water fountains, and wealth of high-tech paraphernalia one would imagine in a twenty-first century nightclub.

Kendra nodded her agreement as she, too, observed the club's vast expanse and the gyrating humanity within it. She noticed that many of the girls were clad in very little clothing, with hair sporting varying rainbow shades of indigo, red, violet, and green, that most of the men wore expensive gold jewelry around their necks and fingers. There were others, too, who wore more formal clothes, workaholic Buppies who'd come straight from their offices with mobile phones and filofaxes, holding in their paunches whilst pretty young things with long legs, short skirts, and straight weave-on manes clasped their arms possessively.

"You okay?" Shay yelled, catching Kendra's hand and then her wrist to lace his warm fingers through hers.

"I'm fine," Kendra assured, welcoming his strong

grip and aware that his fingers were stroking softly against hers, protectively.

"Well, you feel as tight as a drum," Shay roared, his voice almost dimmed by the music. "Just relax."

Kendra didn't feel she would have a problem doing that, not as long as she was with Shay Brentwood. But she reminded herself that it had been nearly fourteen months since she'd last attended a nightclub, and that was a long time by any young woman's standards.

Since her mother's untimely departure and the onset of her dating Selwyn, she'd always requested to go out to dinner, or was happy to accompany him to some black-tie function. He was often invited to them. It was only at Selwyn's suggestion that they'd scheduled a visit to Millennium Two thousand, and she was sure she would've connived some excuse to release herself from going at the eleventh hour. In truth, since her mother's passing, she'd wondered if she would ever be able to dance again.

"Come on," Shay urged, pulling her past traffic of brown legs under velvet and leather hotpants and into the heart of the dance floor, where heated, swaying party troopers were twisting their bodies in permutations of visible, unadulterated craziness. "Let's dance."

Kendra instantly wanted to protest, but Shay had already gripped her by the waist and was pulling her to his rigid frame, firmly fixing her against the contours of his body so that she was able to feel his warm, firm chest. They were moving among too much laughter, she thought wearily. Loud, bawdy, pointless laughter. And there were too many disjunctive conversations swirling around her head, meaningless talk booming off her eardrums as everybody competed to be heard.

Then suddenly the music changed. The bass became heavy, the tune became mesmerizing, and as if by rhythmic consent, everybody quietly slowed down to steadily waft their bodies to the reggae drum's hypnotic beat. Kendra recognized the song to be a dancehall favorite, a Jamaican import which had recently swept the charts, placing yet another Caribbean newcomer among the top ten recording artists vying for the number one spot.

She felt Shay pull her closer, aware of a warmth enveloping her as she instinctively reciprocated by locking her arms firmly around his neck. The music demanded physical response; movement of the feet, shaking of the torso, twisting of the body in time with the lax rhythm, and Kendra obliged by allowing Shay to guide her through the idyllic pulsations.

"Tell me about this dress," he whispered into her ear, his hand moving tenderly against the soft, blue velour fabric.

"Selwyn didn't approve," Kendra whispered back shyly, feeling a little inhibited as she realized that Shay liked her in it.

"You're kidding?" he gasped, pulling her closer. "A man can forget himself seeing you dressed like this."

Kendra licked her dry lips, disbelieving that this man was making her feel so feminine. Then the vocal harmonies, the brash, drugging percussion which often consisted of an abrupt jump from one beat to the next, the intricate electric bass in which the accents fell in the most unexpected places but in which the heavy drum was never lost, all produced a most curious effect. They began to work a magic inside Kendra, as if a bewitching cabala held her spellbound so that she felt she was about to groan and encourage the DJ to do his worst with the club-mix rhythm.

He was manipulating the sound, causing octaves to rapidly shift in runs and jumps off the beat, playing with it like a radical activist looking to cause havoc. And he was succeeding. Kendra had never felt so free and suddenly uninhibited. And Shay was incredible at keeping pace with the animated rhythm, anticipating every diversion in the music so that by the time it fell into an intoxicating dub, he was steering her with consummate ease to where every risqué beat fell.

While he did so, his exploring hands roamed around Kendra's waistline, up her back, down her sides, and then settled on her hips, coaxing her to move seductively against him.

Kendra was perspiring as her body worshiped the euphonic, lyrical, melodic adaptation of original reggae truly stylized into another dimension of Afrocentric interpretation which the music scene simply called "ragga". She marveled at the way she was enjoying herself, delighted at the week's pressures falling from her quivering limbs, but secretly she knew that it was being with Shay which was causing this turnabout. Nestled against him, she felt good. Superlative. Perfect.

"Enjoying yourself?" Shay whispered against her ear, his tone coarse and huskily taut as though he required some form of assurance. It seemed to stroke all over Kendra's skin, enlivening her nerve ends as he familiarized himself with her waistline once more.

Kendra didn't know whether he meant being with him at the nightclub or being in his arms, but she whispered back a positive response. She felt rather than heard the slight expulsion of Shay's breath as she leaned back against his chest, molding the fullness of her body to the firm, pectoral muscles she detected beneath his clothes.

"Good." Shay sounded more relaxed.

Kendra suddenly wondered whether he'd been worried that she might not find his company to her liking. After all, she thought, they were still technically enemies.

She looked up into his face, expecting to see some reservation there, but Shay's gaze was boring a direct appeal into her, a silent invocation commanding her to react. She couldn't stop herself from treacherously responding to the warm wickedness reflected in their dusky, brown depths. Surely there was no harm in playing along with him . . . for a while, she thought, reminding herself of the truce they'd pledged.

His intention was crystal clear to her, and the erotic demand in his caramel face shattered all her disciplined resolutions about never allowing him to kiss her again. She felt his lips imprint a gentle kiss across her forehead, over one eyelid, then across her cheek, telling her how exquisitely feminine he found her. Then, slowly, they moved over her lips in pliable, supple persuasion as their bodies cruised with the music.

Kendra exultantly surrendered herself to the oblivion she was plunged into where nothing existed except this man, the dub rhythm, and the explosive, raw passion between them.

His tongue plunged inward for a sweet, arousing taste of her, and suddenly the music was dimmed as she heard only the dictates of her heart drumming madly against her rib cage at a discordant, rampant pace. She could feel Shay's heart thumping as madly as hers, and yet Kendra knew he was restraining himself.

Everything within her rebelled against his struggle for control. She didn't want him to retreat, but to feel as reckless and needful as she did. Provocatively, she slid her tongue along the softness of his lips, playfully allowing it to retreat and then probe teasingly into the pink, wet flesh of his mouth.

A low, guttural sound broke from Shay's throat. "Baby . . ." It was a deep, sibilant groan of wild desire, and his grip tightened around her waist.

Satisfied with the pleasure she'd evoked in him, Kendra drew his lips to her own, yielding as Shay took them in a succession of slow, tempting mouthfuls. She couldn't remember a time when she'd taken so much pleasure in a man. Not even with Selwyn had she behaved in so . . . risky a way. Shay was so relaxed, attentive, strong; only he brought out something infinitely wild inside her, and she wanted more. For this one evening she would allow herself to fall in love . . . a little. Only a little, her mind cautioned before the music suddenly came back and Shay's hungry, insistent lips were abruptly being dragged away from her.

"Come up for air, Bro," a voice interrupted, throwing Kendra back into the world of reality.

"J B!" Shay reluctantly greeted his brother with a firm hand gesture, his forehead creasing into a frown as he suddenly remembered that he was to have met Joel's wife at the restaurant he'd just left. "Where's Rhona?"

"I don't know," Joel Brentwood dismissed casually, looking intently over his younger brother's shoulder at Kendra. "I'm here solo."

Kendra felt herself flinch at his cool, calculating observation, though she realized he didn't seem at all surprised at seeing her with his brother. His wife, Rhona, was U.S. Senator Morgan Layton's daughter, she thought, referring to the new memory files stored in her head, thanks to Trevor. J B had married into influential power, as Morgan Layton was part of the new wave of African-American senators to take office in the current administration. Joel was also two years older than Shay, thirty-six, and possessed his own attributes for attracting murmurs of approval from the female sex. He was an inch shorter than Shay, she noted, and he had the same raven hair and same complexion. He was mustached, wider in the chest, and he had his father's eyes. He was also currently engaged in talks about cutting in on a disabled English cable TV channel, hoping to extend his father's monopoly by syndicating their U.S. cable network on the channel to broadcast across Europe.

"Arlisa didn't tell me you were a party animal, too," Joel suddenly said above the rhythm of a new beat.

"J B told me you two had met," Shay acknowledged.

"Briefly, at a British Black Networkers function in Birmingham," Kendra roared in explanation. "You were flexing a little managerial muscle," she told Joel as she fabricated a shallow smile to disguise her loathing of how he'd betrayed her sister, choosing her words diplomatically. "We all enjoyed your speech on money dispersal and how we should all endeavor to find more ways to encourage spending within our own community."

"I remembered you leaving shortly after we were introduced," Joel responded drily, as though he'd been offended.

"I had to catch a train back to London," Kendra yelled above the music. "I had an early morning meeting."

Joel had opened his mouth in readiness to add something further when another man approached them; short, stout, wearing densely dark sunshades and flagged with an entourage of women decked out in zebra-patterned dresses. "Shay," the newcomer croaked, skipping with a two-step gait toward them. "So, what d'ya think of my new nightclub?" he inquired with a Chicago accent.

"Great," Shay answered with a huge smile, though his eyes displayed his resentment at yet another intrusion.

"This your girl?" the man with the heavy voice asked as he dipped his sunshades to make a judgment of her. "She's got it going on." He nodded in approval. His voice lowered slightly. "Listen, Man, I have to thank you for what you did—you know, being in my corner the other day." Turning immediately to Joel, the newcomer challenged, "I've a bone to pick with you, J B.

Where's that advertising agent you promised to hook me—"

"Come on," Shay urged, seizing his opportunity to pull Kendra away from the two men. "I didn't come here to spend time with them." He took her across the dance floor, through the bottom grinding crowd, past the sheer yardage of humanity impaled at the bar, and then called a halt when he'd reached the other side of the club. Guiding Kendra back into his arms, he held her against his steely chest.

They danced silently to the slow tune, their bodies reacquainting in a communion Kendra was reluctant to break. She realized that she'd never felt this way with Selwyn. He was always much more reserved in the way he kissed her. There had never been fiery, unrestrained passion between them. Probably she wasn't being fair to him, she thought, being sensible. She'd never given him an opportunity to take liberties with her. There'd been other men, of course—two to be exact—but Selwyn had unfortunately caught her at a time when most of her emotions had been spent mourning the loss of her mother.

Now, as she felt new, masculine hands embrace her slithering body, and lips planting attentive little kisses down her neck, inflaming an uncomfortable craving for deeper intimacy, Kendra lost all thought of Selwyn Owens.

During the next two hours, they danced, ate, drank, and kissed their way through Calypso, Ragga, New Jack Swing, Hip Hop, Jungle, House, New Classic Soul, and even a little old-timers Ska—a rhythm which transported Kendra back to her childhood days when her mother played the two-tone beat on the gramophone as she cleaned the house.

By the time she'd finally begged Shay to leave the dance floor, dehydrated and totally exhausted, he was laughing heartily at her for being a stick-in-the-mud and being unable to keep up with him.

"At the advent of ragtime in the nineteen twenties," he was telling her, "you would have had to at least get through the Shiver, Lindy Hop, Black Bottom, Grizzly Bear, Humpback Rag, Eagle Rock, Turkey Trot, Bunny Hug, Texas Tommy, Scratchin' the Gravel, and Ballin' the Jack before anyone would've allowed you to leave the floor."

"Are you really that old?" Kendra joked, admiring his knowledge of the many dance crazes which she knew had shaken Harlem.

"Just a little history lesson," Shay said, laughing, as they walked toward the main exit door for fresh air.

"Really." Kendra giggled, made drunk by the music and a little dizzy from the amount she'd consumed in drink. Slipping her hand through Shay's elbow to steady herself, she laughed, "You'll be telling me about Thomas Dorsey next."

"The Godfather of Gospel," Shay clarified. "Gospel was where it all began. Everything. Even the Civil Rights Movement had its roots in that."

"Another history lesson?" Kendra asked sweetly.

"I like black history," Shay admitted. "I like to read a lot of that cultural stuff. Helps me know where I'm from, and to define myself as a person."

"To be reckoned with." Kendra smiled wickedly.

Shay adored that curled-lip smile. It captivated him in ways he couldn't begin to explain. "Lady, you're incorrigible. Come on." He laced his fingers through hers. "The rain has stopped. Let's take a walk."

"Now?" Kendra breathed. "It's one o'clock in the morning."

"Just a block or two," Shay said persuasively.

"I don't know what you Americans mean by a block," Kendra protested, already feeling Shay gently pulling her along. "Is it ten yards? Twenty-five? Do I have a choice?"

"No." Shay chuckled, taking her around a corner.

The night stars twinkled above her head, and as Kendra cast her eyes down the long, commercial street filled with its galaxy of streetlights, which were bouncing like shimmering rhinestones against the wet sidewalk and camouflaging all the scars and flaws that were normally present in the glare of day, her sense of closeness to Shay intensified.

"Nighttime always makes a city look better," she said, casually peering around at fashion shops lighted up to show off their wares, at furniture and interior houses exhibiting their finest for the home-conscious, at the jewelry merchants parading treasures in their security-protected windows—the most exquisite accessories for the financially stable.

"Looks like Milton did his homework," Shay surmised, admiring the Canary Wharf Tower which loomed up in the night sky. "This is one of the better parts of London, right?"

"Newer parts," Kendra amended. "Canary Wharf is still relatively young . . . about six years old. All the big companies are moving here . . . banks, restaurants, investment companies. . . ."

"How long is the Thames River?" Shay inquired, noting its close proximity to where they were as his fingers closed ever more tightly around Kendra's.

"I'm not sure," Kendra admitted, enjoying the delicious rush of feeling she felt as she, too, tightened her fingers. "It runs right through London, though."

"Too long for us to walk along?" Shay joked.

"Don't even think about it," Kendra teased.

"You must do something to keep that incredible figure." He laughed.

"I don't exercise. I hate it."

"You're not a vegetarian?"

"No. I like my meat too much."

"Well, your meat is agreeing with you," Shay assayed warmly, appraising every part of her slowly before his eyes met hers. He was amazed to find that she was treating him to that curled-lip smile that made him believe her the most remarkable creature he'd ever met. "There's not an ounce of fat on you. Has Mr. M.P. discovered that firsthand yet?"

Some of the warmth left Kendra's eyes. "Shay, that's really none of your business."

For a moment, Shay's gaze danced merrily into hers, then he said, "You're here with me, so I was just wondering."

"I'm here because we've called a truce, remember? I don't ask you about your girlfriends."

"Ask me anything," Shay openly invited.

Kendra looked at him, finding herself accepting his offer. "Okay. Were you serious about any of them?"

"No. Should I have been?"

She looked at him more steadily as their gait slowed a little, thinking of analyzing him but deciding against it. "Only you can answer that."

It hadn't been her imagination. Shay had straightened his shoulders noticeably, as if he were holding on to a breath. It made Kendra feel awkward, and so they walked for a while, until she was unable to take the silence. Her mind feeling around for another subject of conversation, she said, "Isn't it odd that we've never met before?"

Shay turned and studied her nonchalantly, then returned his gaze to the street. "Yeah, considering what you must've heard about me from your family."

Kendra tensed, aware that Shay had felt it in her fingers. "My family never talked about you, specifically. More your father."

"Well, now that we have met," Shay taunted, "there's nothing we can do about that." Then, as an afterthought, he added, "Sometimes destiny follows no rules."

"You think it's destiny that your father is after my father's newspaper?" Kendra started, certain that Shay had become irritable because she'd refused to answer his earlier probing question.

"The fact that we're even talking right now is a miracle, considering," Shay cautioned, stopping in his tracks and letting go of her hand. "We have a truce, don't we?"

Kendra stopped and heaved a shaky breath, disliking the loss of warmth she experienced at the release of his fingers. Tipping her head slightly, and allowing a newborn smile to play upon her lips to persuade him to hold her again, knowing that she really didn't want to argue, she said, "Yes."

Shay touched the end of her nose with one fingertip. "Okay." He laced his fingers through hers once more and they resumed walking. "So tell me. Where did you go to school?"

"Right here in London," Kendra answered easily. "Then I studied journalism and photography for four years at the College of Printing and Distributive Trades."

"Here in London?"

"Yeah. And you?"

"I graduated from high school in New York, then was an undergrad student at Morehouse College, where I chose Mass Communications as my major."

"Morehouse?" Kendra thought for a second, recalling that she'd heard of this institution. "Isn't that an Atlanta school for African-American men?"

Shay nodded. "Built in eighteen sixty-seven for making men out of boys. In fact, I met Milton Fraser there. He was doing an architecture program. He always wanted to do something with buildings—universally.

He got a lot of local opposition here, though, with his nightclub. Nearby residents complained to their M.P."

Colin Parker, Kendra recalled. "Selwyn mentioned it. Is that why you threatened him?"

"Shoop." Shay scowled, shaking his head, his eyes fiery. "Mr. M.P. leveled some . . . disobliging remarks at me when I went over to Milt's club to see if he needed any help before the big night," he explained. "Selwyn Owens was there, making accusations. Somehow, I got embroiled, and . . . well . . . I saw him to the door. What is it with that guy, anyway?"

"I'm not sure," Kendra confessed uncomfortably. "He lost his wife a few years ago. She died suddenly."

"I see."

"I don't know if she was sick . . . I never asked him," she explained. "But her name was Katherine, and he told me how ironic it was that her life insurance policy enabled him to become a full time M.P. Most other M.P.s work, you see."

"Which political party is he with?"

"Labour. They won the election last year."

"They're like the Democrats, right?"

"I suppose so, if Conservatives are like the Republicans."

"So, is he good at what he does . . . being an M.P., I mean?" Shay grinned.

"Selwyn's a good M.P.," Kendra chirped in response. "He's with the Brent-South constituency in Middlesex, North London, and was the first black M.P. to be elected there."

"Yeah?"

"Yeah," Kendra confirmed. "He spends much of his time on local bread-and-butter issues, rather than on national ones like the European Monetary Union. He's not a Euro-sceptic but he's not a Euro-fanatic, either." She laughed nervously, only to forget that she was referring to a man who had that night made her a proposal of marriage. "In fact ... he's so neutral on the subject that for weeks I've been trying to tie him down to an opinion on whether Britain should lose its sovereign pound to a single European currency."

"I can see you admire him a lot." Shay grimaced.

Kendra flinched, knowing that she'd never thought of herself as a politician's wife. Understanding the pressures of Selwyn's work and of the society to which he belonged, where importance was attached to social class and title, she acknowledged that he was part of a world she could never accept. What she felt wasn't so much admiration but silent recognition that Selwyn still held the "old school" set of values. "He has his own qualities," she murmured quietly. "They may be different from yours or mine, but he has them all the same." Tactfully moving from the subject, she quickly asked, "What was your childhood like?"

"It had its downside," Shay intoned, "like being on Pops's coattails when I was a kid. There were always people sucking up to me to get to him."

"So you always knew you were going to work with him?" Kendra probed shamelessly. "Maybe take over one day?"

Shay shrugged. "Like a sense of vocation? Who knows? Pops wanted nothing less than to revitalize the black media. Instead he revolutionized it. J B and I, we just hopped on board with the knowledge of everything he'd taught us. I did originally want to play basketball."

"Professionally?" Kendra inquired with surprise. "Like for the Bulls or something?"

"Yeah," Shay admitted. "Sometime during the summer between my sophomore and junior years at Morehouse, I developed a love for it. I used to play point guard for an amateur team back home."

"What's a point guard?"

"My job was setting up plays and moving the ball down the court so the scoring guard could take a shot at the basket."

Kendra raised a well-marked eyebrow. "I would've thought you'd be more interested in pitching the ball into the net."

"I used to play scoring guard once," Shay began, "but I got into an accident with another player and dislocated my shoulder. Pops decided he didn't want me out there dodging team players, so now I indulge that fantasy by sponsoring my own team."

"You have a team?"

He shrugged, non-committal. "I like the idea of supporting young talent. I was lucky, but not many kids with dreams have someone in their corner."

"I was wondering what you meant about putting your team's basketball trophies in the cabinet at my office," Kendra said wryly. "For now, I think they're best where they are. I wouldn't appreciate them in the same way you do, since I don't understand the game."

"I'm going to have to take you to a ball game sometime," Shay offered. "After watching, you'll understand its attraction."

"You Americans really know how to sell a sport." Kendra smiled, considering exploring the mystery, and knowing that the stylish rituals and hoop techniques were reasons enough as to why the game had found such a special place in the hearts of players and spectators. "That's why it's so popular and not elitist, like cricket."

"Cricket's a drag," Shay drawled. "I once watched an ICC Trophy Final between Kenya and Bangladesh and decided that I didn't like the responsibility placed on the batsman. Besides, the game lasts too long."

"Not quite like partaking of the ballyhoo at the opening of an NBA season, right?"

"Right."

They had reached the end of the street and Shay aptly turned and directed them back toward the club. When they'd established a steady stride and had walked a while in communal silence, Shay ventured, "So, you haven't told me what you wanted to be?"

"Would you believe I always wanted to work on my father's newspaper?" Kendra began proudly. "Do you know, he still has an original copy of the very first edition he ever published in Britain way back in nineteen sixty-three? It was only like a newsletter back then, but I feel really honored knowing that it was an indispensable information sheet to all the men and women who came into England from Jamaica to find work in the service industries. It's quite an eye opener to compare it to the present *Nubian Chronicle.*"

"Pops still has the original Jamaican editions," Shay said in response. "All three of them."

Kendra flinched. Wasn't there ever going to be a time without constant reminders of what Benjamin Brentwood had lost to her father? It seemed ludicrous to her that he should have kept keepsakes of his childhood dream, having entrusted all of it, and its mounting debts, to the responsible hands of her father. "I suppose your father saw that as valid justification to take the *Chronicle* back," she aimed at him, unable to hold back the remark.

"Ouch," Shay quipped as though her words had wounded him. He instantly forced a smile to his lips the moment Kendra looked at him, concerned. "Truce?"

Kendra smiled gingerly. "Truce."

"Okay," Shay ventured carefully. "While we're on the subject, tell me how did you handle becoming editor of your father's newspaper?"

Kendra studied him, hardly imagining that Shay Brentwood should care at all, under the circumstances. But he'd asked, so she offered truthfully, "Badly, at first.

There was bold and blatant resistance to my appointment, both inside and outside the *Nubian Chronicle*'s offices. Those outside had justifiable concern about whether or not I could maintain the newspaper's high editorial standards. To them, I was inexperienced. I hadn't worked as a freelancer, hadn't done radio broadcasting to widen my scope. I never trained with a national daily paper. So how was I to handle a weekly? I was simply a graduate who'd fallen into her father's footsteps."

"But you had worked on the *Chronicle* before you became editor?"

"Yes," Kendra admitted. "I was fashion editor. But that wasn't enough for some people. Many still felt I was a long way from being short-listed for the Race In the Media Award. It was hard."

"Did you make any changes?"

"I changed a lot of things," Kendra declared passionately. "I had my own vision for a new *Nubian Chronicle* and I hired the smartest people I could find. Soon, the objections turned to applause, and despite what you think about our editorial I quite like what I've achieved."

"You have tremendous spirit," Shay admitted. "I can see why you're so tough."

"Well, your father's untimely interference hasn't made things much easier," Kendra remarked with caution. "Doesn't he have enough?"

She noticed a momentary mask of guilt cross Shay's delectable features. "My father always liked a good incentive to work hard to get what he feels he deserves," he told her calmly. "When he began to broadcast on TV in nineteen eighty, he was only doing two hours a week, because not many homes had cable. Now look where he is. He feels he's in a deserving position."

"But many people have gotten hurt," Kendra reminded. "Doesn't he have any compassion, or love for anything?"

"My father's a lobbyist," Shay explained. "What time is there for love when you're building an empire? He had to lobby the National Cable Association, appeal to Congress and the Regulatory Commission to support the embryonic cable industry. He thought that every racial group should have its voice, and if he'd become vulnerable over whose toes he was treading on, he wouldn't have gotten very far."

"I wonder what all that power has cost him, personally." Kendra pondered aloud, almost absently.

Shay glared at her. "I don't know what you mean," he told her, his voice pained at her interpretation. "You seem to be implying that my father isn't human. I think it takes a special kind of human, particularly a black male, to raise seventy-two million in his first public offering on the New York Stock Exchange. October, nineteen ninety-one will always be a special year in African-American history for that."

Kendra breathed raggedly, aware that she was talking objectionably about this man's father yet unable to forget that she had an admirable one of her own. "I'm glad that you feel so elated by what Benjamin has done," she conceded. "I can see now why you respect him so. But my father is deserving, too. He's a man of integrity, and he would be wholly satisfied with just knowing that his being here had made a change. A good change."

Shay stopped in his tracks and faced Kendra. For a moment, their eyes locked and held, betraying the unquestionable fascination each held for the other. Something compelling and all encompassing seemed to shine between them right there, a certainty that what had happened between their families, and presently between them, would change them both in ways neither wanted or welcomed.

"Look," Shay said warmly, "I'm not going to waste time arguing the night away about two old men when this time belongs to us. We had fun tonight. Let's keep that, okay?"

He bent his head toward her, then paused. Shay knew he was hovering on the brink of something he felt it wise not to begin, but when he looked into Kendra's face and again watched as she curled her lips in that slow motion smile that captivated him so, whispering an impassioned, "You're right," he couldn't help but dip his head and gather her lips into his.

The kiss was deep and unhurried with come hither invitations which each implanted on the other. Kendra felt that she was swimming out of her depth, and shivered as a night breeze swept up against them.

"Cold?" Shay asked, dragging his mouth away, trying to keep his heart from ramming in his chest like a jackhammer.

"Yes," Kendra breathed, failing miserably to stop the fluttering in her stomach. Strange, she thought, that she hadn't felt cold before.

"Here." Shay took off his blue cashmere jacket and put it around her. "Let's go back inside," he urged. "There's about half an hour of dancing time left."

"We've done enough dancing in there already," Kendra chimed in as they hurried back toward the entrance door. "The Donkey, The Butterfly, The Boogle. And I'm sure that Kingston Shuffle you showed me has done my back in."

"Maybe I should take you home and give you a back rub you'll never forget," Shay suggested seductively.

Kendra was feeling totally dazed by the thought of what that might entail when a harsh voice suddenly caused her face to freeze in profound shock. Selwyn's solid, grim frame was illuminated in front of her, his physical presence plainly and incredibly real.

Six

"This isn't for real," Selwyn raged furiously, disbelieving that he was actually seeing Kendra wrapped in Shay Brentwood's jacket. He rushed over to her, his right hand raised in a threatening manner, as if intent on striking her.

Shay instantly blocked the move with his left hand, but Selwyn caught his arm and twisted it round, pushing Shay up against a wall and pinning him there with such brute force that two framed pictures—one of Fats Domino, the other Ella Fitzgerald—fell crashing to the floor, splintering into pieces.

"If you're spoiling for a fight, Mister, then I'll give you one," Selwyn spat out murderously.

"You looking to take me out?" Shay growled in challenging response. "You're going to have to do better than this."

Before Kendra could even blink Shay had released his hand, punched Selwyn in the stomach, then knocked him to the floor with a heavy thud. Her throat released a terrifying scream as Selwyn quickly rose to his feet and felt the side of his mouth where the second punch had landed. It'd begun to bleed.

"Oh my God," Kendra screeched as three men walked unsteadily out of the club laughing. "Stop them," she appealed to the youngest of the three, her voice raised to a high crescendo as she observed Selwyn taking a menacing step forward.

"Get a load of this," one bellowed in amazement, his voice tinged with uncontrollable excitement. "Stu," he immediately ordered, "you referee. Brendon, go pass the word."

As two stood guard and the other rushed back into the club yelling, "Fight in the house . . . fight in the house!" Kendra's innards churned into a sickening knot. Within seconds, she watched incredulously as prospective spectators began to file out of the club, intent on encouraging the two men to engage in a fistful onslaught.

"Check this out." A young man wheeled around, suddenly pulling a stash of crisp, paper money from his trouser pocket. Holding the handful in his palm, he told a friend, "Hey, Brotha. You wanna piece of the action? I put fifty on Shay Brentwood. I heard he's a slam super dunk when it comes to pitching a ball through a hoop."

"I'll cover it," another man quickly yelled, deal crazy and looking to profit from the situation.

"No," Kendra roared, disbelieving that she was actually witnessing such a colossal exchange of sterling. Her gaze moved in desperate search around the number of unfamiliar faces for someone who would help. Someone who would stop them before Selwyn decided to make a bad career move and hit back. When she finally saw Joel quickly pushing his way through to the front of the small crowd, she felt overwhelming relief. "Stop them, please," she appealed, tearful and earnest.

"You stay here," Joel commanded, sidling his way around the two men, careful not to disturb them as they glared at each other. When he reached a point where it looked as though he could strategically intervene,

Kendra was starkly amazed to hear another assurance drop from Joel's steely lips. "Okay, Bro," he coached. "I got your back. Take him on the left."

Kendra couldn't prevent the tears which fell as her anxiousness gave way to unbearable anxiety. The wall was covered completely with framed pictures of all time greats; Duke Ellington, Billie Holliday, Nat King Cole. Any more breakage and they could get seriously hurt, she thought, fearful of the awful truth that she was the only one who wanted this dreadful thing to end. And it was all her fault, she accepted. How could she possibly have done something so selfish to a man who'd just hours ago proposed marriage to her? The devastation on Selwyn's face on his seeing her with Shay reflected in her tormented mind, even as she caught sight of Shay taking a retaliatory step forward in readiness to accept Selwyn's challenge, when it came.

"Shay, don't!" she cried, dissolving into guilty tears as she jostled her way through the crowd and deliberately wedged herself into the small space between them. "Selwyn, I'm sorry. I'm so sorry," she apologized, deep repentance and remorse etched in her voice.

"Get away from me, Keisha." Selwyn bristled offensively.

"Keisha? Her name's Kendra," Shay amended arrogantly, gripping Kendra by the waist and bodily removing her from what he considered to be imminent danger. Forcing her behind him, his eyes narrowed sternly. "Have you forgotten her name already?"

Selwyn's expression was dejected but incredibly fierce. "I know all about her." He bristled harshly, his voice full of irony and deceptive scorn. "She likes to play guys like us against each other. It's a sport with her."

Kendra's mouth fell open in consternation. "That's not true!" she screeched. *Why was he saying this?*

"Shut up, Kendra," Selwyn fumed with contempt. "He doesn't believe you."

"Oh God," she murmured.

"You'd do well to call on the Almighty," he hissed bitterly. "You're going to need him."

"Guys . . . guys." A nervous Milton Fraser came running to the scene, dread planted across his frightful expression. "Shay, Buddy, don't do this to me," he prayed before his eyes fell on the broken pictures. "Geez, look at the glass." He began to fidget with a thin, gold chain around his neck as he moved slowly among the broken pieces. "Do you realize I could get sued for this?" he ranted. "Some idiot's gonna say they fell on the glass and—"

"Shut up, Milt," Shay demanded. Milton gulped as he watched his friend glare combatively at Selwyn Owens. "One of your . . . guests is just leaving."

"You imbecile," Selwyn blazed in return, brushing himself down and wiping the side of his mouth, recalling he'd received a punch there. "I'm going," he jabbed, fixing the tie beneath his jacket preparatory to leaving. "But I'm warning you, Shay Brentwood. By the time I'm through exposing you and your family for what you are, you won't have a tin pot to piss in or a window to throw it out of."

The silence was at breakneck level when Selwyn walked boldly out of the building. Kendra lowered her head. Every part of her was shaking like a leaf in winter, cold and fragile, and easily broken.

"I guess that makes two people out for me. You and Mr. M.P." Shay breathed, coming face-to-face with her. Taking a firm hold of her arm he commanded, "You're going to tell me what all that was really about."

Kendra shivered. "Not here," she pressed, too petrified to look at him. Reaching into her handbag, she found her coat ticket and handed it to him.

"I'll be right back." Shay threw an annoyed look around the group of people as he pushed his way back into the building to retrieve Kendra's overcoat. He then grimaced when they began to block his exit, each delaying his departure to hail his victorious conquest and exchanging paper money in their excitement.

It seemed hours before they were able to inch their way out of the building undisturbed. Even as they'd reached street level, where the cold night air greeted them with an unpleasant slap of blustery wind, Kendra could hear Joel's voice, like a whisper in the wind, heralding his brother and taking delight in what had happened. *"I taught him everything he knows,"* echoed softly against the starlit stratosphere.

"Over here," Shay said tersely, directing Kendra to where he'd parked his Maserati.

Seating herself in the familiar car's plush, cream interior, Kendra listlessly removed her sapphire and diamond clip-on earrings and almost threw them on the dashboard, along with her blue velvet handbag, not caring where Shay took her. As long as it was far away from that dreadful place she would be fine, she told herself, unconvinced.

The Maserati surged into the sparse, late night traffic, along neon lit streets, past bawdy, drunken night troopers, and through the noise which bellowed from round the clock burger parlors. Kendra remained silent the entire time, not daring to look at Shay, not daring to even speak to him.

It was a while before she decided to risk averting her gaze to study his profile. From beneath her wet, mascaraed eyelashes she could tell he was angry and distant, and she observed, too, that he was fighting to keep calm. She desperately wanted to know what he was thinking. Did he blame her? Did he really believe her to be playing some kind of game with him, as Selwyn had suggested?

Then she saw something, a small raw graze above his temple, something she knew hadn't been there previously. She felt her body quake, knowing that she was the one ultimately responsible for it. "You're hurt," she whimpered weakly, her mink-almond eyes spilling unwilled tears of stupid, shameful emotion.

"Really?" Shay rasped, oblivious to Kendra's emotion and the graze.

"It's all my fault," Kendra wept, the tears now washing down her face. "I made him do it."

Shay glared at her, caught in a trap of heightened concern. Steering the car off the road to a secluded side street, he cut the engine and pulled a tissue from the glove compartment, handing it to Kendra as he brushed back a strand of hair from her damp cheeks.

"Kendra," he began easily, planting a kiss against her forehead. "Mr. M.P. was a well-meaning amateur trying his luck. So what if I got hurt a little?"

Kendra closed her tear-glazed eyes, and instantly the consoling pressure of Shay's lips were against them. She was reluctant to accept the whirling dervish kind of excitement he was inducing and fought a silent battle to deflect her emotions, turning her head away from him to suppress the ripples of anticipation along her nerve ends.

In the recesses of her troubled mind, a voice nagged at her conscience. *You shouldn't be doing this, not yet, not now. You're not ready,* it cautioned. And the circumstances which shadowed that thought made her feel compelled to explain.

Unknowingly, she felt herself pull away from Shay and sensibly positioned herself in the car seat. "Shay, don't," she blubbered quietly as she used the tissue he'd given her to carefully blot the inner corners of her eyes. "I need to apologize . . . for Selwyn. I need to explain."

"What?" Shay stared at her incredulously, crazy yearning held within the depth of his dusky brown eyes.

"He had his reasons for behaving the way he did," Kendra began shakily, aware that Shay immensely disliked her shift in concentration.

His expression clouded. "You're apologizing for him? Kendra, the guy wanted to hit you."

"I know," she blurted, "but . . . you see . . . tonight Selwyn proposed to me. He wanted us to get married. But instead of giving him an answer, I went to Millennium Two thousand with you. I shouldn't have done that. I should've given him an answer."

Shay looked at her sternly, his eyes registering something Kendra felt unable to decipher. "What are you going to tell him?" he inquired, leaning back abruptly in his seat, frustrated and annoyed.

"I haven't thought about it yet," Kendra told him truthfully. "But I think I should've made him realize that I'd taken it seriously."

"Well, he's a fool wanting to imprison himself with one woman," Shay snapped irritably. "And you'd be a bigger fool taking him."

Kendra's mouth dried out. "What?"

Shay eyed her coolly, comprehension masking his face. "Don't tell me you believe in all that lifetime commitment thing?"

"Yes I do," Kendra said simply. She lifted her face then, to observe Shay's unsmiling one.

Shay didn't flinch from the issue. "Why?"

Kendra could sense that his whole being was intensely concentrated on her . . . waiting . . . anticipating a logical answer. Perversely enough, she couldn't think of one. All she knew was that marriage was one of the highest compliments a man could give a woman, and that Selwyn had offered her that. In retrospect, she felt flattered, uplifted, reassured by it, but in truth there had been no onus on her to reciprocate. Her heart ached to realize that Shay could reject the same thing so completely.

"Well, I believe in children," she started, reaching blindly for a reason to convince him of the validity of marriage. "And I think that two parents are better than one."

"You don't need to be married to have kids," Shay argued, translating her point into a social reality. "In my opinion, marriage exists as that old bastion of morality to legitimize them."

Kendra grew alarmed. "Well, on a subconscious level, children are happier when their parents are in love," she insisted.

"You're confusing sexual need with love," Shay analyzed. "Love is a word people put to work when they want to use somebody."

"I don't believe that," Kendra protested sharply. "Your brother must've been in love with Rhona Layton when he married her."

"J B married Rhona to keep Pops happy," Shay derided knowingly. "It was a handshake deal between Senator Layton and my father."

Kendra struggled against a dreadful feeling as she reassessed Shay's single-minded attitude. She sensed an iron-rock determination behind the soft caring in his eyes that she knew was impossible to break. How could she even attempt to try to hack away at it when she knew Shay had been raised by a unscrupulous tyrant? If only Benjamin Brentwood knew what he'd done.

"It seems your father demands that *he* find your life's work and your life's mate," Kendra bleated wildly.

"Are you capable of even knowing what you want for yourself?"

"From a woman?" Shay cackled. "I know what I want." He leaned forward and allowed his fingers to trace a line against the hollow of her throat, moving downward until they settled into the cleavage between her breasts.

Kendra's chest heaved at the unexpected delight, but she took control and clasped his fingers against her chest. She faced him squarely. "Tell me."

Shay eyed her warmly. "I'll tell you," he whispered, slowly releasing his hand to delve deeper into the soft, velour fabric of her dress until he found what he was looking for. "I like a woman who is physically fit, experienced, and sexually self-aware." Within seconds, he'd exposed one of her nipples to his shadowy gaze, taking the soft, budding flesh into his mouth and sucking it ardently until he felt Kendra arch against him in frantic supplication.

"And?" Kendra whimpered softly, trying desperately to keep her mind on the issue.

Shay raised his head. "What?"

"What else do you want?" Kendra probed weakly.

Shay shrugged, curiously wondering why he should feel so reluctant to answer. Was it because he knew all his answers would be so superficial? "Attractive, great legs—"

"All surface stuff," Kendra whispered hoarsely.

Something in Shay's eyes darkened, Kendra noted. Then his voice altered suddenly and she began to feel captivated by what he was saying. "I once told you that you disturb me," he admitted huskily "I find your beautiful eyes disturb me, the way you smile disturbs me, and . . . Girl . . . the body beneath this dress, which I've done nothing but dream about touching from the moment I first saw you, disturbs me to a restlessness I can't begin to—"

Their lips met and Kendra melted. Shay was awakening every nerve inside her quivering body, invigorating every hidden pressure point she felt sure he would discover. She knew she'd begun to yield to his overpowering persuasion, because she'd become weightless, almost mindless, spurred into darkness where there was nothing but the pleasure she was feeling.

When Shay cupped the womanly curves of her breast and playfully aroused an ardor too strong to resist, she felt ready to accept his greedy invitation without question. His warm mouth was provoking her to react, and she'd never responded to passion before in this rampaging, insistent way. It was all-consuming, all-devouring, almost frightening. She felt almost unable to stop reveling in its primitive savagery, like a starving tiger having discovered fresh bait. But a tiny voice of conscience in her head surfaced, warning, *You shouldn't be doing this.*

"Shay." Kendra reluctantly broke free, hating herself for being so principled. "This . . . tonight . . . it's all going too fast for me."

"What are you frightened of?" Shay questioned, his warm breath coming in small, hurried gasps.

"If you must know," Kendra confessed quietly, "you frighten me. Everything you stand for and believe in frightens me."

Shay glared at her, then braced his right arm against the car's steering wheel. "Is this about your father's newspaper or my views on marriage?"

Kendra refused to answer because she suddenly felt unsure. Shay's kiss was still causing havoc inside her, while her mind was trying hard to focus on the truce they'd pledged and the turmoil of her having been proposed to that night. Such confusion rendered her silent.

"Look," Shay reasoned, unnerved by it. "I'm no hypocrite. That sacred union you praise so well is for those who want to give more than fifty percent of themselves. And if more than fifty percent is called love, then I respect those who want that."

"But you don't want that for yourself?" Kendra judged, finding her tongue.

"I didn't say that," Shay breathed, irritated. This was all new territory for him. In fact, he'd never approached the subject of commitment before in such a probing, analytical manner. And if anyone was frightened right now, it was he. He felt frightened that Kendra had found something in Selwyn Owens that she wouldn't find in him. "I suppose you've discussed all this with Mr. M.P.?"

Kendra dipped her head, toying with the damp tissue in her hand. "We both have values," she acknowledged almost sadly. "They're different, of course. His are placed more in the crumpet eating, fox hunting world of class, politics, and titles. Mine are more simple. My mother always raised me to be someone who would find a unique role in a man's life. She had these old-fashioned West Indian slogans . . . *'Learn at home before you go abroad.'* " *Kendra crooned lightly.* " *'A man who sits at the head of the table has to earn his place there.'* I never quite knew what she meant until Selwyn came along and offered everything she talked about. Responsibility . . . respect . . . security."

"But no roses or romance," Shay rebutted jealously. "Roses are red, Kendra. Does he know that? And your name *is* Kendra, right? Or does he think it's Keisha?" He gently caught her hand and placed it against Kendra's heart so that she was forcibly aware of the discordant thudding still present from the way Shay had kissed her. "And you're a red-blooded woman, as I've told you before. So tell me, how does he make you feel?"

"Stop it," Kendra pulled her hand away. "You're confusing what I'm saying."

"Am I?" Shay's voice was laden with tension. "You're prepared to spend the rest of your life with a man to insure yourself against your own insecurity. Dammit, Kendra. You're living an illusion."

A dull ache took hold of Kendra's heart. "I don't have any illusions about you, though." She swallowed, disliking the way he'd correlated everything she'd said. "Your only obligation seems to be to your father. You're like him, aren't you? You can't love anything. Life is all about little game plays with dear Pops laying out all the strategy moves. Maybe he sent you here tonight to try to win me over."

Shay adopted a blank expression. "What are you talking about?"

"You turning up at the restaurant like that." Kendra's suspicions were roused. "So timely, so precise."

"Actually, I went there to meet someone," Shay declared, remembering Rhona.

"Who?"

"A woman."

Kendra tensed, jealous, blood rushing into her face. "Why didn't you wait for her?"

"She wasn't there, but you were," he told her, his own jealousy forcing him to skirt over an explanation. "So I left with you."

Kendra's heart fell heavy and weak into the depth of her stupidity. So he did have a date. What an idiot she'd been. It was obvious to her now that Shay had singled her out as a replacement. Whoever the woman was, she deserved a medal, Kendra thought murderously. Unlike her, this woman had obviously recognized Shay for what he really was; a handsome, conceited, playboy user interested in satisfying his own pleasures. And hadn't *she* known it?

Trevor's research files had thrown up a little more than just factual evidence. Speculation and tangible conjecture were in there, too. She'd noted his romances with Pauletta Weston, public relations guru to many top African-American stars, Fatonia B. James, novelist whose book *A Tide in Cuba* had hit the best-seller list, Nori Ark, world-famous athlete, and, more recently, Shanice Khone, renowned talk show host on one of their syndicated cable networks.

Shay was a highly physical man, not slow in taking what he wanted, she admitted. Love would never be a consideration. Men like him could have sex without their emotions being involved, without even having feelings for the women they were with. Besides, it would be strange if Shay had reached the age of thirty-four without having been involved in several sexual relationships, she told herself. He'd probably intended to take her to bed, too, she thought, horrified at how easily she'd been following his trail there. He was good. So damned good.

The tragedy of it all was that she'd ruined a perfectly amicable relationship with a man who'd helped her through so much the past year. There was no relief in her at hearing Shay's honesty, only deep-seated anger, hate, and fury. "I hope you're not still considering me fair game," she retorted coldly, attacking his assumption that she was his for the night. "I told you already, you're never going to have me, present circumstances considered."

"I don't want anything you're not ready to give," Shay chortled flatly. His eyes were hooded, preventing Kendra from knowing what lay in their dusky depths.

"Good. Then take me home."

Seven

Kendra dragged herself out of bed at precisely eight A.M. and slowly hobbled downstairs to answer the firm, persistent knock at the front door. Where was Arlisa? Where was Dad? Where was the damned hired help? she croaked to herself, rubbing at her throbbing head as she carefully navigated the long stairway downward. She had an headache. Correction. A hangover.

Wrapping her brushed cotton nightdress around her craggy, sleepy body, she reminded herself that it was Sunday, the hired help's day off. That meant Arlisa had still probably not come in yet from her Saturday nightclubbing, and her father would still be in bed. At least they were blissfully unaware of the conflicting turmoil she was in presently, she thought dismally.

Last night had been a nightmare; a perfect evening gone disastrously wrong. She remembered every last shameful detail. Kendra flinched, scowled at her guilt, and grimaced at her unfaithfulness as cruel memory came flooding back to haunt her. She should have had more sense than to fraternize with Shay Brentwood, her mind scolded. And she should have told Selwyn long ago that she could never love him. In many ways he'd been almost like a godsend to her: patient, understanding, considerate. But she'd known from the outset that he wasn't for her. Her heart ached knowing what Selwyn now thought of her.

I'm an idiot, she mused wretchedly. *I never see the line until I've crossed it.*

She stood slouched at the front door, a wretched human being in desperate need of more sleep. Then, suddenly, a terrible thought struck her. What if her early morning visitor were Selwyn? It was just like him to seek out a private explanation from her. Then again, it might be Shay Brentwood, bringing back the earrings that she'd left in his car last night. Her eyes widened at the prospect of him coming there. They'd parted in the early hours of the morning with all guns blazing. She could still sense the smokey after effects swirling around in her tormented mind.

His dusky, brown eyes had been uncomfortably watchful as he'd driven her on the silent journey home. She'd detected him studying her expression every time the car had slowed to wait for a break in the traffic, and she knew it was because he'd been unsure whether to believe her dismissal of his male virility. She could tell it frazzled him.

By the time the Maserati had pulled into the curved driveway of her father's house, her instincts were on red alert, warning that the mitigating relief of having arrived there would be disturbed by him exacting equal punishment for her rejection of him. And she'd been right.

Releasing the clasp of her seat belt, he bristled. "I take it all battle stations will be manned when I come for my money on Wednesday?"

Kendra remembered glaring at him, startled by his conjecture. "You just don't give up, do you?" she antagonized, seizing at her velvet handbag.

"You've got that right," Shay rebuffed, his expression strained and disgruntled. "I'm only a humanitarian when I'm not working."

She could still feel the sharp, sensitive stab of regret which had penetrated her heart. The blissful time they'd spent together had been all but forgotten. There was never any truce between them, not really. Just make-believe farce.

"The next time you ask me to bury the hatchet," she said, seething, pulling the car door open and stepping out for blessed, consoling relief, "remind me to bury it in your skull."

Shay didn't let her go easily. He lunged forward and caught her wrist, pulling her back into the car until he could see her shadowy face. Kendra remembered his face well enough; darkened, disheartened and . . . confused. Yet there had been a shallow warmth there, too, an unwillingness to let her go. "You can't stop the hand of providence," he'd told her simply, as if some divine intervention were at work: a destiny, a fate, a certainty of sorts.

"Then let's hope it's not in the habit of leaving any fingerprints," she'd remarked, releasing herself from his grip and slamming the car door. She could still hear the hum of the engine in her head as it whisked him away.

Another firm, clipped knock superseded the humming, reminding Kendra that she had yet to answer the door. "Okay, okay, I'm coming," she roared, aptly punching at the motion detector release buttons before she turned a gold key in the white Chelsea door. Bracing herself for trouble, she swung the door open and stared dazedly as her sister tumbled over the threshold.

"I'm going to make that miserable toad sorry he ever crossed me," Arlisa babbled tearfully, stumbling into the hallway. "I want Jerome Morrison's affair with

Judge Crossland's daughter plastered all over this week's edition of the *Nubian Chronicle*."

Kendra caught Arlisa by the arm and held her up, studying her fretful, intoxicated expression as she used her other hand to close the door behind her.

"The hateful rat," Arlisa slurred, abruptly releasing herself from Kendra's grip. Slowly, faltering on her feet, she made her way across the hall to the sun den, unaware of whether Kendra followed her or not. Kendra was in slow pursuit, sighing deeply as she watched Arlisa head straight for the wine cabinet and pour herself a large glass of Scotch. "I don't know why I couldn't get the key into the lock." She was whimpering shakily, pulling back her long, braided hair. "Must be broken or something."

"What's happened to you, Sissy?" Kendra demanded, seizing the nearest available chair and frowning as her own voice echoed loudly in her head, adding pain to her hangover.

Arlisa slumped into another of the pastel-colored chairs and offered Kendra a look of anxious misery. "You remember Jerome, the barrister?" she drawled in explanation. "Well, his worldwide knowledge of law may be en-en-encyclopedic, but when it comes to in-infidelity, he's out of his subject. I caught him blue . . . redhanded with Bernadetta Crossland." She winced. "And do you know what Ms. Thang said to me?" She panted heavily. "She said, *'I'm the one he reaches for in the middle of the night, or did you think that was you?'* Who does she think she is?"

The question hovered unanswered in the atmosphere, punctuated by Arlisa's hiccups and sniveling gestures. Kendra's reaction was to simply close her eyes, feeling for her sister yet wishing she could alleviate the throbbing headache which had begun to bore its way to the forefront of her head.

"Anyway," Arlisa lisped, "I told Ms. Thang that the fact that she's sleeping with Jerome didn't fazzle . . . frazzle me. He'll never let me down. He owes me." Arlisa sunk, dejected, deeper into the chair. "It turns out Jerome didn't think he owed me anything." She winced. "He said my honesty couldn't be sub-substantiated in a court of law, that the auditors of the BPCF and Association of Black Journalists would no longer be satisfied with my handling of the trusteeships so I'd done the right thing by resigning, and that he wasn't going to risk his career by helping me to cover up my mis-misappropriation of funds."

"Oh, Sissy." Kendra sighed, disbelieving that she was hearing such dreadful news. Aside from the shortfall they had, that being the interest she'd promised Shay, they were still in the predicament of having to find one hundred and fifty thousand dollars, and there were only two days left. "What about whatshisname . . . Brad? Did you manage to reach him in the Bahamas?"

"Don't talk to me about Brad, the little twerp." Arlisa took a large gulp of whisky to drown her sorrows. "Do you know he cares more about that lowbrow, West Indian comedy he's working on than he does about me. Anyway, he found out about me and Jerome, so he's refusing to give me any money."

"I knew it," Kendra chortled, suppressing the sudden anxiety in her bosom. "I warned you that your past would one day catch up with you."

"Well, you're not a par-paragon of virtue, either," Arlisa snorted in return. "I heard all about what you did to Selwyn Owens, that so righteous, upstanding Minister of Parliament you were always singing about. Well, don't worry about it. Shay's a better prospect . . . worth ten of Owens."

Kendra stared at her sister. "How did you know about that?"

"It was the talk all over town last night," Arlisa snarled with a hiccup. She eyed Kendra speculatively. "You dating Shay—is that all part of the pan-plan you were telling me about? Because if it is," she said, winking, "I'm undressed."

"Impressed," Kendra corrected wearily.

"Yeah, that's it." Arlisa sighed. "I'm glad you've discovered that when it comes to men, money has to definitely talk."

Kendra ejected a weary chuckle, knowingly aware that her sister was tired, but not too tired to impart some personal wisdom in her insobriety.

"Men are seldom useful unless they have money," she slurred, serious. "And there's one thing I've learnt about them lately. When anything goes wrong, it's a woman they want to lay the blame on. And another thing," Arlisa pursued recklessly, "forget love. Men don't understand what that means, so they never dish it out. Those of us who've seen the light, we know not to chase for that like it was sweet nectar from God, 'cause we're never gonna find it." Raising her glass in a salute to Kendra, she pronounced, "So here's to enlightened women and to the enlightenment of men."

Kendra didn't wish to debate her sister. Arlisa had been betrayed, humiliated, passed over for another woman—all deserving retribution, in her opinion, yet all cause enough to make Arlisa cynical and embittered, lashing out at all the unacceptable facets of double standard behavior men were renowned for the world over. She knew that not all men were like that. Their father wasn't. He'd loved her mother as if she were the rare black opal *Empress of Glengarry,* too prized to part with. He was brokenhearted when he lost her to pneumonia. She'd often wondered whether he'd ever recovered.

She wondered, too, about Arlisa. Gone was her usual sparkling charm, her cheerful bubbling chatter. In its place was sheer misanthropy, painful, hardened, and vindictive as it could come.

Then, in an abrupt shift of mood, Arlisa was giggling, as though something had struck her to be screamingly funny. "Do you realize you had two men fighting over you last night?" She chuckled frantically, her big fawn eyes filled with the sheen of tears. "I should be so lucky."

"Come on." Kendra had heard enough. She walked over to her sister, removed the glass from her hand, and raised her to her feet. "I'm taking you to bed. You need to sleep off your troubles."

Arlisa laughed again, though Kendra failed to see the joke. "Bed," she giggled sardonically. "Is there a man in it?"

Her eyes focused on Kendra, and suddenly nothing was funny anymore. Forming a faint, self-condemnatory line between her eyes, she rasped, "I've messed up everything, haven't I? I always do. I've gambled away a fortune, our inheritance . . . well, yours, really . . . I was never interested in Daddy's newspaper. I don't know what's happening to me. If only Momma had never died . . . if only she was still here . . . none—"

"Arlisa, don't," Kendra squealed, holding her sister's body in a consoling embrace. For ten long minutes she shared Arlisa's agony, sobbed with her a little over her own stupidity. And when at last they'd expended their emotions, when at last the final tears of despair had fallen, she sat her sister down and stared at her weakly.

Arlisa had regained much of her composure, but she was still upset and depressed. Expressionless, she whimpered, "When are we going to tell Daddy?"

Kendra tensed, trying to form a suitable scenario in her head. "I'll get round to it."

Somewhere behind them, in a voice that could have frozen a volcanic lava flow, someone said, "Tell me what?"

Kendra's body jerked in stunned surprise as her head shot round and her thunderstruck, mink-almond eyes settled on her father. She sucked in her breath, her spine rigid, as she began to anticipate his reaction.

Ramsey Davenport did not look like the sort of man who could be manipulated. Standing a little less than six-feet tall, he was still, at fifty-eight, lean and hard-muscled, his mocha cheeks stretched tight across prominent bone structure. His hair had thinned in the same manner as Bill Cosby's, but he still wore a size thirty-nine jacket, still maintained a thirty-three inch waist, and still retained an alertness that could often catch one off guard.

He had never lost his steely-eyed authority, but there had always been a gentleness of character about him, too. Ironically, in the tough world of journalism, that one trait had been his salvation and the springboard to his success.

Kendra was aware of all this as she met his inquisitive, no-nonsense gaze. She opened her mouth, about to speak, but Arlisa rushed in first, intent on accepting full responsibility for her own actions.

"I'm sorry, so sorry, Daddy," she sniveled, ready to turn on the waterworks again.

"What for?" Ramsey Davenport arched an eyebrow, displayed his even white teeth in a shallow, disbelieving smile.

"I've done a terrible thing." Arlisa couldn't bear to look at him. "We're going to lose the *Nubian Chronicle* on Wednesday if I don't find a hundred and fifty thousand dollars. U.S currency."

Ramsey's voice sharpened like ice. "What?"

Arlisa crumbled. Over bawling and wailing, weeping and requiem, she told her father of the terrible things she'd done. Throughout it all Ramsey stood rooted at the doorway, too angry, it seemed, to venture into the room for fear of causing his youngest daughter some great harm. Kendra could see it in his face, watched as it intensified at the mention of Benjamin Brentwood and his sons. Just when she felt her father was about to explode like a firecracker, Arlisa placed her hand across her mouth and rushed out of the room, forcing back the vomit which was about to erupt from her gut.

Kendra had silently, impassively, listened to everything without comment, too exhausted, fatigued, too damned sorrowful, to add her own account to the tragedy. And it was a tragedy. She'd never seen her father so crestfallen.

Yet all she could think about was Shay Brentwood. Her heart performed a peculiar, sinking somersault as an image of him was projected in her mind. She wanted to wish it away because he'd won, and because he had no right to intrude in her family's despair, but his enigmatic, brooding profile wouldn't budge. Instead, the craziness of it being there made her skin begin to prickle with sensual awareness, reminding Kendra of how deeply he affected her. Even now she wanted to feel . . . to know again . . . the power of his kiss.

It was her father's voice which dislodged her musings on that heady subject. "Are you going to deny any of this?" he blazed furiously.

Kendra drew a deep, painful breath and compressed her lips to disguise the swift run of erotic turbulence she was feeling as Shay's wistful image faded. She'd known everything, of course, but the motion of her lips didn't go down well with Daddy.

"Don't push your mouth up on me," he snapped, his

face contorted in fury. "You're not too big for some old-fashioned discipline. What did I do? Put a fool in charge of my newspaper?"

"Daddy, I didn't know," Kendra whined, knowing her father probably didn't believe her. Her pulses suddenly pounded a quick, fiery rhythm, and any minute now she would forget that she was a grown woman, not a child never too old to receive some good, old-fashioned licking, after all.

"Wort'less! I know Arlisa is wort'less, but you?" Ramsey addressed her savagely, his eyes fiery red and full of rage. "It's you I did work so damned hard for. Me and your momma work hard to keep that newspaper. And why? Because from when you were a little girl you always told us you were going to become editor one day." He raised his hands helplessly, then paused for breath. "I outlived them all, Kendra, for you. When the *West Indian Gazette* folded in sixty-five, the *Nubian Chronicle,* only two years old, took its place, and me and your mother watched as we rose above the *Caribbean Weekly Post* and the *West Indian World,* both folding because they couldn't meet our pace. Now you're here, telling me that one of Benjamin Brentwood's boys is going to take my newspaper? Benjamin Brentwood can go to hell. I'm going to tell him that. No one takes my newspaper."

Kendra shuddered as her father's raw rage filled the room, coming down like a sledgehammer on her painful, throbbing headache. She was expecting to hear more, but realized that Ramsey had suddenly stopped. The room had fallen into such silence that she quickly looked at her father, almost panicked. A calculated, pondering expression was etched across his face, telling Kendra instantly that some chain of thought was turning like a wheel in his head. She recognized the pattern from her childhood days, especially when her father had been struck by some great inspiration or idea. Now, his eyebrows were arched in amazement. His eyes had widened to startling proportions, and his stony face was no longer cracked with frustration. It had softened surprisingly.

"But kiss me neck back," Ramsey yelled, incredulous. "I forget all about you momma's will." He began to pace the room with menacing excitement. "Me never tell you?" he bellowed loudly.

Kendra shook her head, too numbed to understand what he was talking about. Naturally, after her mother's passing, she'd left all her mother's memorabilia in the care of her father. He'd discussed what they should do with certain things, but beyond that nothing further had ever been decided.

"Of course I didn't tell you," Ramsey uttered, his voice struggling with amazement. "When I incorporate the *Nubian Chronicle* in England in nineteen sixty-three, I had to divide up the shares. Your momma got forty-eight percent in her name and I take the rest."

Kendra nodded away, understanding so far what her father had said.

"When she passed away, God rest her soul in Heaven," Ramsey continued, "she leave all her shares to you in her will."

Kendra gaped at him, her eyes going very wide, her lips drooping open like those of a fish. For a moment, she was in shock. She simply couldn't believe what she was hearing; that her mother had left a will bequeathing her shares. "Why didn't I know about this before?" she asked her father finally.

"You were not supposed to know until you were married," Ramsey explained. "You momma made me promise not to tell you until then."

Kendra's eyes glazed over with bittersweet tears, mindful of what a wonderful wedding gift her mother had intended to give her. Now Shay Brentwood and his hateful family would get them, she thought bitterly.

As though tapping into her mind, Ramsey said, "Benjamin Brentwood can't touch them shares. Those shares are yours and they cannot be sold, transferred, exchanged, or disposed of in any way until after you have married. That's the provision of your momma's will, and Benjamin Brentwood will have a hard time contesting that legally."

"Oh, my . . ." Kendra's head was spinning. "That means they only get fifty-two percent of the *Nubian Chronicle* for bailing out Arlisa? The Brentwoods can't push a paper clip around my office without telling me about it?"

"Right." Ramsey laughed heartily. He walked briskly over to the wine cabinet and poured himself a liberal dose of cognac. Raising the glass to Kendra in a toast, he announced, "I'm coming back to the *Nubian Chronicle,* Kendra. God bless your momma."

Eight

Kendra gave a long sigh of contentment as she lay back in the scented bathwater and watched the warm, soapy bubbles burst softly against her ebony skin. If only they could remove the morning's tension inside her, she thought, reminding herself that it was Wednesday.

Tension. It was an odd word to use. There shouldn't have been any tension attached to taking a long, hot, relaxing bath, and Kendra knew very well that there wouldn't have been had the bath not been in preparation for the confident persona she would need to project when she joined her father to meet Shay Brentwood at the *Nubian Chronicle* that morning.

Her stomach churned sickly as her mind conjured up an image of her arch enemy's handsome, brooding face. She remembered everything about him—the way his raven black curls were cropped around his chiseled, caramel face, his dusky brown eyes, watchful . . . penetrating, and the smell of his tangy, expensive aftershave, so erotically aromatic that she wondered whether it had been created especially for him.

She tried to anticipate how he would take the news that he had not acquired complete ownership of the *Nubian Chronicle,* tried to remember exactly how her father had said he was going to handle him, and realized that she was dreading the confrontation terribly.

Her father had called Rugg Brown, his long-standing lawyer of twelve years, to be sure he would be in attendance to witness the outcome—more precisely, to explain the terms of her mother's will. He'd even gone through the company's accounts, ascertaining that the Brentwoods could not touch any other subsidiary operation linked to the *Chronicle*.

Though no formal agreement had been struck in writing between her and Shay stating the terms under which he would be taking over the paper, Kendra realized that her father was very much aware that he had to protect Arlisa, that there would be enough evidence to expose what she'd done, and that he might have to strike some other amicable arrangement to pay off the debt if Shay didn't agree to the terms of the will.

She felt her head begin to ache at the prospect, as if there were a million warring thoughts in there, all battering around, looking for a way out. Suddenly a wave of nausea attacked her. What if another deal couldn't be struck? What if Benjamin Brentwood intervened and decided he would rather see Arlisa in jail than share the *Nubian Chronicle* with her father?

She felt sick with apprehension as she let herself out of the bath. Her father hadn't discussed a contingency plan. In his mind, he had all the cards and he was going to play an ace. Perhaps, she thought wearily, he was too old to realize exactly what he was up against.

Selwyn's voice suddenly infiltrated her head. *"If Shay is anything like what I've heard about his father, you can kiss good-bye to the Nubian Chronicle,"* Kendra shuddered as she registered the silent words. Dear Selwyn. He was probably right. Shay's intention to take over the *Chronicle* was like a single-minded ambition that had never faltered from the moment she'd met him.

The conditions of her mother's will might well spur his determination on further, her astute mind warned.

Sitting at her dressing table, she began to pin her relaxed auburn hair up into a loose bobtail, second-guessing what Shay would do. Unused to devising unscrupulous tactics, she wondered what measures he could employ. He could force her into signing legal papers stipulating that upon the advent of her marriage she must sell her shares only to him. Or, he could contest her mother's will.

Applying translucent powder to her cheekbones and forehead to enhance her ebony complexion, off-black eyeliner and mascara to define her worried, mink-colored, almond shaped eyes, and then plum lipstick to her trembling lips, Kendra mused over the last tactic. In her mind, that was exactly something Benjamin Brentwood would do.

He must have plotted and connived with his lawyers for years to find some way of getting his hands on the *Nubian Chronicle,* she thought. Why else would he have waited thirty-five years from the year her father began publishing in England to launch a bid to get it back? And so why not contest her mother's ownership of her shares at the time she wrote the will?

Wearily, she rose to her feet and padded across to her wardrobe. Selecting a mauve pant suit and a silky, white blouse, she slipped into her underwear and then into her clothes, recalling that her father had wanted them to leave directly after breakfast in order to avoid the flotsam of early morning bumper to bumper traffic from St. John's Wood to Fleet Street.

She paused to reflect on her appearance in her dressing table mirror, then disciplined her profile to one of serious intent. Quickly stepping into patent, brown, leather ankle boots, she inhaled deeply and picked up her briefcase from the bed. She would stand by her father and lend him her full and loyal support, and she would forget that his hostilities would be directed against the very man who almost stole her heart.

Flanked by a squadron of six male lawyers, Shay Brentwood and his father marched regimentally into Kendra's office at precisely 11:30 A.M. Kendra was at her desk, compiling data on her computer terminal for the Black History Month supplement to the *Nubian Chronicle*, when she noticed their noisy arrival.

Leola had rushed in behind the squadron, screeching like a mother hen, wide-eyed and clearly startled. "I went to get your father," she said, panicky, eyeing all the men, with one exception, with total distaste. "He's on his way."

As she hurriedly left the room, Kendra instantly put her computer screen on hold, deciding that she was not going to lose one iota of professional stature as she rose to her feet to confront Shay and his ensemble head on. Yet the moment her cool gaze swept across Shay's enigmatic features, Kendra wanted to curse wickedly. The window of her mind saw nothing but handsome virility and she felt a flash of irritation as her heart skipped an erratic beat, irked that this man could so easily affect her in this way.

She observed that Shay did not blink. The office itself might have been falling down around him, but from the moment he entered the room never once did he allow his eyes to wander from her. The simple action successfully served to weaken her resolve even further. She knew that Shay was aware of what he was doing to her—what he probably did to every woman—and that he was deriving deep pleasure from the way she was looking at him, exposing her feelings entirely.

She felt hypnotized, embroiled in an emotional morass, and an unfamiliar feeling crept up on her, rather like she imagined airsickness to be. She willed herself to regain some control, but when Shay strode coolly across the expanse of beige carpet toward her, his hand in one trouser pocket as his eyes regarded her from the opposite side of her wooden desk, Kendra knew that her reserve had crumbled completely.

"Hello, Kendra," Shay drawled smoothly, his eyes taking in her bands of hair, held up by a simple bobtail, and the breasts he knew so well, which were at the moment heaving up and down slightly under her white, silky blouse. And as Kendra looked at him with bedazzled eyes, his voice lowered seductively. For her ears only, he added hoarsely, "You're wearing your hair like that for me?"

Kendra trembled. She'd done no such thing. Or had she? She hazily realized that she had worn it exactly how he'd wanted her to, true to Shay's request, and that annoyed her. She hadn't given a thought to what he'd asked of her the previous week, nor to what she was doing that morning, and so her subconscious had played a trick on her. Now Shay was under the impression that she was trained to his command, and that thought heightened her annoyance even more.

As his lazy eyebrows rose in curiosity as he waited, expectant of an answer, Kendra wondered what to say, for in that moment a crazy, melting sensation weakened her limbs. But, miraculously, she smothered the emotion well by thinking of their meeting. "Gentlemen," she proclaimed, shifting her gaze from Shay to his entourage, "we shall come to order when my father and our family lawyer arrive."

"One lawyer?" Benjamin scoffed, as though the solitary number was obscene.

"One is all we need," Kendra rebuffed.

Luckily, her father made a timely intrusion, aborting

anything Benjamin could possibly have thought to reply. "You think you're going to take my newspaper?" Ramsey blazed on announcing his entrance.

Kendra instantly felt a ripple of something akin to terror run over her skin as she risked looking at her father and then at Benjamin Brentwood. She could tell that Benjamin was made of vinegar and grit, and that he, like her father, was in no mood for any fooling around.

"Long time, Rammy," Benjamin began gruffly, helping himself to one of the guest chairs stacked in an obscure corner of the room. Swiftly planting his heavy body in it with an agility that made a mockery of his years, he added, "So, Pretty Feet filled your prematurely departed shoes?"

"Kendra looked after things for a while," Ramsey confirmed roughly. "But now I'm back, to see you to hell."

As Benjamin lit up a cigar, Kendra gazed helplessly at Shay, who had also helped himself to a chair. Seemingly unfazed, he seated his casually dressed frame alongside her desk, the chair strategically angled so that he could glance over in her direction at any time and make a clear appraisal of her.

Kendra knew that he was being arrogant, as was the way in which he was dressed. Shay was wearing a pair of faded blue jeans, a pale blue shirt opened to reveal dark hair on his chest, and a camel wool jacket, all in blatant contrast to the army of men stood to attention like corporate soldiers, fitted out in expensive executive-type suits. Even the way he straddled his chair, his arms leaned across the chair's back with his chin resting against them, seemed a casually gross indication of just how little her father's life's work meant to him. He could just walk in there, dissect her life, and then run along to a basketball game, it seemed. Didn't this man have any scruples at all? Her mind seethed stupendously.

She contemplated the entourage of men he'd brought in with him, with their watchful expressions and determined, cool eyes. Then she glanced over at her father's deepset ones—savage, ruthless—and Benjamin's strange, triumphant ones—violent, alert, the darker rims around the irises giving him a hardened look. Then she looked at Shay's. His eyes held a sense of playfulness, danced with a sense of menace, and Kendra suddenly realized that he was having fun. He was enjoying the situation he'd brought about, and she felt sudden anger.

Overcoming the nervousness and the delicious shock waves which had first plagued her when confronted with this formidable individual who held her future in his relentless hands, Kendra moved slowly around her desk and towered over Shay, ignoring the impact of his devastating masculinity as she rapped out, "I want all your men out of my office, now. If you want them to play at being lawyers, have them do it on their own time."

Six pair of male eyes shifted immediately to Shay and acknowledged his brief nod of acceptance to Kendra's request as if he were the highest authority in the room. Kendra fumed as each one in turn filed out of her office. Then she felt Shay's hand on her wrist, sending a gigantic, electric nerve sensation right up her arm. She removed her wrist instantly, but the presence of Shay's touch remained.

"Delbert stays," he told her calmly, inclining his head toward an older, more senior member of the squad whom she imagined ranked in superiority to the others.

"You Americans," she dared, meeting the gleam that might have been amusement spread across Shay's dusky brown eyes. "We don't falter at your scare tactics here."

"Always full of fire," Benjamin Brentwood noted bluntly.

Kendra shot him a murderous glance. "Enough to burn down the house of Brentwood," she admonished furiously. "Just when are you going to give up your crusade against my father? Daddy got all your letters after Momma died, and your lawyers know you have nothing to gain by coming here today."

"Is that a fact?" Benjamin countered sternly, allowing his eyes to flicker with disapproval round her small, fashion-dated, cracked ceiling office. "Girl," he promised, sucking in a mouthful of cigar, brown fingers closing around it as if they would mold it to his will, "my son intends to transform this wreck of a newspaper so that it's ready to make a major collision with the twenty-first century. And when my son says he is going to do something, believe me, Girl, he does it for a very good reason, and it stays done."

"This your boy?" Ramsey suddenly inquired, his expression slightly puzzled. "But I thought he was Selwyn. It was him who come to me house."

Kendra quivered at the mention of Selwyn's name, but quickly explained to her father, "This is Shay Brentwood, Dad. He did come to the house, to tell me what he'd done for Arlisa."

"You mean to blackmail you," Ramsey said scornfully.

Offended, Shay remarked sternly, "Any one of your daughter's infractions could have led her straight to jail, Mr. Davenport. I saved her from that."

"You're asking a high price, Boy." Ramsey chortled in return. "The contention I have with your papa is between me and him. What do you have to do with it?"

"I want to end it," Shay stated tersely. "And today, it's going to."

Kendra's eyebrows rose in sudden surprise, even disbelief. She'd always thought that Shay's motivation to get her father's newspaper was caused by an inbred obsession driven by childhood conditioning, parental encouragement, and the sheer will to win a battle his father had started. Now, here she was, listening to that same adversary profess how much he sincerely wanted the dreadful feuding to end.

She leaned against her desk, her hands behind her for blessed support. Could she be dreaming? Was she imagining what she'd heard? It was Rugg Brown's late but timely entrance into the room which reminded Kendra that she was living the reality. Within seconds, he'd introduced himself as the executor of the estate of her mother, Mrs. Merle Davenport. He briefly explained the contents of her will relating to the newspaper, and then motioned with his head that Kendra should take up the gauntlet.

Disciplining her features to a mask of indifference, Kendra added, "I don't wish to disparage your assessment of the situation, but Mr. Brown is right. I have shares in the *Chronicle* which simply cannot be bargained over for my sister's unfortunate . . . indiscretions."

To Kendra's annoyance, Shay smiled. Perhaps it wasn't exactly a smile, but just his long, curling eyelashes giving the impression of one. He was looking at her keenly now, and Kendra wasn't sure he was serious. "We know about the will," he clarified softly. "We . . . anticipated that your mother had made one. Our lawyers had a fair idea what the provisions would be."

"And they've considered every angle?" Kendra asked stiffly.

"Exhaustively," Shay replied.

"Then they will appreciate, on sight of course, that it is a carefully worded document," Rugg Brown interjected knowingly. "Quite . . . explicit in fact. Simply put, Miss Kendra Marie Davenport cannot dispose of her forty-eight percent share ownership until after she has married."

"Forty-eight percent!" Shay raised an inquisitive brow.

Rugg ignored the brief interruption. "I grant it's unconventional. However, the intent of the late Mrs. Merle Davenport is clear. She wished to protect her daughter's financial interests by imposing the restriction that disposal of the shares cannot be entertained until after her daughter had married. There's no doubt that she was of sound mind at the time of its execution, and I find no basis for contesting the provision or her right to ownership of the shares in question at the time she wrote the will."

"We're not going to contest," Shay declared with a mild hint of irritation.

Kendra glanced at the straight back, at the squared shoulders and the sudden hard line of Shay's mouth, and detected that in the handsome austerity of his authoritative features there was something being left unsaid.

Then, almost as if cued to play his part, the lawyer Shay had asked to remain in the room suddenly stirred himself into motion, reaching for a set of papers from his briefcase and promptly handed them over to Shay. "As I said before," Shay reaffirmed tightly, "today we're going to end this." His gaze rose to Kendra and sparkled almost menacingly as he in turn offered the papers to her. "You wanted my deposition from God. Here it is."

Kendra stared down at the set of papers in Shay's hand which provided a fragile link between them. Shaking, she took them from his outstretched hand, mouthing a simple, "What are they?" as she opened the transparent folder which housed them. Her voice sounded odd, different, and Kendra realized that she'd verbally sounded out her perplexity as her mind whirled curiously over what she'd been given.

She fought back the awful premonition that it was something dangerous, something that would bring about a sudden change to her life. And as she recognized that the papers included the deed to her father's house, her heart plummeted into total despair. "What are you doing with these?" she demanded hotly, her tongue feeling thick in her mouth as her eye caught her father heading straight toward her.

Shaking herself into some semblance of normality, she looked into Shay's determined eyes. They were hard . . . concerned . . . gentle? She was unsure what interpretation to make.

Benjamin's voice followed her father like a shadow in tow. "You should never re-mortgage your house, Rammy," he derided. "It makes it a lot easier for guys like me to make a move. We bought out that tiny Barbadian finance company you approached for the loan. Two point four million was a good investment to get me what I wanted."

His voice echoed as Ramsey snatched the papers from his daughter and perused them slowly. But Kendra was already reeling off her reply. "Let me get this straight," she roared, disbelieving what she'd just heard. "Are you telling me that you paid over two million dollars to get your thieving, conniving hands on our house?" Her eyes diverted to Shay and for an instant she felt blind rage. "In a pool of sharks, you swim with the best of them," she chided icily. "Well, you've wasted your money with that little contingency, because my father doesn't have a second mortgage. The house in St. John's Wood is paid for."

"Was paid for," Ramsey amended weakly. With pain

in his eyes he looked at Kendra. "I took out a loan secured against the house, Kendra, three months ago, to set up a university scholarship fund for black journalists." He paused forlornly. "I couldn't forget what those students at the British Publishers's Awards said to me. They were right. I wasn't thinking ahead. So me set up the money for forty education grants which I was planning to launch at Christmas. The newspaper would have paid for it over time," he told her, his eyes turning murderous. "But I never knew that this . . . lizard was going to get him hands on my deeds first."

"What . . . what did you call the scholarship fund?" Kendra asked dazedly.

"The Merle Davenport Foundation," Ramsey answered, shaken.

Kendra pressed her hand against her mouth.

"Limited by guarantee with charitable status," Benjamin intruded into curls of smoke from his Cuban cigar. "Made things real easy."

Kendra wanted to weep. Her father was truly noble. Despite his frail years, he was esteemable to a fault. There was so much dignity in him, so much pride. It was a striking, visible contrast to Benjamin Brentwood, who instead possessed every form of vanity which contributed to self-glorification. She hated him, and from the look in her father's eyes, she knew he did, too.

His reaction was ultra quick. He squared up to Benjamin with all the rage of ten men and vented over thirty years of aggression and unadulterated rage. Both men exhibited a direct cutting quality, cussing in their native Caribbean tongues, dredging up the past as if it were yesterday, accusing each other of disreputable behavior, and more. It was a powerful argument that could be likened to a pit bull fight.

Kendra's eyes flickered anxiously toward Shay. She expected that he would do something to stop the two old men, but he simply sat in his chair like the umpire of a tennis match, scoring up the serves and adding the points.

Deuce came when her father, finally out of steam, sank himself into a vacant chair by her cabinet. "Why?" he snapped, panting for air.

"Because the *Nubian Chronicle* was my idea, Benjamin blazed, the emotions he'd brought to life after long years of atrophy still evident in his voice. "It was always more mine than yours."

"But I made it what it is today," Kendra heard her father say. "I molded it, nursed it, shaped it up. And me pay for it, too."

"That's right," Kendra suddenly seethed. "Now you have fifty-two percent of the shares for bailing out my sister. Pretty damned cheap, in my opinion."

"Mr. Brentwood wants complete ownership," the senior lawyer rooted at the door suddenly interjected. "We're looking to acquire the rest of the shares in exchange for the deed to your father's house. If there's no agreement, we will be forced to call in the loan and evict."

"But wait," said Ramsey, his face full of scorn. "You're forcing my daughter to marry her boyfriend... Selwyn Owens, so she can exchange her shares for my house?"

Benjamin Brentwood's cigar seemed poised triumphantly. "No, Rammy. You get back your deed after your daughter Kendra marries my boy Shay."

Kendra's eyes bulged with shock. Grabbing at her composure, she diverted her eyes to gauge Shay's expression. Knowing his feelings on marriage, she expected that he would be furious at the suggestion, that his face would be blazing her non-admittance into his life, but he was strangely silent, as quiet as he'd been throughout the fighting between her father and Benjamin.

During the commotion he'd glanced over at her twice, his brooding, dusky eyes penetrating, probing, skirting across her entire being as though he'd needed to know that she was all right. And for the most part she had been, except during the times when her father had seemed about to hit Benjamin.

Now, she was truly shaken. Everything was too . . . planned. That was it. Too orderly, too decided. And that frustrated her. It seemed Benjamin Brentwood always got what he wanted. She opened her mouth, about to protest with a firm *"To hell I am,"* when her father's face caught her eyes.

His brown eyes were tired, old, pleading that she end it, too, and she felt pressured. Pressured into agreeing with his hateful enemy so that he could keep the one material thing he had left. The house he'd shared with her mother. She heard Benjamin's voice infiltrate her mind, dropping, *"There's nothing like family,"* and *"I want my grandchildren legitimate,"* and suddenly she realized that Benjamin Brentwood wanted a dynasty.

Incredulous, she realized, too, that her father's eyes had softened at what Benjamin was saying, as though they had both reached a sudden meeting of minds. *Two powerful families—married,* they were saying to each other. She panicked, feeling caged in, needing air. Lots of it. Pushing past the lawyer, who was still stationed at the door, she made straight for the elevator and was about to summon a car when Shay's proprietorial hand clasped her arm.

"Wait," he restrained softly.

Kendra's reply was one of heated fury. "Another handshake deal done The American Way? First Joel, now you. I didn't know your father was still nursing two puppy dogs."

Shay's grip hardened. "You ain't looking at no underdog on a leash." His voice stiffened. "I'm all bark, with plenty of teeth. Pops may be the big wheel steering the company, the main man that everyone sees, but never forget for one minute, Baby, that me and J B are right there behind him, calling the shots." He paused as Kendra dissolved into silence, then said, "Pops had nothing to do with what went on back there. I did."

"You!" Kendra wavered.

"Our fathers are both old men, Kendra," he assayed sensibly. "They *needed* to get all that feuding out of their system. Look how it'd eaten away at them. They said things that even I didn't even know about. I love my Pops and—"

"And you'd do anything for him, including getting married to me," Kendra screeched, forcing back the painful tears in her eyes. "What annoys me is the huge stunt you've pulled to get this newspaper, and that you have the unmitigated gall to actually believe that I would accept this . . . this marital merger." She pulled her arm away from Shay's grip, her mind recalling everything she'd witnessed in her office. "Well, I'm going to be a thorn in your side, a splinter in your finger, a blister on your heel. I'm going to make you regret the day you ever take me for your wife."

"Kendra, stop it," Shay ordered. He looked at her furiously and then gripped her wrist, and Kendra found herself helpless, being propelled into one of the photo processing rooms Shay had spotted across from the elevator. Pulling Kendra into it, he slammed the door shut and placed her against it while he switched on a light. Red rays of light bounced off Kendra's defiant face as Shay looked down into her adoring, angry eyes. He surveyed her in silence for an age, then said softly, "Pops is from another generation. He speaks his own mind and he's a damn stubborn man, just like your father. All I wanted was for them both to realize that they could one day die hating each other."

Kendra flinched. "What you wanted was the *Nubian Chronicle* to settle a score," she amended scornfully, her mind taking her back across a week of turbulence which had led to the inevitable round of confrontation where two old men's memories had surged. For them, the decades had fallen away to that long ago moment when they had been young, when life was full of dreams and hopes. When the fate of two best friends had been settled in a little coffee shack in uptown Kingston, Jamaica.

"Maybe," Shay admitted coolly, his gaze intensifying as it met hers. "But what I want more than anything is you."

Kendra averted her own gaze. She wished she didn't know Shay's face could soften into such unexpected tenderness. She should carry on mistrusting him, a voice warned, yet she couldn't help being enveloped into the gentleness of his face. She found it unnerving, because only a few minutes ago she'd sized him up to be a callous brute.

Now Shay was looking at her with fond, appreciative eyes, and Kendra felt as if the ground were being cut away from under her feet and there was a deep abyss in front of her ready to swallow her up. But she pulled herself together sufficiently, common sense and something more—a feeling that she was really out of her depth with this man—cautioning her to stay on her guard.

Leaning her back into the hard wooden door, she chortled. "How do you manage to stay so cool?"

Shay eyed her, uncomprehending. "What are you, the weather girl? Didn't you hear what I just said?"

He was much closer now, closer than he'd been seconds ago, Kendra realized with delicious alarm, his face only inches above hers so that she could feel the warmth of his breath stirring her hair. It was not only her hair that stirred, either, but with supreme effort she suppressed her acute excitement with miraculous calm. "I heard what you said, but I don't believe you," she admonished vigilantly. "And you know why?" She forced her eyes to narrow with scorn. "Because I don't think you, like your father, felt anything for me or my father back there. I don't think you feel anything for anyone."

Shay shrugged, unconcerned. "So I'm not given to outward shows of emotion."

As I've gathered," said Kendra. "Do you think that because you don't get hurt, nobody else does?"

Shay grimaced as his hands came down to rest on Kendra's shoulders. "If I've hurt you, then I'm sorry," he offered with a note of sincerity. "I know you think I'm dangerous, that I'm the epitome of a child who's been visited on by the sins of his father, and you have every right to wonder whether you're safe with me." His voice came against Kendra's hair, sending tiny shock waves of sweet anticipation down her veins. "Well, Kendra, you're *not* safe with me," Shay mouthed in earnest, his head coming down to lean against Kendra's forehead, his hands absently caressing her shoulders, every brush, every stroke, inciting a heady, hectic motion inside Kendra that made her feel that the very space between them was vibrating. "Every time you look at me with your eyes, I know you'll never be safe with me until I have you," he declared ravenously in his American accent.

Kendra closed her eyes, reveling in the closeness of this man who had the power to turn her bones to water. She knew Shay was going to kiss her, and the urgency of her need for it to happen was almost shocking, considering what he'd put her through—was still putting her through. Yet, somehow, she didn't care. In that moment, all she wanted was for Shay to feed her need. She began to tremble, and her lips parted thirstily, invitingly.

"Kendra, I'm sorry," Shay muttered, looking down into her warm, beautiful, oval face before he pulled her strongly against him, forcing Kendra's head back as his mouth came down on hers greedily.

His wet lips were demanding yet gentle, grazing her mouth in deep, meaningful movements. Kendra was spellbound. Shay was so warm and alive against her, his heart beating in tune with her own, providing a craving she'd never before experienced.

He kissed her with every pretext of an apology, his lips in silent redress, sampling, relishing, making amends. Then, drawing a labored breath, he probed deeper to find the essence of her fire.

Knowingly aware of her actions, Kendra tipped her head farther back to welcome his soothing requital, accepting the tongue that had driven into her mouth, a fevered need for more intimacy causing a smothered moan to eject from her soul.

Incited by it, Shay pulled her closer to his hardened rigid muscles, whispering a soft, tangible appeasement that speeded up the motions inside her aroused body. "I'll never hurt you again," he gasped against her lips before he ardently took them again into his mouth and languorously explored them with such tormenting and persistent slowness that Kendra was driven wild with torturous passion.

She could hardly breathe as his hunger provided her with renewed appetite. He caused butterflies to flutter in her stomach, snakes to run up her spine in tingling sensations, scorpions to jab with great frequency at her heart, for it pulsated with more than its usual rapidity.

Jarred by her frantic, sensual longing for him, she

indulged in Shay's amorous reconciliation, forgetting the agony of her recent ordeal with him, forgetting, too, how their fathers had fought and the god-awful things they'd said to one another.

He was the most forceful, dynamic and compelling man she'd ever met, and she couldn't get enough of him. She leaned against Shay's muscled, hard chest and savored the sizzling heat of atonement that had built up between them. She felt the bold rising of Shay's passion and mindlessly rubbed herself against him, taking delight on hearing his deep, pining groan in frenzied response. She delved her own tongue into his mouth to tell him of her yearning for him. And still she was unsatisfied.

"Girl, you're on fire," Shay rasped, reluctantly pausing to look at the red-blooded woman in his arms who had turned him into a wild, insatiable animal. "I'm so crazy for you, too," he whispered hoarsely, allowing his hands to familiarize themselves with Kendra's body again, his fingers deftly reaching to unbutton the flimsy, white blouse she was wearing. "I've been walking around like a kid with hoop dreams thinking about you, carrying around in my pocket those damned sapphire earrings you left in my car because they'd been part of you."

Kendra smiled, unable to disguise the immense joy which tugged at her strained heartstrings on hearing Shay's musical confession. "I thought you didn't believe in love," she breathed shakily, gasping as his hands came up against the softness of her breasts. "Love is a word people put to work when they want to use somebody," she said.

Shay's eyes shadowed and Kendra realized that some of the warmth had fallen from their dusky depths. "Who's talking about love?" he murmured, raising his hand to trace a shaky path across her cheek. "I'm talking about that hot, crazy, sexual thing that's been eating away at the two of us, that fire that we're both eager to release. I'm talking about taking you to bed."

Kendra's body shook. Shay's admission startled her, excited her, appalled her. As he planted another kiss against her lips the recesses of her mind told her that to him she was nothing more than an alluring challenge, perhaps the biggest challenge of his life. It wasn't enough to pursue her father's newspaper. He had to include her in the package deal too, and for what? Benjamin Brentwood got the *Nubian Chronicle*, would get his dynasty. And Shay? He would get sex and plenty of it, judging by his physical prowess, she thought.

Love. *Where is love?* a tiny voice pressed. Arlisa's words surfaced in her confused mind. *Those of us who've seen the light, we know not to go in chase of that like it was sweet nectar from God, 'cause we're never gonna find it.*

Strange, Kendra mused as she felt Shay plant kisses against her neck. *Selwyn never used the word* love, *either. The closest he could come to it was* happiness. Was she being naive? she wondered. Was she really the only one in search of something there was no hope of finding? It dismayed her somewhat, for as long as Kendra could remember she had always thought that she would one day find that sweet nectar from God.

She was aware that Shay had detected some change in her. Ever alert to her moods, he raised his head and studied her face with concern. "What is it?"

Disturbed at what she was thinking, Kendra seized upon a conciliatory tone. "Nothing," she lied quickly, though privately she still felt staggered by what she'd been drawn into.

"Nothing?" Shay repeated. He didn't believe her. He looked down into Kendra's face and experienced a distinct tug as his heartstrings pulled against his lungs. He'd had this feeling before—every time she smiled at him. Only now it was different. More intense.

She looked so beautiful, so fragile . . . so vulnerable. Yet he knew only too well the fireball personality temporarily hidden beneath the moody visage. Oddly, it was that combination, that mixture of brown sugar and spice, which had attracted him so. Lifting his hand, he gently touched her shoulder, playfully allowing his fingers to stroke gentle circles of persuasion against the flesh exposed through the unbuttoned white blouse.

"You know," he confessed. "when I was a kid about ten, maybe eleven, Pops took me and Joel to Jamaica to meet our grandfather, Amos Brentwood. He was a bear of a man, but he was real gentle and he read the Bible a lot." He rolled his eyes in reminiscence. "Anyway, one day he sat me and Joel underneath a mango tree and told us how, when he was a young man, he went in search of a virtuous woman. It's a term mentioned in the Bible."

"I know." Kendra nodded. She'd heard the term before, too.

"Well, he told us that this . . . virtuous woman . . . would know her value because, like Eve, who was made from the sensual bone of Adam, she would find her place in his life." His hand traveled along the side of Kendra's neck, tracing slow, nerve-tingling circles just beneath her ear. "Well, from that sensual bone, close to my heart, I realized what you were telling me in the car last week."

For an instant, Kendra felt some inner self shake. "I . . . I find that rather hard to believe," she mumbled weakly, the words practically falling out in an unwilling jumble. Kendra knew some cynical thought refused to let her conjure up a meaningful reply to such a spiritual revelation because only a week ago this man had been so explicitly against making any sacred union. "I'm at a loss in trying to understand you," she explained. "Why are you doing this to me?" She told herself it was because he'd fallen in love with her.

Shay drew in a calming breath. Why should she believe him? He'd made a judgment call by pressuring her into marriage. Not to please his father or to end the feud between their families—he could have found some other way to settle that. He'd done it for something inexpressible that he couldn't quite fathom without displaying some honesty about how he was really feeling.

It was truly unlike him. What did he know about commitment? Perhaps he'd behaved this way because Selwyn Owens had offered her it. Yes, that was it. He was jealous, he told himself. Jealous that Selwyn had offered her emotional stability, had offered her loyalty and security, all the things he'd always thought irrelevant until he remembered his grandfather. Yet as he looked down at Kendra, intent on telling her all those things, he realized he didn't know how to express himself without betraying something he had yet to come to grips with.

"I need you," he whispered quietly, annoyed because there was so much he wanted to say. "I need you like I've never needed a woman." His lips came down again and smothered hers in delicate, aqueous motions. Kendra was instantly swept away by their fluid, moist invitation, too emotionally caught up in Shay's magic to deny herself the phenomenal vitality she was feeling. Too overawed even to realize that she was tasting that sweet nectar from Heaven.

A sudden knock at the door harshly disrupted the delirious dream they were both in. Shay's head shot up and he muttered a sharp, nasty word. "I could easily kill whoever is standing on the other side of that door," he croaked.

Kendra sighed and pressed her head against his chest, still dazed as she sensed that Shay reached for the door and wedged it open. Leola's voice echoed into the room. "I thought I saw you come in here," she began meekly. "Your father told me to find you. He says he's ready to go to the airport now. Shall I tell him you're on your way?"

Shay frowned irritably. "Yes." He scowled. Sliding his gaze over to Kendra, he felt his face soften. "My father is going to New York to take care of some business. I'd better go." Pulling Kendra toward him with his free hand, he took one final taste of her sweet lips. "I'll come for you later," he promised wickedly. And then he was gone, leaving Kendra wondering what the hell her father's newspaper had gotten her into.

Nine

"You all right?" Ramsey Davenport inquired of his daughter as she drove toward St. John's Wood from the office that evening.

Kendra was not fine. She was disappointed. Shay hadn't come back for her as he'd promised. Instead, he'd left a message with Leola that he had gone to meet his brother and would see her in the morning. He had forgotten about her already. She sighed wearily, careering the car down a quiet road which led toward their home in North-West London.

Residential and office buildings loomed up against the night sky as she traveled, and the dim streetlights served more to cast dark shadows from the sparse trees littered there than to offer ample help to guide her along. But Kendra persevered, enjoying the one control she had, that of navigating the car in her smooth, calculated manner, hoping it would disguise her malaise. "I feel . . . numb," she admitted to her father forlornly, knowing she couldn't fool him.

Ramsey gritted his teeth. "Kendra. If there was something I could do . . . I don't want to lose that house. Not when so much of your mother is still in it."

"I know," Kendra said weakly, understanding his need to hold on to the memories. "I'll be fine. It's not as if that newspaper were the be all and end all in life. No doubt Benjamin Brentwood will give it all the global appeal it deserves. I suspect he and Shay will probably plan to circulate it in the United States as well as England."

"So the man tell me," Ramsey confided calmly as he began to repeat Benjamin Brentwood. *" 'The past is the past. What we are offering is the future. Consider the glowing picture we can paint. An international communications network the centerpiece of a dynamic conglomerate. A newspaper that could triple its billings in less than two years.'* The man's son has plans, Kendra. Big plans."

Kendra eyed her father momentarily. He seemed to like the idea, she realized. That it was mirrored across the tired lines in his face, adding a curious zest to his features she hadn't seen since her mother had died.

"So, Shay is spearheading all this, I take it?" she queried oddly, returning her eyes back to the road.

"Ben tell me so," Ramsey admitted lightly. "You know, Shay not such a bad boy. Yes, he blackmailed me, but I think things could have been worse. He didn't let my girl go to jail, and I have to thank him for that. But I'm going to punish Arlisa for what she do. So," he added, probing carefully, "you think Selwyn is going to mind when you marry Shay? And how come I haven't met that there boy yet? Is he frightened of me?"

Kendra flinched at the mention of Selwyn's name as she changed into fourth gear and steered the car into a smooth cruise around a bend and into another street. There was a time when she'd wondered that, herself. Selwyn knew her father had been at the cutting edge of black journalism for over thirty years, had met all the political dignitaries from South Africa, Ghana, Nigeria, for official state interviews, and he was probably an authority on every influential black person throughout England for the past decade. She'd thought those were all reasons enough for any man to be eager to meet her father, but instead Selwyn had declined all her invitations to have dinner at her home.

There was no chance of him coming there now. It was all she needed on top of everything else, having to tell Daddy about her own behavior with a man he knew almost nothing about. It would be far easier if she simplified the truth, she decided quickly, despising the thought of lying to him about how she and Selwyn had parted company. But, she argued, the less he knew the better.

"Selwyn is very career-minded, Daddy. He has very little time for domestic introductions," she answered, choosing her words carefully. "And he understands what he wants in terms of happiness, which is far off the mark from what I want, so I think his career will compensate him adequately."

"I see," was Ramsey's noncommittal reply as Kendra sensed him leaning back into his seat and comfortably pressing his limbs into the soft, leather upholstery. "Well, Ben say he's going to pay for everything, so I'll just wait to get the deed back to my house," Ramsey added sternly. "But Kendra," he said, his voice softening, causing Kendra to instantly glance over at him, "if you don't want to stay married to that boy, just say the word. If it's Selwyn you really want—"

"Dad, I'll be all right," Kendra shivered, unconvinced. Would she be all right? And if so, why was her heart flapping around like a lost bird? She wasn't prepared to think more on the topic. Too nervous to continue the discussion, she turned on the car's compact disc player and inserted Sam Cooke's "You Send Me," and as the soft music bellowed from the low stereo monitors she guided the car along the shadowy road, thinking only of Shay Brentwood.

* * *

Arlisa was waiting impatiently in Kendra's bedroom when Kendra kicked off her brown boots and sank onto the chair by her dressing table. "I want all the fine details," she demanded hastily. "Did Daddy hit Benjamin Brentwood?"

"At his age!" Kendra remarked, startled. "Don't be silly."

"Well, what happened, then?" Arlisa flung herself onto Kendra's bed and glared murderously at the ceiling. "I told you I wanted to be there."

"Daddy didn't want you to be," Kendra answered harshly. "It was embarrassing enough for him to know you'd been the cause of this horrible mess without sporting you off to the enemy." She caught Arlisa's dejected reflection in her mirror and surrendered to her sniffling. "Okay Arlisa. If you must have it. The lowdown is that Rugg Brown is drafting an agreement which states that after Shay and I are married my shares in the *Nubian Chronicle* will be transferred to Benjamin Brentwood so that he can give Daddy back the deed to this house."

Arlisa shook her head in confusion, the enormity of her actions weighing heavily upon her in slow, calculated kilograms. "But . . . but . . ."

Kendra fully explained and watched as every expression of amazement was reflected in her sister's shocked expression. "All on account of your gambling shenanigans," Kendra finished, tossing the words carelessly over her shoulder.

"I said I'm sorry," an exasperated Arlisa lashed out. "It wasn't my fault entirely. Raymond told me to always bet on black, but well, red seemed—"

"Raymond! Who's Raymond?"

"I met him in Monte Carlo," Arlisa said, quavering,

knowing she'd let something slip inadvertently. "He's fluent in French, Spanish—"

"Dozens—no *hundreds,* of men," Kendra exploded loudly. "Your life revolves around them like a bee to a honeycomb. When are you going to stop, Sissy? One man. That's all you need."

"All *you* need, maybe," Arlisa snapped. "Besides," she added spitefully, "I'm sick of you being so disapproving all the time. What do you dislike? My hundreds of men? Or do you simply envy me the amount?"

"That's below the mark, and you know it," Kendra hit back bluntly. "I want you to take care in what you do, in who you see, in the caliber of men you date. You're wayward, Sissy, and because of it I have to marry, or have you forgotten that already? Every time you do something, someone else has to pay for the consequences of your actions. You were like that in school, in college, at home, too. Like that time our cousin Nellie came over to spend summer vacation with us. You made her lie to Momma about Cory Robinson being her boyfriend and not yours, and so *she* got grounded instead of you, remember? Everything you do affects somebody. As of now, you're free to create more mayhem, to cause chaos elsewhere, to disrupt someone else's life. I'm sick of it."

Arlisa's lips trembled as she rose abruptly from the bed. "Well, I'm sick of you always winding up with everything." She frowned. "You're Daddy's favorite girl, editor of the *Nubian Chronicle,* a media power player who even lands an M.P. in her bed. Now, I discover Momma left you *her* shares. Me, I do something wrong and what happens? You get Shay Brentwood, joint heir to Benjamin Brentwood's publishing enterprise and his prime time cable television network, broadcasting twenty-four hours a day to over forty million households in twenty-five hundred markets. You're mistress to a fortune, and I have zilch."

Kendra didn't know what to make of Arlisa's tearful, statistic laden outburst except to recognize that twenty-five years of accumulated resentment lay behind it. "Listen, Arlisa." She turned in her chair and attempted to reason with her sister. "I don't want to be hard on you, even though I have every godgiven right to be." Her mind traveled back to a time so long ago. "But . . . I still remember the day Momma brought you home from the hospital." A smile creased her face as she watched Arlisa retake her seat on the bed. "You were so tiny, only five days old. I didn't even know how to say your name, so I called you Sissy. The first thing I remember Momma saying to me was that I should help her look after you. Somehow, maybe it's a big sister thing, I always felt that I had that responsibility."

"But I'm a grown woman now," Arlisa protested sharply.

"I know that," Kendra relented. "But just because Momma's gone doesn't mean you have to behave irresponsibly. Daddy never knew us like she did, and I know that's not how she would've wanted you to behave."

Arlisa's shoulders dropped as some truth of what Kendra was saying sunk in. "I always felt she loved you more than me," she admitted tearfully.

"That's not true," Kendra clarified quickly.

"Maybe." Arlisa seemed unsure. "I think that's why I've always deliberately gotten myself into trouble, to see how she would react."

Kendra raised a brow. "Did she ever hate you?"

"No."

"Well, then," she said in clipped tones, drawing back from the precipice, "I think it's time you started behaving like the grown woman you say you are. And I'm sure Momma left you an equally treasured gift for when you marry. As for me marrying Shay," she told Arlisa, diverting her attention back to her own dilemma, "that's just a cruel twist of fate. Now that he owns fifty-two percent of the *Chronicle,* I'll have to look up to him—literally. Remind me to invest in a higher pair of shoes."

"I *am* sorry," Arlisa breathed.

"I know you are." Kendra sighed heavily, thinking of Shay. "Destiny has no rules," she repeated absently.

"What?" Arlisa rasped.

"Oh, you know what they say, Sissy." Kendra shook herself. "Marry in haste, repent at leisure."

"Repent." Arlisa suddenly laughed. "With Mr. Cool Lover? You have to be kidding. He's so sexy that every woman who read the "Best Bachelors Ever" in *Ebony* magazine will be weeping. Just do me a favor. When you throw your wedding bouquet, head it in my direction, and make sure it's big enough to knock me out. Maybe he has a cousin I can hook up with."

Kendra smiled, even chuckled somewhat. The old, loving Arlisa was back, adorably mischievous, high-spirited, and exhibiting all the sparkling, vivid, animated power that would always remind Kendra that she had the most cheerful, foolhardy sister in the world. And how she loved her so.

Kendra arrived at the *Nubian Chronicle*'s offices the following morning to find it in chaos. Mindful of the fact that she would be seeing Shay there, she'd decided to arrive at her usual 8:30 A.M. time to get the newspaper ready for its regular Friday morning print run.

Resolving in her head that she would still have editorial control, she'd already planned exactly what features would run with the Black History Month supplement, and how the paper's image that week would reflect on five decades of heritage and cultural diversity within the community it had served since the advent of the Second World War.

Yet as she strode confidently out of the elevator car, briefcase in hand and dressed immaculately to camouflage a restless night, two workmen in blue overalls struggled past her, their arms wrapped around her big wooden desk, evidently having removed it from her office.

Fretfully removing the coat which had protected her against the harsh elements of the October morning, curious, she walked over to her office to find it a mere shell of a room. Her cabinet had disappeared, as had the chairs, the coatrack and the word processor, and all her Egyptian statuettes were sitting on the bare floor, along with the telephone and boxes of her work, the carpet having already been stripped and rolled, ready for removal.

"Wait a minute," Kendra ordered sternly as one of the workmen paused to reposition his hold on her desk. "What in the hell are you doing? Who instructed you to move all this?"

"You'll have to speak to me gaffer, Love," the man told her in his broad, London cockney accent, his breath giving evidence of him having drunk a pint or two of lager that morning. "We just take our orders."

Kendra folded her arms beneath her breasts, suspecting that Shay Brentwood had lent a hand in all this. "Who exactly is your boss?"

"Mr. Grahame, McCain Removals," the man answered, inclining his head toward Leola. "Your girlie's got our instruction sheet. The number's on the top, Love."

Kendra stalked briskly toward Leola and deposited her briefcase and coat on her desktop to pick up the clipboard the man had indicated. Annoyed, looking into the younger woman's green eyes, she inquired, "What time did they arrive?"

"I don't know," Leola stammered. "They were already here when I came in."

Kendra looked puzzled. "Is Shay Brentwood here?"

Leola shook her head. She hadn't seen him.

"Then who let these guys in?"

"Maybe someone of the staff," Leola guessed weakly, her expression sending out signals that she'd taken on a fair amount more than what had been listed on her job description. "Miss Davenport—" she began, her voice holding enough conviction to tear Kendra's gaze away from the clipboard.

"Anything important in my mail today?" Kendra asked, oblivious that her secretary wanted her specific attention.

Leola looked alarmed. "No."

Kendra gazed at her, puzzled, recalling she'd seen a man on a motorcycle leave as she'd entered the building. "I thought I saw a courier downstairs on my way in."

"Not this floor," Leola confirmed, hesitating.

"Oh." Kendra sighed with guilt. "I was worried that maybe Selwyn had a note sent over. I owe him an explanation about something I did, and—"

"Miss Davenport," Leola firmly impressed, cutting Kendra off midstream. "We all want to know what's going on." Her voice lowered slightly as Kendra stared at her. "I don't know if you've realized, but everyone's uneasy here. The staff are all coming to me with questions I can't answer, and . . . well . . . we're all feeling quite ignored."

Kendra grimaced. It was her own fault, of course. She should have held a meeting with all the *Chronicle*'s staff members—to whom she affectionately referred as "the people"—the day her father had made his untimely return to the newspaper.

She quickly recalled their startled faces, their furtive glances, their bewildered expressions, and scolded herself for not having said something sooner. Everyone had just gotten used to doing things the Kendra Davenport way; gotten used to the new page format and design she'd introduced to the paper, the new publishing software she had installed, the fresh arts, film, and entertainment sections which she'd expanded, and the addition of a world news page for which she had brought in two experienced overseas correspondents from Trinidad.

Her father's sudden return must obviously have been unexpected for many of them, she thought suddenly. Even his old aides—Lynton, Tony, Irvin—seemed to stand in resentment as he walked around the editorial floor, reacquainting himself with the old place. Strange, she thought sadly as she dialed the telephone number detailed on the clipboard, that her father should gravitate to something he'd built and find that there was nothing there for him anymore.

An engaged tone rang out in her ear and she madly slammed the receiver back into its cage. "Call that number every five minutes until you get through," she told Leola firmly. "And don't worry, I'm going to talk to the people now. I'll fill you in later." She looked over at the two men. "Don't let those guys take anything else, and if Shay Brentwood arrives send him to the conference room. That's where I'll be."

Asserting all the requisite gloss of her profession, Kendra clicked her heels together, smoothed the crease in her burgundy dress and jacket, then deftly strode over to where she knew her journalistic staff would be waiting for her.

"Okay people, let's get started," she began, coming up against the crew of twenty men and women seated in a semicircle around the room in anticipation of her arrival.

Kendra knew the instant she saw them huddled together in solidarity that a covert early morning meeting had transpired in her absence. She suspected that it had more to do with the team of lawyers who had arrived there yesterday than with her father, and, perhaps, from the odd rumor and speculation which had escalated into fact. Sensibly positioning herself where she could see them all, she asked, "Are we done?"

Lynton, the oldest member of the team, who had served on the *Chronicle* for nearly fifteen years as the financial director, rose bravely to his feet, an indication that he'd been elected the group's spokesman. "Kendra, you know we all respect your father," he began, his face hard and serious. "When he retired, we were all sorry to see him go. A few of us here remember you when you were a kid, running in from school all the time to watch him work. We always knew you'd learn the ropes one day." He hesitated, then pulled up the courage to say, "We saw the lawyers come in here yesterday. We figured your father must have sold us down the river for a good price. In our opinion, you were doing just fine. We had a few problems with you in the beginning, but—"

"Lynton, Lynton," Kendra interrupted, eager to put his mind at ease. "The paper hasn't been sold. We . . ." It was her turn to hesitate, realizing astutely that she would have to tell her people sooner or later about the new ownership plans. "Yesterday, Dad and I agreed to a partnership deal between the Davenport Publishing Company and the Brentwood Communications Group, Inc. in New York," she began in part, truthfully. "My father came back to bring about a smooth transition during the minor changes which will affect us all, but there is nothing for any of you to worry about."

"I told you it was Benjamin Brentwood I saw," Kendra

heard Irvin, her assistant editor, say to a member of the crew. Ignoring him and deciding that she just couldn't tell them about the Brentwood's plans to acquire complete ownership, she added, "Sometime soon, Shay Brentwood and I will be getting married and—"

"Getting married!" The whole team became excited. *"That means we won't be losing our jobs?"* one boomed in anticipation. *"You'll still be running the paper, right?"* another asked.

Kendra swallowed as she saw the relief on their faces. She felt understandably guilty. Working on the *Chronicle* was their livelihood, too, and, as in the case of Tony, who'd served the longest, as the senior production controller, their life's work. How could she possibly tell them she had no idea what ultimate changes the Brentwoods had in mind, when she herself was unsure what was happening to her own office? "As I said, you have nothing to worry about," she prevaricated uneasily, "so let's get to work, people. We have a paper to get to press."

As the team began to disperse to their relevant workspaces, laughing and bantering in their progress, Kendra heaved a sigh of relief. For now they were satisfied, though for how long she had no idea. Discontentment would eventually resurface above the troubled waters, she mused. When that time arrived, she would no longer be present to explain to her people what went wrong. It was an unsettling thought, for Kendra had always believed that she would never leave her father's newspaper.

Pivoting on her heels, feeling saddened and dejected, she was about to return to Leola's desk when Trevor rushed from behind her, panting heavily and throwing out words in a quick succession of panic and apprehension.

"What do you mean, there's a virus in the computer network?" she bellowed after digesting his running dialogue. He was using disturbing words like sabotage . . . deliberate . . . intentional, and Kendra suddenly realized that her momentary relief on having dealt with her staff was dissolving as a new wave of anxiety washed over her. Heading in Trevor's direction, she hurried behind him to the computer terminal he'd discovered was the trigger point of destruction. It was in his office.

"Everything's going down," he told Kendra somberly, shaking his head in disbelief. "I tell you, Kendra, whoever did this knew exactly what they were doing. All that research data we collected on police street justice, it's gone. The files on the number of immigrants dying in custody, wiped out. We've even lost all those statistics on the frequency of inner city male homicides." Trevor paused, the two second silence sending a shaft of trepidation down Kendra's spine. "If I didn't know better," he told her sternly, "I'd say this was the work of someone who's out to take control of the *Chronicle*. Either that, or they're looking to take us down, because as of now we've got nothing to get this paper to press."

"You're kidding!" Kendra mouthed in amazement. "I just pieced together the entire Black History Month supplement yesterday. Don't tell me we've lost that. Please?"

"Along with everything else," Trevor answered. "This is a very sophisticated piece of work, Kendra. My guess is that they loaded it in from here, triggered the program with an access code, and allowed it to do its worst. I figure it must have been planted within the last twenty-four hours."

"What are we going to do?" Kendra said, weakened. "This is Black History Month and . . ."

"Someone mention Robert Starling Pritchard?" Kendra's body stiffened as her head shot round in time to chart Shay Brentwood's entrance into Trevor's research room. "Black History Month!" he added, observing the shocked, almost blank expression on Kendra's face. "Pritchard invented it, or was it Carter G. Woodson, the Father of Black History?"

"Forget the U.S.," Kendra retorted, erecting a cool, aloof barrier to deflect her pleasure on seeing him. "We're in England," she reminded, "and right now, I'd say you have some explaining to do."

Her voice was harsh, but she couldn't help herself. He made her so damned angry, standing there like that, staring at her with those warm, dusky brown eyes, looking like something fresh off the cover of *Ebony Man*. He was dressed in black denims and a black, designer, signature sweatshirt with a navy blue, nylon windbreaker. His tooled leather boots had been elegant once, but were now worn and scuffed from months rather than years of battering.

Shay's brow furrowed. "What'd I do?"

"Spare me the pretense," Kendra accused hotly, a corner of her paranoid, skittering mind telling her that she'd seen something in his eyes that betokened some secret victory over her as the ignorant foe. "Trevor's discovered the virus you've implanted in our network. Everything's gone. Another contingency of yours, I believe?"

She half expected him to explode at her presumption, but Shay merely looked at her, twisting his car key around in his hand as he reined his instant urge to respond. Then he growled his reply in the careful manner of a man who was exercising supreme restraint. "You believe me capable of destroying the nerve center of this newspaper after having done so much to get it?"

Kendra shrugged sullenly. The question was unanswerable in the present circumstances.

Shay was silent. In fact, he was silent for so long that Kendra was finally driven to blurt, "Who else could it be?"

Shay's eyes clouded, as sullen and opaque as a winter sea. "You gonna tell me why you think that is?"

"To expedite a quick takeover," Kendra assaulted. "So that by the time dear Pops gets his shares you will already have installed your people and your equipment. Isn't that why you've moved everything out of my office?"

Shay's body suddenly took on a stillness that to Kendra appeared menacing. "What . . ." His jaw sagged as though the blow had come from a totally unexpected direction.

His puzzled innocence was very well done, Kendra surmised ruefully. Shay was the epitome of deception, and she was angry that her blind absorption with how he'd kissed her had almost camouflaged his consolidated conquest, which he was obviously now exercising to the fullest.

Now she felt mindful of exactly what was going on, and it terrified her. "Perhaps you and Pops forgot to trade notes," she jabbed knowingly. "I guess his trip to America caused you to overlook your battle plans."

Shay's eyes narrowed as he turned to Trevor, his face rock-hard, his muscles banked with tension. "Leave us alone." The three words exploded with the force of a gunshot, nearly blasting Kendra's ears.

As Trevor skittered out the door like a rat, Shay's voice sharpened to a lethal cutting edge. "You're playing a dangerous game, Lady. Blowing hot one minute and cold the next. I hope you're prepared for the consequences."

"I . . . I." Kendra's voice died in her throat. She was mortified. She *wasn't* playing any games. *He* was. He was the one who'd financially covered Arlisa's embezzlement, who'd wanted the *Nubian Chronicle* in return, who'd brought in a team of expensive lawyers to overturn her mother's will. Who'd then gotten hold of the deed to her father's house to force her into marriage, so that his father could definitely obtain complete ownership of their newspaper. And of course, he would have to make sure that she married him, in order to take over the shares. This latest escapade made perfect sense to her, considering all the stopgaps he'd activated to get so far.

Yet Kendra was more frightened by what he'd insinuated—that she, by virtue of her womanhood, was able to jest with her emotions with deadly intentions. The sarcasm was as insulting as it was effective. How could this man even think that she could so easily abandon every nuance of passion he had evoked in her amorous limbs—and could still evoke in her, even without the power of touch?

They were yards apart, yet her skin was supersensitive, absorbing every part of him and translating it all into a tingling sensation that spread over her entire body. Then he was walking toward her, and Kendra gritted her teeth at how dazed she felt.

"If this is your idea of revenge," Shay remarked indignantly, "then you're wasting your time." His hand came up and touched her cheek, his finger sliding downward across her swollen mouth before he slowly dropped his hand. "I'm still going to marry you, and we'll all get what we want."

Kendra's fascination turned to aversion. It pained her to know that this man had so much power over her life, that he could control and manipulate people with such ease. "You have no qualms at all about me being in your bed under sufferance, have you?" she demanded harshly, as every motive she'd devised in her head to convince herself that he loved her paled into insignificance. "You're just like your father, who has to have everything he wants. Well, as far as I'm concerned, our marriage will be a simple business arrangement, a technicality to enable the transfer of my shares to your father. As handshake deals are your forte, I trust we can accept that amicable agreement."

Shay's gaze seemed to crawl over her face. It was just too cruel that she thought him so insensitive, and he knew it was his own fault for putting the idea into her head. He wasn't prepared to defend his actions or argue semantics, because she was right. He felt as twisted as a spiral stairway; bending, curving, shaping every situation for the sake of having her. She didn't know it, but from the night she'd stood in the rain under a flash of lightning which had illuminated her lustrous oval face, he'd wanted her.

He'd never known a woman like her. There had been many, but none had possessed the vivacity, the intelligence, the serenity, all rolled into one attractive lady. Without knowing her intimately he'd offered her marriage, something he'd never really expected to offer anyone. He recalled his jealousy over the way she'd responded to Mr. M.P.'s offer of it—that babbling baboon who couldn't even remember her name. It'd made him damned angry, but when it came down to it he realized that he'd been angry with himself.

He was angry because he'd never been able to put up that invisible wall between himself and Kendra which he'd always been able to build with other women. He was angry because he'd told himself she was everything his grandfather had ever spoken about in a virtuous woman. And he was angry because he could not deny the way she was making him feel; so alive, so masculine, so hopeful.

But he'd behaved unreasonably because he'd been afraid that she would run back into the arms of Selwyn Owens. The thought made him uneasy. He was wrong in thinking that she thrived on risks, because now she was fighting back, and he felt unsure how to react.

"Shall we shake on it?" he heard her say abruptly, his gaze lowering to her outstretched arm.

"Fine," he answered simply.

Kendra almost died as he accepted her hand and asserted a firm, steady agreement, an unceremonial baring of their souls. "Okay," she breathed shakily, slowly releasing her hand. "Now that we know where we stand, maybe we can sort out this newspaper."

"What day do you go to press?" Shay inquired solemnly.

"Tomorrow," Kendra murmured, knowing that there was much to be done to get the entire computer system back on line, hardly what twenty-four hours would allow.

"Right," Shay relented, snapping into action. "I'm sure there must be people we can call to get temporary equipment and software up here?"

"I can get on to the systems analyst who installed our operating program," Kendra said after thought. "Maybe I can get him to come right over if we pay him top rate per hour."

"Okay," Shay agreed. "While you do that, I'll stop by Leola's desk and look into what's going on with your office. I assume the editorial staff can rustle up a makeshift issue."

Kendra nodded, relieved that he seemed resigned to sorting out what she now guessed to be Benjamin Brentwood's doing. "They're all professionals. This is as good a time as any for them to prove their worth. I'll go and talk with them now before I make some phone calls."

"Good." Shay made for the door, then stopped. Kendra noted his hesitation as he dug his hand into his trouser pocket before he strode back toward her. "You forgot these," he admonished tightly, dropping her sapphire and diamond earrings into the palm of her hand. Kendra shook as he purposely curled her fingers around them before he returned to the door. "By the way," he added, bracing his hand on the doorknob, "that man who was in here? Fire him." Without giving her an explanation, he left the room.

Kendra immediately rushed to the window and opened it for blessed air. She breathed deeply, uneasily, as if unable to get enough oxygen into her lungs. The beginning of October was always dismal. Even the elements rejected her as they blew cold, blustery wind against her ebony skin. She felt stifled and stymied by what she'd done, but she took respite in it.

With the progress of events, she knew that Shay would eventually hurt her. She hoped that by the time that had happened she would be secure enough to accept that the pleasure of knowing him would far outweigh the pain. She recalled that pleasure, the feel of him against her, the tiny rough sounds that he had moaned into her mouth, the way he'd held her. If she'd taken much more, had accepted him and every part of him, the pain of leaving would be as devastating as the pleasure.

No. She'd done the right thing. From here on in she should count on the normal modicum of detachment she usually exercised when confronted with the postman or the janitor. It would be her only saving grace if she were ever to save herself from suffering a broken heart.

Ten

From the moment Shay Brentwood occupied Ramsey Davenport's office, Kendra noted that there were new buzzwords circulating along the grapevine of her editorial staff. *"The Nubian Chronicle, A.D."* had aptly spread like wildfire from the lips of everyone on the pressroom floor; hushed secretly in corners, spoken in soft, subdued undertones at lunch, and whispered confidentially as though the cryptic initialed code words, *"After Davenport"* signified a new, exciting era.

Kendra sat behind her wooden desk in her freshly furnished office, uneasily contemplating the changes that had taken place in the six weeks since Shay had been there. He had not returned all her things. Except for stopping the departure of her desk with the assurance that he would retrieve every article that had been removed from her office, he had ordered its complete refurbishment, which encompassed a new lick of paint, upholstered guest chairs, deep pile blue carpet, new cabinets, and all the hardware modern technology demanded for one to keep abreast of the world's media market. She had yet to discover how to use them all.

They'd also succeeded in reaching press time with a makeshift issue of the *Chronicle* following the virus scandal; that being how it was termed after the news hit every televised and mainstream tabloid in the country. Trevor had been fired, much to her annoyance, so she suspected that he had made the leak to get a foothold in another newspaper.

She'd realized that the disclosure had irked Shay thoroughly, but he was never daunted by it. He quickly settled into working on the *Chronicle* with such speed that the pace of the newspaper suddenly became more hectic. Her people—the half dozen reporters, the handful of columnists, the small core of contributing feature writers who lent their expertise on special topics, factcheckers, copyeditors, proofreaders, and overseas correspondents—were all encouraged to become more idealistic about their opinions, and it'd all begun when Shay started to attend the early morning conferences.

Prefacing his entrances with a jolly "What's up?" before he straddled a chair and digested the concepts that were lobbied with enthusiastic eagerness, he'd been able to bring out the best in her people. Despite the renowned dominance that she was known to assert, she was suddenly reduced to a position of obscurity, yet on occasions she'd been happy to sit back and watch, bedazzled, as Shay extracted confidence and talent.

The *fait* was *accompli,* she'd even told herself, realizing that Shay belonged to the American culture, which was more gutsy, savvy, and more ambitious in its actions, and she'd never been able to boost self-esteem and morale in her work force the way he had.

The work had become more demanding, too, despite her own demonic pace, and she went home exhausted each evening, mindful of the fact that she was learning a lot more than she had when under the tutelage of her father. Shay possessed a rare mixture of sharp senses which at the very least included an ear for hearsay, a nose for investigative journalism, and an eye for priority selection. By the sixth weekly issue under his proprietorial guidance, sales of the *Nubian Chronicle* had elevated by degrees.

Leaning back into the uncomfortable leather chair, which had not yet molded to the curves of her body, absently jotting down lead marks of irrelevant patterns in a notebook, Kendra now imagined that it would be impossible to ever get close to Shay again. While other people got his attention, she did not. Even Leola, who seemed more interested in reporting to him, was able to demand some of his precious time, forcing her to almost unforgivingly fire the woman as she wallowed in her own jealousy.

It had become blatantly clear to her from the day he had installed himself in her father's office that Shay was treating her with the same level of courtesy that he would the cleaning lady, though there was always a measure of respect in his dusky brown eyes whenever he did consult her. She'd almost thought he was worried about her, because he'd always made a point of asking her if she was all right. It was silly, she thought, but she'd thought he cared.

But she realized his concern had more to do with her workload and the way she kept a tight rein over the activities of her sub-editors—ensuring that they were on top of their tasks—than anything to do with their personal feelings for one another. His keeping her at arm's length constantly reminded Kendra that he was unapproachable, except on matters relating to the newspaper. And so for the most part she saw very little of him, his time spent taken up with meetings in his office or elsewhere, proving that whatever they'd once shared was now severed.

Not strictly. There had been times when, in spite of his care to avoid it, a moment of intimacy would overwhelm him, taking shape in the form of a caressing glance across the conference table or an endearing leer in the pressroom, but this was always quickly suppressed, killing the joyful emotions stirred within her.

It meant he'd taken her seriously about their marriage contract being a stern and strictly business one, she mused dismally, flicking the page of her notebook to add further meaningless scribbles. It was the getting married part which now bothered her. Benjamin Brentwood had decided to call her father with his suggestion for a December wedding, and she'd detected the stress lines of anxiety across her father's face as he agreed to everything Benjamin wanted. It seemed even her father's strong will was diminished under the power of a Brentwood.

The quandary she'd been flung into was deep and inescapable, though Kendra had long since realized that she had no wish to escape. The idea of *being* married to Shay was beginning to grow on her, even as her mind warned time and time again that there would be no future in such a legal conjugality.

Their union would be solely about power, about pounds and pennies, dollars and cents; who was controlling whom, and what gains were to be made. Mentally, she'd felt oversensitive and disagreeable about what she had been pledged into, but inwardly, where her heart ruled supreme, she was wholly accepting of every nuance of what their alliance would hold.

Her mind was riveted keenly on what it would be like; the media parties, life in the fast lane, transatlantic travels . . . It would be a ball, she thought, pencil poised over her notebook as she began to contemplate an entirely new wardrobe. But her mind's eye reflected on something much more tangible, something she knew had irrevocably transcended the money and lifestyle Shay would have to offer. She wanted his love. She wanted the kind of love her parents had, where loyalty and trust, family values, and a sense of duty to each other would be the foundation from which they could build a lasting union of love and friendship.

But she was painfully aware that Shay was more interested in their physical attraction than anything spiritually binding. Perhaps that was why she'd accepted Selwyn's pragmatic self-discipline. He lived by rules and he also didn't rush her, though she was conscious that he'd expected to know her intimately, eventually. And, he'd also been married before, which gave her knowledge that he took that vow seriously. But his values in life were not hers. She could never have spent a morning with the Beaufort Hunt, chasing a fox into its hole on horseback, only to scare the life out of it or slaughter it. And though she'd been fond of Selwyn, she could never have loved him. Staring blankly, she wondered why he'd called her Keisha.

She blinked, propelling her thoughts back to Shay. The knowledge that he could never offer her the kind of love she really wanted because he was just like his father quickly pulled Kendra back to the decision she'd made. They were to have an amicable business agreement which would swiftly bring about a transfer of shares. Then they could both do as they damn well pleased.

Placing her pencil atop her desk with that resolve firmly planted, she glanced at the dial face of her watch. It said 9:30 P.M. Horrified that she was still in her office so late on a Friday night, Kendra packed up her things to prepare to leave. She would go home and wallow in the misery of her thoughts by immersing them and her tired limbs in a steaming hot bath.

Expelling a yawn and knowing that a positive frame of mind was sadly lacking, she walked lamely toward the door and threw on a heavy cashmere coat to protect herself from the harsh elements of a mid-November evening. Then, reaching for the lights, she switched them off and braced her hand on the doorknob.

As Kendra made to leave the safety of her office she felt the door click from the other side and found herself freezing as it began to inch open. Only the night watchman should be on the premises, downstairs, so she was justifiably nervous as to who was on the other side as the door opened and streaks of light invaded from the enclosed hallway.

"Who's there?" she demanded, her limbs shaking, frightened of confronting her intruder.

"Kendra?" Shay's voice instantly allayed her panic, and Kendra smiled cautiously as he made a slow entrance, his sturdy, practical appearance displaying a cool indifference to seeing her there. "Burning the midnight oil?" he ventured, taking another step into the dark room. "I thought you'd gone home until I saw the light go off beneath your door."

"I was just leaving," Kendra said, sucking in her breath as she looked into his shadowy face and wondered at the mysterious, faraway expression in those compelling, dusky eyes. From under her eyelashes she studied Shay's firm lips, now moving ever so slightly as he chewed gum, the lean jaws which were already showing signs of nearly a full day's stubble, the strong chin that had once nestled in the hollow of her shoulder as they'd danced. Dressed impeccably in a navy suit, though the white collar button of his shirt was open and the silk tie was askew, she suspected that he'd just concluded a meeting somewhere elusive, but she couldn't understand why he'd come back to the office.

"Did you need to see me for something?" she inquired as she motioned him outside into the hallway.

Because Shay hesitated for an age before he spoke, Kendra had the feeling that his words were modifications of those he'd originally intended to speak. "There's no immediate hurry for this," he said finally, handing her a large white envelope which contained papers. "You can read it, whenever."

Kendra felt a stab of apprehension as she took it. As it came from Shay, she had every right to be wary. "What is it?" Her voice stumbled.

"Rugg Brown had it sent over today," Shay clarified. "There are two copies in there which require your signature."

"For my shares after I marry you?" Kendra asked flatly, less in query and more as a statement of fact.

Shay looked at her in silence, his brooding face absorbed with every part of her with such familiar appraisal that Kendra was instantly reminded of the way he'd first scrutinized her under a torrent of rain and electric current. That now seemed like aeons ago... Then he blinked as though he had remembered something. "I want to talk to you," he said quietly. "Have you eaten?"

"No," Kendra answered immediately, before realizing that she should have said that she was going home to eat because—as she suspected he would—Shay seized the opportunity to ask her to dinner. She accepted, only because she felt obligated to discuss the few matters related to the newspaper to which he'd made reference as an additional persuasion for her to join him.

Seated in her car and following the red Maserati as it traveled at cruise speed in the cold, blizzard-like weather through the city of London, Kendra wondered whether she should have accepted his invitation. She felt almost resentful that he should choose that precise moment, disgusted with herself that she hadn't had the foresight to decline, because in truth she was still so mistrustful of the man.

One minute he'd be her gentle prince, the next a robber baron settling a score, and, as always, he left her feeling as though she'd stepped off a pirate ship's plank and into the abyss of the unknown. Beeping her horn at an intruder who rudely inched his Ford Kia in between her car and Shay's, she began to realize that Shay was also making it very hard for her to clarify her thoughts. She hadn't forgotten his steely, unfriendly gaze when he'd given her back her earrings, nor the accusation he'd leveled at her door, echoing Selwyn's view that she was an expert when it came to toying with males. And when she added his consistently cool, courteous behavior toward her while working on the newspaper, she began to feel uneasy altogether about being with him.

Observing the flash of his left indicator, only just, she followed his car as it curved around a bend, frustrated with herself and almost swearing under her breath as yet another driver edged his way in front of her. She tailed the Land Rover Discovery for half a mile, then panicked as she realized she might miss Shay making another turn. Furious that London drivers always managed to dampen her mood, she flicked on her left turn indicator and decided that she would overtake the two road hogs by pulling into the left lane, a move not allowed by British traffic standards. But as she got into lane and saw Shay's red Maserati ahead of her, she also found herself swallowing hard as a road sign marked Wimbledon loomed up near the windscreen of her car. Shay was taking her to his home. Her mind reeled in alarm, her senses wondering whether she should slam on the brakes and make a U-turn or continue.

Choosing the latter, Kendra decided to behave like an adult and not in a childish, skittish manner about crossing the threshold of that frightening mansion house where Benjamin Brentwood had once ordered her to leave.

* * *

An hour later, she was sitting in an empty room across from a large, open fire warming her freezing feet as her eyes roamed and checked the shelves of books, the snowy white, soft furnishings against a rich, melon-colored carpet, the elegant, dimly lit fittings and Edwardian curtain arrangement, all of which bespoke the delicate planning of a talented designer.

It was a lovely period room, one even a most unfamiliar house cat would find comfortable and lazily soothing. Leaning her back into one of the white sofas, she amended her thoughts about coming there. She felt thoroughly relaxed, having not been confronted with any unpleasantries, though she wondered where everybody was. The house had been empty on their arrival but the heating and the lights had been left on, and the flickering embers in the hearth, which fanned a blazing roar, indicated that someone had recently been in the house.

The sound of the door behind her opened with a squeak and Kendra turned her head to find Shay briskly entering the room. "I've ordered Creole food," he told her, making his way across the room toward her. "I hope you're hungry."

Kendra held out under the steady regard of his dusky brown eyes for a few brave seconds, mindful of the fact that his words, though sounding perfectly innocent on the surface, held a potent, underlying suggestion that was unmistakable.

Lowering her eyes demurely to avoid him seeing how suddenly vulnerable she felt, she muttered a simple, "I'm starved," delighted that she'd tossed the words back as equally suggestive banter.

She did not miss Shay's raised eyebrows in response, nor the wicked slant of his mouth, indicators that he was in full understanding of her chain of thought. As if to tease her, he urged, "Wouldn't you like to kick off your shoes?"

"No." Kendra swallowed nervously, aware that she'd already begun to feel too comfortable for her own good.

Shay's face seemed to attract the light from the fire and took on a gleam of burnished gold as he came and sat down beside her, his arm spreading companionably along the back of the sofa behind Kendra. "What's the matter?" he inquired softly.

Kendra shook her head. "You know, it's ironic that I'm even here," she declared blankly. "Why *am* I here, and where is everybody?"

"Pops is still in the States," Shay answered, allowing his hand to settle on Kendra's shoulder as briefly and lightly as a butterfly descending on a flower. "He comes back tomorrow. J B and Rhona have gone out to a nightclub. The domestic staff don't work after 8:00 P.M."

"I see." Kendra nodded, a sixth sense alerting her to exactly why she had been brought there. "So we're not here to talk?"

Shay's eyes narrowed. "Would you believe in a little honesty?"

"No," Kendra answered, poisonously sweet. "Are you sure you would even recognize it?"

"Try me," Shay challenged.

Kendra drew a breath. "Okay." She nodded again. "Why *am* I here?"

"Would you accept an abject apology from someone who has a lot to learn about English girls?"

Kendra ejected a shallow laugh. "You're apologizing?"

"I'm apologizing."

"And that makes everything all right?"

"No," Shay admitted, shifting his body to face her more directly. "Tell me about Selwyn Owens. How intimate were you two?"

Kendra gasped, feeling ridiculously nervous, knowing that her composure had slipped a notch. "I . . . I don't want to talk about Selwyn."

She quickly began to get up, but Shay pulled her back down again. "Have you slept with him?"

"No!" Kendra cried, pained by the very subject of their conversation, but even more taken aback by Shay's probing questions.

"But you wanted to?" he asked, curious.

"No!" Kendra insisted harshly.

"Then why did you stay with him?" Shay demanded, clearly confused.

"It was . . . it was out of puppy-like love and an exuberant wish to please," she stammered, her mind spinning as to why she was subjecting herself to such interrogation. "Selwyn's a perfectionist. He is obsessed with high standards and morality. I told you all that. Protocol is an important issue to him, and he liked things just so. I got used to it."

"How did you meet him?"

Kendra grew annoyed. Shay wasn't going to rest until he'd worn the topic of Selwyn Owens threadbare. "We were doing a piece in the *Chronicle* about repatriation . . . should people be given money by the government to go back to Africa?" she stated firmly. "He was kind enough to give us his views when we asked, and then I accepted his offer to lunch. Are you going to give me a reason for this damned embarrassment, or am I going to have to leave?"

Shay sighed, lifting his hand from Kendra's shoulder, leaving a trail of warmth in its wake. "The London Borough of Brent Council normally place all their public sector job vacancies with the *Chronicle,* right?"

"Yes," Kendra acknowledged warily. "A large portion of our readers are government employees looking to take different career options."

"Our advertising manager told me today that they've canceled all their previously booked slots indefinitely," Shay informed her wryly.

"What?" Kendra was alarmed, her brain suddenly piecing together a puzzle that didn't make any sense. "Are you saying that . . . Selwyn had something to do with it?"

"I don't know, but it's revenue we can't afford to lose." Shay sighed, shifting his head on hearing the doorbell. "That'll be the food. I'll be right back."

As he left, Kendra grew worried. She hadn't detected any character trait in Selwyn during the time they had been dating that indicated a vindictive temperament. He had a proficiency for arriving exactly on time—a dead giveaway that he was a man who lived by a schedule—and an eye for detail which made him slightly possessive about how she presented herself whenever they were going out, but she couldn't fathom any peculiarity in his manner that would force him into coaxing a local council to cancel their advertising budget with the *Nubian Chronicle*.

Yet she guessed that even the most stable person, when jilted, could do something bizarre to overcome the shame of being let down by someone they'd trusted. Perhaps he was getting back at her, she thought wildly, regretful that she'd already witnessed that tactic firsthand at Millennium Two Thousand. Yet the more she thought about how he embodied the picture of wholesome, exemplary character, the more unbelievable it became. Selwyn's life was far too demanding for him to waste time concocting childish attempts of revenge, she decided, so there must be some other explanation as to why the Borough of Brent Council canceled. She would call them at her earliest opportunity.

That thought was abruptly interrupted when Shay reentered the room with eight small, delicately designed boxes on a tray, each allowing the escape of an appetizing, steaming vapor which tickled her senses with scents of jerk chicken and prawns, lobster in oyster sauce, and fried basmati rice.

Five minutes later, both sat on the floor, the tray on a coffee table nearby, downing medium sweet white wine and sampling each box in turn with the same measure of concentration a gourmet chef would employ when tasting the inaugural food presentation of an apprentice.

Kendra noticed that Shay had removed his jacket and his shoes, and suddenly she found herself relaxed enough to remove her own shoes, enjoying the warmth of the rich pile carpet against the softness of her panty hose.

Swallowing a piece of chicken, she looked at Shay, knowing herself to be a little unsettled but confident enough to pick up on the subject he'd begun earlier. "What you were saying about Selwyn," she began nervously, "do you really believe him capable of jeopardizing our advertising?"

"I was hoping you could tell me that," Shay responded drily. "You're the one he proposed to."

Kendra detected a measure of coldness in his voice that surprised her somewhat. Not quite understanding why he was behaving so irritably, she answered, "I think there must be some other explanation."

"Public sector advertising keeps the *Nubian Chronicle* economically buoyant," Shay noted, taking a bite of his food. "So let's hope there is another explanation, and he isn't out there coaxing them all into doing it. The regular advertising we get from the U.S. hair and cosmetics companies and the music industry are not enough to support the paper entirely."

"I'll call the Borough of Brent Council on Monday," Kendra said, certain that Selwyn wouldn't pull favors from councillors and other M.P.s to wreak revenge. "I'm sure it's an oversight on their part." When Shay chose not to respond, the silence left Kendra feeling nervous. Searching for a conciliatory topic of interest to make conversation, she declared, "This is really a lovely house. I can understand why your father bought it."

Shay looked around him, swallowing the food which occupied his mouth before he spoke. "Pops didn't buy this house. I did." Shrugging, he added, "It's a lot cheaper than renting in the long run, and I'm told it's a good investment because of the international tennis games close by."

"It's yours?" Kendra said in surprise. "I thought your family lived here."

"We like to stay together a lot, and I like it here," Shay explained. "We all still live in the big house back home, but J B and Rhona are looking for a place of their own now, and Pops, he's all American. God, Coca-Cola, blue jeans, and honor. He even has the stars and stripes on a pole behind his desk in the house back home. Most folks don't even know he's a native Jamaican."

"Is your mother from the Caribbean—originally?" Kendra inquired, suddenly eager to learn more about Shay.

"Ma's from New Jersey," Shay declared warmly, licking his fingers in satisfaction and leaning his back against the foot of the sofa, his face relaxed, even offering Kendra a smile. "Her name is Clara, and she has a family history that goes way back to the Africans that came with the Dutch settlers."

"Wow," Kendra exclaimed, buoyed by the sudden closeness she felt toward him.

"Yeah," Shay agreed. "There's all kind of blood on Ma's side. I guess that's why she's so interested in culture and art."

"I don't know a thing about my ancestry," Kendra admitted, ejecting a soft chuckle that made her aware that she'd relaxed to some degree herself. "Maybe one day I'll discover that I'm an African princess or something."

"I'd believe it," Shay proclaimed, his expression misting over seductively.

Kendra's mind felt ravished by the needful look in his eyes, but she quickly looked away from their compelling depths and picked another topic.

"What do you do in your spare time, besides reading?" she asked.

Shay smiled lightly. "I like to play one on one basketball."

Kendra chuckled. "And besides basketball?"

Shay's warm eyes appraised her. "I like to rent movies on a Sunday night and order in pizza. It sorts of gears me up for the following week. You?"

"Mmm. I read too," Kendra said. "Novels, mostly Victorian stuff. Charles Dickens, Emily Bronte, Jane Austen . . . all the old classics."

"Victorian?" Shay laughed. "You're English, all right."

Kendra nudged him on the elbow, feeling embarrassed yet understanding how comical that must seem to a man of his background. "There's nothing wrong with that."

"I know."

"Well?"

"I'm sorry." He laughed, attempting to adjust his

face to one of seriousness. His lips quirked. "I guess everyone has different reading habits."

"Yes, they do," Kendra affirmed. "I happen to like period pieces. In fact, here in England we get a lot of Victorian melodrama on the TV. It's just great knowing what that bygone age was like."

"I take it you enjoy the museums, then?" Shay queried more seriously.

"Castles, stately homes, cathedrals, art galleries. Maybe I should take you up to Derbyshire sometime to visit Chatsworth House, in return for that ball game offer you made me," Kendra invited, recalling the breathtaking country views and freshness of air for which the North of England was fondly known. "The present Duke and Duchess of Devonshire open it to the public every year, and their gardens are noted for their roses."

"You're incredible." Shay laughed again. "You'll get on well with my mother."

"I was hoping to coax *you* into taking interest in English culture." Kendra smiled, enjoying the way Shay laughed so heartily. "I do live here, you know."

"I know," Shay relented, trying to calm himself. "Please tell me you have some other interests."

"Swimming," Kendra offered reluctantly.

"Mmm . . . that's good," Shay approved, leaning on his elbow as he reached for his glass of wine, his eyes firmly trained on her. "Do you swim well?"

"I think so," Kendra returned, reaching for her own glass of wine. "It helps me vent my frustration when things get tough."

"At the office?"

"And out of it."

"You must have been swimming a lot lately," Shay said absently. Then, pulling himself up short, he amended, "Sorry, did I hit a nerve?"

"The only nerve here is yours," Kendra said. "And you've got one hell of a nerve, reminding me, what life has been like these past couple of months."

"Aries," Shay remarked quickly. "You must be an Aries. They have fiery tempers, right?"

Kendra looked into his direct gaze. *God, he has devastating eyes,* she thought. She loved looking into those dusky eyes which always seemed to dim her temper. "I'm an Aquarius, actually—sixteenth of February."

"Leo—twenty-first of August. Pleased to meet you." Shay observed her smile before Kendra took a sip from her glass. *God, I love the way she smiles,* he told himself honestly. "So, do you swim for fun, too?" he asked, going back to the subject.

"Yes," Kendra admitted, sinking into his gaze.

"Maybe we should swim together sometime," Shay drawled, leaning over to place his wineglass on the coffee table before he took his position again—this time, inches closer to Kendra. "I can't remember the last time I swam."

"Maybe." Kendra inhaled sharply as she felt the warmth of his body as he reached out to her. Then Shay removed the glass from her hand and placed it on the coffee table. Within seconds he was back next to her, his very closeness beginning to cause exciting flutters of apprehension inside her body. Then, lifting one hand, Shay began to knead the tight cords in the column of her neck in slow, gentle motions.

Kendra immediately relaxed to the terrible sweetness of his touch. She even felt a sudden, soothing comfort as the apprehension faded, but when she felt deeper flutters within that spoke of her arousal she became nervous as to where it was all leading. Shrugging her shoulders gently, she hoped that Shay would stop the motion of his hand, but instead he began moving his fingers lightly against her soft skin, making caressing, circular movements around her neck, his fingers stroking the hairline just above it.

"You feel nice," he intoned huskily.

Kendra shuddered, and a shaft of liquid fire darted through her loins. "I shouldn't be here," she whimpered nervously.

"I want you to be," Shay whispered softly against her ear.

Kendra's body quaked in response. Shay's gaze was fiery, hypnotic, and intense as it snared hers, and she felt something stir within the pit of her stomach as their gazes held. His fingertips trailed a fiery path down to her raised shoulder and pulled, a strong, steady motion that slowly brought her face close to his rugged one.

Kendra was suddenly deathly afraid that this wasn't real, that the man who only hours ago seemed unapproachable and was now within her reach was the dark, shadowy lover of her intimate dreams. Yet her mind was replaying a resolution she'd made to herself, a silent pact that she felt obligated to uphold. Closing her eyes, she sighed weakly, "I can't."

Shay placed his right forefinger beneath her chin and tipped it upward. "Stop me," he said faintly, brushing a warm kiss against her lips, "and I'll stop."

Kendra felt a rising fever, a heat that was so warm in its intensity that she felt helpless to deny it. "Shay—"

His mouth covered hers, smothering all words with passion and need. In the name of seduction, he kissed her smoothly, wantonly, grazing her lips in rapid succession, absorbing her uncertainty in one fell swoop. He was waiting for her to surrender to him, concede to his sexual persuasion, but she was afraid to.

A part of her held back, and Shay felt it. He released her and surveyed her angelic face. He saw the ardent expression in her eyes and felt her shallow breath against his neck. She wanted him as he wanted her, yet she refused to submit. "What is it?" he rasped softly.

The past eight weeks rose up to torment her. "We made an agreement—"

"This has nothing to do with what we agreed, and you damned well know it," he jabbed in interruption.

He shocked her with his sharp perception, and to her chagrin Kendra couldn't explain why she had an uncanny urge not to lie to him. "When my momma was ill . . . after she . . ." Kendra hesitated "I've been celibate for nearly two years," she blurted finally, annoyed that he had the power to force such a personal admission from her. It had never bothered her before, not even with Selwyn, but with Shay she'd always accepted the certain knowledge that he would be the one who held the key to releasing the wild, imprisoned, and uninhibited desire she'd kept locked in for so long.

She expected him to be surprised, even staggered, but Shay's dusky eyes slanted wickedly as he looked into her adoring face. Prepared for her swift recoil, he restrained her by taking hold of her wrist and drew her hand across his chest, letting her feel the rapid thud of his heart. "I'm not going to rush you," he murmured silkily against her lips. "I'll take as long as you want." His finger touched her mouth, tracing the trembling contours. "We're going to do this together."

His devoted reassurance, whispered like soft strokes against Kendra's lips, subdued and seduced her so subtly that she was hardly aware she'd submitted to Shay's amorous invitation. With an enthusiasm alien to her, she covered his mouth with the sweet pressure of her own, surrendering to the swift crosscurrents of desire that only Shay seemed able to drag from the hidden depths of her soul.

She heard his moan of acceptance, felt his strong, hard body yield toward her, and knew that in his overpowering presence she was going to lose control over her body's response at the magical touch of his hands and mouth.

His lips covered hers, devouring the ebony pink flesh with eager movements of relished, hungry insistence. Kendra felt submerged in an ocean of desire, and when Shay's tongue plunged inward for a refreshing taste of her arousal, she knew she was truly drowned by the inevitable tide that had washed over every niche of her weakened body.

And she kissed him back with a greedy satisfaction that was equally ravenous, deliciously aware that Shay had lowered her to a reclining position on the carpet, his weight supported on braced arms so that he didn't crush her.

Erotically, he ground his hips softly into hers, enticing Kendra with his erotic actions as his hands began to deftly attack the buttons on the front of the warm, green, woolen jersey she'd thrown on that morning. Removing the soft angora from her shaking limbs, his hands slipped into the deep vee of her neckline and closed over the soft swell of her breasts beneath the delicate silk fabric of her blouse.

She heard Shay's breathing quicken and felt deep elation, even power at having caused such a savage reaction. And then sanity left her completely as he found the pinnacle of her breast, circling the soft, brown bud between his fingers as if she were being shaped and formed as a living sculpture beneath his talented hands.

As wave after wave of ecstasy coiled through her, a tiny voice crept from the recesses of Kendra's mind to the forefront, where reality was hovering indecisively. *You're ready for this,* it told her as Shay's tongue moved deeply into the interior of her mouth. *Accept everything.*

She groaned, weak with longing, as something in her subconscious acknowledged her silent voice moments before she felt herself go under once more. As if enticed by the soft, whimpering sound she'd ejected, Shay grew bolder with his movements, his hand quickly, urgently, snapping open the buttons on her blouse, his fumbling fingers breaking open the fastening on her bra until the glow of the fire glimmered against the bronzeness of her bare, womanly flesh.

Shay took delight in what he saw, finding nothing disappointing to his exuberant gaze as he gently pulled away both items and dropped them absently to the floor. "You're beautiful," he groaned, stroking tentative fingers against the sides of her breasts, across the heaving of her chest, and then down to the navel that was delicately embedded like a precious pearl.

Teasing, he bent his head and nuzzled at the lush swell of her breast, his faintly abrasive jaw drifting caressingly over their satiny tips. The wetness of his tongue followed, outlining the budding contours, drawing them tighter until Kendra was positively wriggling beneath him with an abandon that shocked her even while she gloried in it.

There was a rising of tension, an urgent expectancy within her to feel Shay's skin against hers. Feeling as wild and as uninhibited as he was inviting her to be, she began to strip him of the impediments to their merging flesh. And Shay allowed her to dominate, surrendering to her fierce, sexual aggression as if he were aware that she needed this freedom to once again assert her sensuality with a man, though Kendra knew that he was the one still very much in control.

He'd reared back, kneeling between her parted thighs to give her full access to him and everything he had to offer her exploring hands. Her lips were dry and her fingers trembled as she sat upright and began to release the tiny, white buttons that closed the shirt around his tapered chest.

She could feel his body vibrating at her tormenting slowness, awed that she'd brought about such exquisite friction in a man who had once seemed unable to display any semblance of outward emotion. They'd kissed before, intensely, pleasurably, but she'd always been aware that Shay lacked a spontaneity, total abandonment, and that had at times left her wondering how quickly he could detach himself.

Now, his violent, untameable passion was as sweetly wayward as her own. As she allowed the white cotton shirt to fall discarded at her feet, she felt the vast expansion of his chest beneath her tormenting lips as she used her teeth to gently, playfully, bite into the smooth muscle that made up the anatomy of his glorious chest.

Ignoring her own moans of delight, Kendra kissed the hollow where his shoulders met his neck, took into her mouth the hardened nipples hidden beneath curls of soft, dark hair, and ran eager, exploratory fingers along the maleness of his body, leaving a trail of heat in her wake.

She felt the shift and drop of first one relaxed bang of her auburn tresses and then another against her neck, aware that Shay had removed the hairpins which had held up the languid tangle of hair crowning her perspiring head moments before his strong, rough hands roamed freely through the disheveled locks, his wide, firm lips a whisper away from her mouth.

"Come here," Shay growled, tenderly pulling her straddled onto his lap, his arms wrapped around her slim waist as his lips brushed hers rhythmically, then closed over her mouth, easing her lips apart, taking his time while his bare chest rubbed erotically against the little hard points at the peaks of her breasts.

Kendra almost squealed at the contact, finding that

her disillusionment was quickly being diminished by the awakening of her dormant sexual impulses. Celibacy had been an easy option for her after her mother had died, and even when Selwyn had come along she'd felt mentally unprepared to deal with the high emotional power intimacy demanded.

Yet in the brief span of ten minutes, Shay was showing her the wondrous image of her thriving female body, of her blissful womanhood that was instinctively capable of giving and receiving every adornment of lovemaking.

Nothing mattered in this whirlpool of sensual discovery. Not the knowledge that she was intimately entwined with her father's enemy, the man who held the deed to her father's house, nor of the forthcoming nuptials she had been forced into to end a feud that had spanned over thirty years.

Instead, she was caught up in Shay's tutoring motions, swept away by the dictates of his coaching hands, of his guiding insistence, proving that he was very much the teacher, edifying her body to accept what no man had ever taught her.

Conditioned to act, she shifted her thighs against his kneeling body, letting the male weight of his hardened arousal beneath his trousers slide exquisitely against the fiery heart between her legs. Primitive grunts of animal passion erupted to echo across the room as Kendra dazedly felt her body being raised and then lowered to a reclining position on the sofa.

Within seconds, Shay had removed the green slacks she'd been wearing, had stripped her of the lacy panties and panty hose which he considered a hindrance to his aim and, as Kendra tried to cover herself, feeling suddenly naive at exposing her naked body entirely, Shay clasped her wrists with one free hand and bent to brush his mouth intimately against the soft curls she'd attempted to hide.

Kendra groaned, moaning a thick, impassioned plea of surrender. Shay absorbed her murmuring as he drove the heat of desire in her blood to a dangerous level of burning, fiery greed. Soon, it wasn't enough for her to lie passively back and shake with submission at his every wish. She was eager for the feel of him next to her bare skin, under her hands, against her lips.

Abruptly, she pushed him to his feet and kneeled into the soft sofa so that she was facing him with longing in her wondering eyes. "I want to take this off," she said huskily, attacking the zipper of Shay's trousers. "I want to feel every part of you."

It was Shay's turn to writhe as Kendra pulled every last piece of clothing from his strong, athletic limbs. For several long seconds she enjoyed every moment of unashamed, blatant, sultry-eyed study of his rising passion. Then, gently, she brushed his hard flank with her lips, feeling a surge of triumph as he moaned in inarticulate surrender.

Moments later, Shay reached to the floor to his trouser pocket where he quickly removed the foil covered item he sought from his wallet, applying the contraceptive protection with impatient fingers before he was back on top of her. Bridging his way between Kendra's thighs, he shifted gently against her until Kendra laxly welcomed him into her silky prison of desire.

Eleven

"Look at me," Shay urged gently as he saw Kendra close her eyes and felt her body tense under him. He did not move, but waited until she gave him what he wanted, until she opened her eyes and looked at him. And when she did as he'd asked her body shuddered as she saw the warmth and impatient yearning in his dark, desirous face. "Baby, it's all right," he whispered against her lips. "Move with me."

He coaxed her gently, sliding his hands under her back, lifting her up to the thrust of him, and suddenly Kendra found herself moaning again with pleasure as each movement, each thrust, brought her body arching closer to him in offering. He took her hand, lacing their fingers together, and rocked against her with an urgency that spoke beyond language his deep need for her. Then, totally unexpectedly, she found her limbs shaking with the violence of her feelings, reacting involuntarily to a fiery, heated sensation deep within that took a hold of her so fast that she felt utterly frightened by it.

"Something's happening," she murmured, almost alarmed, her voice alien to her as it filled the air like a maddening groan swelled with exquisite pleasure.

Shay was stilled, his dark, glittering eyes staring down into her face, confused, uncomprehending. Then, as though he'd understood something she evidently didn't, he murmured deeply against her trembling lips, "Let it happen."

His sedating, trustful voice was kind to her ears, caressing every part of her skin, enlivening Kendra's senses so that she felt her body begin to search erratically for a place she did not know. Her grip tightened against Shay's hand and her breath was fierce. She was panting, almost grunting, like a wild animal. It was so tender, erotic, wild, gentle; she felt close to tears.

Shay was speaking to her now, murmuring her name over and over again, whispering soft, words against her ear, "Reach for me, Kendra. Come on, Baby, reach for me."

What did he mean? Kendra wondered blindly in the recesses of her mind, her subconscious knowing that he was taking her some place high and she needed to reach to get there. Obediently, she followed his whispered command, taking delight as Shay sought her lips and captured them in a raw, devastating kiss.

She felt her nails bite deep into his skin, felt her heart slam in her rib cage as his fingers squeezed ever more tightly against hers, and somehow, instinctively, she knew she was nearly at the place he was taking her. His body shuddered against hers, spurring the sudden, uncontrollable trembling of her own. It was new, all new. She'd felt nothing like it, and she wondered why.

It had not been like this, never like this. On the two occasions she'd been with a man, it had been painful, with only a minimal feeling of pleasure. Now, her body was flooded with all kinds of feelings; wondrous, heady sensations that made her understand at least why she'd craved Shay so much, why she'd hungered so desperately every time he'd kissed her.

He knew where to take her; he knew how to get her there. And she was reaching as he'd told her to, and she was nearly. . . . His movements intensified above her and suddenly, convulsively, she screamed. A climactic, powerful pleasure erupted inside her, ripping her body into such gigantic splinters of frenzied passion that she felt herself about to faint from the sheer shock of it. She was there.

Shay crushed her to him with a fierceness that had him calling her name moments before his body convulsed violently against hers.

Kendra's heart was beating like wild drums when she descended from the highest place her body had ever been. "I . . . I needed that," she gasped absently, holding Shay's shuddering body next to her own as her limbs still wept from the volcanic eruption which had sent her into another axis in time.

"I needed you," Shay rasped in reply, dropping soft, satisfied kisses against her earlobe before he nestled his face in the fragrant softness of Kendra's hair.

As they lay still for a while, slowing the pulsing of their hearts, allowing their blood to gradually ebb to its usual frequency, Shay suddenly found himself thinking how nice it would be to wake up every morning with Kendra beside him. He realized that his life had felt stale and purposeless of late, that it did not surprise him that he should seek adventure by pursuing his father's conquests. Had it not been for that he would never have met Kendra.

His lips curved upward as he smiled at the memory of the unlikely circumstances which had brought them together. If his conscience had pricked him before about how he was deviously forcing her into marriage, it didn't now. He liked the way Kendra responded to him—shyly, softly, lovingly—and it was impossible to deny the emotions he was feeling toward her. She made him feel incredible, and it was even more incredible that he'd found himself marveling over the way he'd made her feel. Surely this was something new to her, too? He wanted to know.

Just as Kendra was about to close her eyes and slip into a peaceful, undisturbed slumber, Shay said, "It's never happened like that for you, has it?"

Kendra shifted nervously. Even knowing what he meant, she uttered, "Like what?"

Shay gently withdrew from her body and Kendra felt a sense of loss as he settled down beside her. "You screamed in my arms, remember? Either you've been out of circulation too long, Baby, or you've been dating the wrong kind of guys."

Kendra felt hot, embarrassing blood rush into her face at his total inquiring invasion. She couldn't handle him knowing such personal details about her, and realized now that she should never have told him why she'd preferred abstinence to intimacy during the time her mother had been ill and long after she'd died, because she knew he wouldn't be able to understand it.

Feeling humiliated by his insensitivity, she started to get up.

Shay pulled her back down. "You're not going anywhere," he told her hoarsely, encasing her by placing a strong, firm arm around her midriff. His voice deepened seductively. "You're full of fire, Kendra, and you've been on fire since I first kissed you. It makes me crazy knowing that you're so hot, and I'm not going to let you leave here tonight without showing you again just how hot that fire is."

Kendra trembled as he spoke, knowing he had analyzed her correctly, feeling the humiliation slip away as her body was stirred by some unspoken understanding that they needed each other once more. This time, Shay held her wrist and pulled her gently from the sofa, leading her slowly upstairs to his bedroom and onto his bed.

The sleep that they both needed was a long time in

coming as she willingly allowed him to steal a touch of heaven first and share it with her, rocking her higher and higher until there was nothing but the burning passion that spiraled between them. And it was everything he'd said it would be; scorching, fiery, and most definitely a furnace of molten, heated ecstasy.

Before Kendra finally sank into sleep she allowed her mind the forbidden luxury of believing that she had tasted that sweet nectar from God, that this was only the beginning of being in love, and that Shay, too, had given something truly irredeemable of himself.

The sound of footsteps awoke her sometime late in the night, when the sky was still dark and the night had not yet paled to day. Kendra bolted upright, muzzy-headed, and glanced at the bedside clock which illuminated a visible 5:00 against its glacial LED screen. Shay was nowhere in the bed, and she was immediately stricken by fear that the whole eventful night had merely been a fantasy.

Only when her body stirred with the reminder of Shay's strong maleness inside her and her eyes took in the shadowy objects in the dim, unfamiliar room did she realize she had not been dreaming at all.

Raising herself from beneath the sheets she pulled the top layer from the bed and wrapped herself in its silken warmth, then plodded with bare feet toward the door, pulling it slightly ajar to the sound of voices which filtered into her conscious mind. She recognized the American accent to be Shay's, but the other surprised her somewhat, for it was alarmingly familiar to her, too.

Without knowing it she silently tiptoed to the top of the stairs and looked down past the newel post, her eyes keenly lodged in the direction from where the sound came in the hope of seeing whether it was really

Rugg Brown who was there, whether it was really his voice that was drumming against her curious ears.

"Do you really want to do this?" he was asking, sounding so troubled that Kendra instantly felt goose bumps travel down her spine.

"I'm sure," came Shay's affirmation.

Kendra couldn't see either one of them, but she heard them clearly enough.

"What about Kendra? Have you told her yet?"

"No. I'll do that after we're married."

"Okay," Rugg concluded. "Just return me the papers. I'll deal with it and confirm with Delbert Jackson, your lawyer."

"Kendra has the papers," Shay verified. "But I'll send them over the moment I get them back."

Kendra heard the shuffle of footsteps and then the hammer of shoes on the parquet floor, and she quickly stepped back into the shadow cast by the bedroom door, her eyes catching Shay dressed in a yellow terry cloth robe motioning Rugg Brown to the hallway where the main door was situated.

The chandeliers above them swayed secretly against the atmospheric current as the door was swept open admitting a mild gust of wind, the fragile crystal droplets twinkling their announcement of having heard something highly confidential that would forever be concealed within their lucid, diamond glare.

Kendra placed shaking fingers against her lips, harshly forcing back the sobbing which was ready to blow from the depths of her chest and out through her mouth. A quick flurry of tears flooded her tormented eyes and her body was shivering, not from cold but from the horrible reaction of feeling fearful and vulnerable.

Her head was spinning, and she felt nauseated and giddy as she acknowledged that she'd just lived through a terrifying nightmare, astonished that the man she loved should still be conspiring against her to ensure that his father would receive the shares in her father's newspaper.

He'd used her, her mind screamed, and it was that thought alone which brought tears tumbling down her cheeks. Frenzied, she groped behind her for the door handle, placing her trembling hands against it for support as she heard Shay's bare footsteps shuffle toward the kitchen. She had to get out of that house, get away from the ugly scene she'd heard.

Suddenly, she was rushing down the stairs as if all the furies were pursuing her. She headed straight for the room where her clothes were strewn across the floor in telltale signs of what had transpired there. As though tormented by the very sight of them, Kendra simply swept up her shoes, her slacks, and her sweater, hurriedly slipping into them before she made a mad dive for her car key, which was sitting dutifully atop a small ornamental table in close proximity to the dying fire.

She was still recoiling in shock when she rushed out of the door and into her car. A cry of misery instantly leapt from her throat when she spotted the white envelope Shay had given her on the passenger seat, containing the very papers which had been the subject of his private, early morning meeting with Rugg Brown.

Tearfully plucking a pen from the glove compartment, she ripped open the envelope, unable to grasp what she was looking at as hot, furious tears fell like rain onto the immaculate copies awaiting her signature. "If this is what it'll take," she whimpered to herself, "then I'll sign and be damned." And sign she did.

Placing both copies back into the envelope, she left the car and stumbled over to the house, which was brightened by a full moon, then aptly pushed the papers through the door's mail slot before she rushed back over to her car.

The engine ignited with the roar of her fury and for the second time Kendra found herself leaving that house in the same way, the rubber of her tires screeching as the white Golf Cabriolet sped down the long driveway and onto the main road.

Such was her hurry to get away that she'd completely overlooked turning on the headlights or engaging her seat belt. Racing down the road, she was almost blinded by the yellow lights ahead of another vehicle coming up in the opposite direction. It struck her as being odd, for it was on the wrong side of the road. As the fluorescent lights advanced nearer, Kendra realized, too late, that it was her car at fault.

Swerving with the dexterity of a rally driver, she steered the car to a grassy verge and slammed on the brakes. The car did not stop. Instead, it veered out of control on the icy grass, and it was an age before it halted with an abrupt jolt as it hit a tree, throwing Kendra directly against the steering wheel.

She blinked once, then twice, and then the scenery began to swim in the gloom. Round and round it went until it blanked out entirely.

Kendra awoke to the feel of warm fingers encircling her limp ones. As the room came into focus she felt a throbbing pain in her head and whined as a further pain, in her foot, brought exquisite rivers of agony to her nervous system.

Shay's face was the first to materialize, followed by that of another man who stood in the room. He was the one who came toward her and tapped Shay on the shoulder, instructing him to move further down the side of the bed, where he was seated. Kendra knew him to be a doctor the moment he shone rays of light into her eyes before he asked, "Are you in much pain, Miss Davenport? I can give you a painkiller."

"My leg," she floundered quietly.

"Yes, you've sprained your ankle against the clutch pedal," he acknowledged softly. "And you have a nasty bump on your head, but happily nothing that won't have you up and around within two weeks or so. You're a very lucky girl."

He turned to Shay. "Can I see you outside?"

As they left, Kendra cast her eyes beyond the sheets and realized that she was back in Shay's bedroom, in his bed. She felt her forehead and found her fingers rubbing up against a Band-aid, and when she propped herself on her elbows to look at her bandaged ankle, she was struck to discover that she was not dressed. She was instead wearing one of Shay's brushed cotton shirts, with only her bare skin beneath it.

Panicky, she looked at the clock. It said 4:30 P.M. A whole half day had practically gone by without her knowing it. She needed to call her father. He would be fretful as to where she was. Prompting herself to a sitting position, she grimaced as a sharp stab of pain slapped against her bone, yet she slowly struggled to her feet.

Hobbling, she made it to the door and inched it open, about to stumble her way through it. But as she began to do so she heard Shay's voice echo down the corridor, causing her whole body to grow rigid as four words struck like hammer blows against her jumbled senses. "Brakes . . . tampered . . . killed . . . police."

The shock weakened her knees and she fell over, screaming, as a fresh wave of excruciating pain enveloped her entire being. Shay and the doctor came rushing in. Within seconds, she was swept up in Shay's arms and placed back down on the bed. "What are you doing?" he barked, alarmed, pulling the covers back over her body.

I'm spying on you, Kendra's thoughts screamed as she closed her eyes, unable to hold back the tears which scrambled from the ducts at their sides. "I want to call my father," she cried, now remembering everything that had happened. "I want to go home."

"I'll give her a sedative," the doctor murmured, concerned. "She'll feel better in the morning."

"No," Kendra whined as a needle was being injected into her arm.

"Your father knows you're here," Shay's soothing voice consoled. "And I'm here. I'm not going to leave you. . . ."

Kendra's mouth was parched when she finally turned her head. It was cradled comfortably in the warmth of something, and when she pulled her neck up she discovered that she'd been nestled against the cottony vest over Shay's strong chest. Her gaze crawled upward to his sleeping face. His eyes were closed, and his breath was feathery and gentle against her disheveled hair.

The clock said 8:30 A.M., and the room was still obscurely dim, but there was some daylight from the fresh morning outside bouncing through the bedroom curtains, giving her enough radiance to study his inactive profile.

In his sleep, Shay looked adorable. His attractive, square jawline needed a shave, but that made him look deliciously rugged. His heavy masculine brows flickered as if he were dreaming, and she wanted to smooth away the motion. His raven, curly hair was silky soft, inviting her fingers to reach out and touch their tiny curls. She felt herself devilishly intoxicated with lust, knowing that he was lying there beside her, so relaxed, somnolent, and temptingly an advocate of love.

She wanted to trace the outline of his face, to touch

his lips and feel his hair, and instinctively raised her hand to give herself that very satisfaction. Poised in mid-air, she lowered first one finger and then another against Shay's cheek, but as she made to lower a third a strong hand instantly snapped over hers and Shay's eyes opened with liveliness that deeply penetrated her soul.

Kendra felt dazed as he searched her face, feeling her heart quicken uncontrollably as he accurately read her expression with an understanding that shook her. Silently, he threaded his fingers in the hair at the side of her face and pulled her amorously toward his lips tenderly in a slow, drugging kiss.

Something exploded inside Kendra the moment his tongue skirted across her own, coaxing her to yield to him, to give to him, to share with him all the passion she possessed as a woman.

He rolled her onto her back and deepened his seductive persuasion, his fingers creeping down to her thighs where they sought and found the core of her desire, exploring her gently until she was gasping for breath. Then he raised his head and looked triumphantly into her eyes. "How's the ankle?" he whispered against her lips.

Kendra was dazed. "What ankle?"

Shay arched an eyebrow. "The one you sprained yesterday morning."

Suddenly a nightmare came flooding back to haunt her—Rugg Brown, the flash of car lights, the screeching of tires, the sound of an explosion, a voice saying, *"You silly girl, you could've gotten yourself killed."* She came to her senses with such force that it was enough to bolt her body upright as every facet of her memory began to assemble itselves in some order of occurrence.

"Who got me out of the car?" she quickly demanded, touching a hand against her forehead where a Band-aid was still present. Fortunately, there was no pain, and surprisingly enough when she wriggled her ankle she was to feel a more bearable level of discomfort from the movement.

Shay sat up beside her, taken aback by her sudden reaction but stroking her shoulder reassuringly, nonetheless. "I got you out," he explained. "I hope it was a company car you were driving, because it's ready for the scrap heap. Are you insured by the newspaper?"

Kendra nodded numbly. "Churchill Brokers, West London. What day is it?"

"Sunday." Shay's voice grew heavy with concern. "Why did you take off like that? You shot down the drive so fast I thought I'd lose you by the time I threw on some clothes and followed you. You didn't have your lights on, so I didn't see you until it was too late." He studied her expression, expecting answers, but when none came he added, "You nearly hit J B's car when he was coming back with Rhona. What were you doing on the wrong side of the road?"

"So stupid," Kendra hissed, absorbing the torrent of questions, the reason for her actions propelled to the forefront of her mind. "I've been a total fool. And here I am again, behaving like an idiot."

Shay studied her for several intermediary seconds before some thought caused him to say, "I don't want you to regret what we did the other night. It was my fault, so don't blame yourself. Blame it on me."

"I do blame it on you," Kendra pounced tearfully, recalling what she'd overheard when he had been talking with Rugg Brown, knowing that she couldn't tell him about it without disclosing that she'd been eavesdropping. "I blame everything on you. You've got guts galore sitting there telling me how broad your shoulders are, accepting guilt. Well, my shoulders are not so broad. I cannot threaten . . . extortion one minute, and then make love the next."

"Is that why you signed the papers I gave you, then

pushed them through the letter slot?" he asked, clearly disturbed by what Kendra was telling him.

Kendra glared into his eyes, remembering, too, that she'd heard awful evidence that her car brakes had been tampered with. "I don't want you to hurt me any more than you already have," she pleaded. "Your father will get his shares as we agreed, and then . . . then just leave me alone to start again somewhere else."

Shay looked at her troubled eyes and heaved a heavy sigh. And then, just as he was about to say something, two brief knocks were hammered against the door and Benjamin Brentwood's heavy, Jamaican-American voice intruded from the other side. "You guys up?" he bellowed.

Shay grimaced murderously. "Come in, Pops."

The door was edged open and Benjamin's tall, majestic frame entered the shadowy interior. "I don't know how your Ma can sleep after six hours air flight," he began absently before his eyes recognized Kendra. "So, Pretty Feet's awake," he acknowledged as he tightened the belt around his robe. "You still want to burn down the house of Brentwood now that you've . . . familiarized yourself with my son's bed?"

Kendra's face burned with embarrassment when she thought of how much more she'd acquainted herself with, knowing, too, that Benjamin Brentwood wasn't fooled on that score. "I got the burner smoldering," she derided coldly. "And that's how I intend to leave it."

"You're not afraid to come up against me, are you Girl?" he said with manly acumen. "People say I cast a very long shadow, but I always did know you'd never get lost in it." He paused, then looked at Shay. "So, when am I going to get me a wedding? I want me some healthy grandchildren around here. I'm telling everyone that December looks good."

Shay expelled a moan. "Pops, not now."

"Tomorrow, next week, as soon as possible," Kendra relented scornfully, not daring to look at Shay. "The sooner the better, so you can set a date whenever you like. My father wants the whole matter sorted."

"That's what me like to hear, the vibes of progress," Benjamin roared. "This calls for a special cigar." He looked at Shay. "Son, get dressed. I'm going to wake you Ma."

As he left the room, Shay grabbed hold of Kendra's wrist, his eyes filled with fury. "Before you start calling any shots and telling my pops how much you set me on fire with that body of yours, I'd better tell you that once we do this there's no going back."

"We have a deal," Kendra reminded, afraid of what he meant. "I'm living up to my end of it. The least you can do is live up to yours. I'll give you the shares, you give me the deed, and that's it. We shook on it, remember? I value my sanity and my *life*."

Shay let her go, her words striking home. "Yeah, I did shake on it, didn't I?" he agreed solemnly.

"It's what you're best at," Kendra scolded sadly. "You and Joel are just like your father."

Shay's expression changed curiously. "In what way?"

Kendra wanted to say *corrupt, impartial, unprincipled, dangerous,* but decided that she'd taken enough emotional turbulence when it came to analyzing her feelings for Shay, and so settled on a simple description. One that wouldn't give away too much. "Self-disciplined," she said uneasily.

"In the most depraved, immoral, disreputable way, right?" Shay scoffed, tapping into her thoughts accurately. "No, those weren't the words you used. Let me think." His mind took him back to when they'd first met beneath a flash of lightning and thunder. "Lying, conniving, deceiving family I think was what you said," he mocked, taking hold of her wrist firmly. "Well, Baby,

Pops isn't like that. Neither am I, or J B." He released her hand abruptly. "Sure, he bent rules, all kind of rules—that's what the media game is all about. Foul play, pitching hard. That's how he got a multi-million dollar cable TV syndicated to all the primary markets. My father will go down in history as being at the head of the first black enterprise to trade on the New York Stock Exchange, and I'm not going to apologize to you or anybody for how he got there."

"And at what sacrifice?" Kendra screeched knowingly. "What has it cost him?" She was thinking now of Benjamin Brentwood's inability to love, and how only he could be responsible for why Shay and even J B accepted his decisions so uncaring and unflinchingly. "I'd be interested to know how he feels about Clara." She bristled with perception. "Because I don't think your father is capable of showing pure, untainted feelings for anyone."

"So he's a man of brawn and steel." Shay shrugged. "Ma's always understood him."

"Yeah." Kendra laughed harshly, tears springing to her eyes. "That's why I'm so glad we made a cast iron deal. I want you to know exactly where you stand."

Shay's face hardened, and the muscles in his jaws tightened so dramatically that Kendra suddenly wondered whether she'd said too much, amazed that she'd actually caused his face to contort so disturbingly. When he finally spoke, she couldn't help but notice a solemnness in his voice that was pitched so low that it instantly caught her attention. "About this deal," he began oddly. "I want to—"

"Bro?" There was another interruption at the door, and Kendra heard Shay swear maliciously before Joel popped his head round it. "Pops is smoking his special brand of cigar," Joel informed him loudly. "I guess that means one thing?"

Exasperated, Shay raked fingers across his hair, disliking Joel's untimely intrusion. "You guessed it, J B," he muttered harshly.

"Well done." Joel smiled, respect mirrored across his face as he offered his outstretched hand to effect a brotherly handshake, his eyes seemingly speaking of all the connotations of a plan well executed. To Kendra, he murmured a simple, "Welcome to the family. I hope your leg feels better." And as she detected the silent honor that transpired between them, Kendra felt certain she was ensnared in a deadly web, its silken threads spun intricately by the man who had stolen her heart.

Twelve

"Half a dozen cabbages and one large egg, please." Kendra beckoned to the fruit shop attendant in High Street Kensington, annoyed that he should look at her with a comical slur on his lips, his face oddly slanted in amusement.

"Blimey, Love." He chortled loudly, his voice heavy with amusement. "I think that's half a dozen eggs and *one* large cabbage."

Kendra stared at him, motionless, then blinked as she realized her mistake. "I'm sorry," she offered quickly, alarmed at how muzzy-headed she'd become. "I haven't been myself lately."

"I know the feeling, Love," the thin, lofty man responded kindly, placing her purchases into a plastic carrier before deftly handing her the bag. "My wife goes the same way when Christmas is around the corner."

Kendra adopted a shallow smile and took the shopping bag, carefully passing over a five pound bill to pay for its contents. As she waited for her change she realized it was the first time she'd smiled in the three weeks since her car accident.

She hadn't forgotten the fateful Sunday morning when Shay had driven her home to her father's house. The ride was quiet. And long. And it screamed with unsaid things.

Breakfast had been a failure, too, for neither was hungry, though Benjamin had scrambled eggs laid out in front of her, at which she'd picked in a desultory fashion.

It was 11:30 A.M. when they pulled into her father's driveway. Neither of them moved when the car came to a stop, but finally Shay asked, "Would you like me to help you in?"

"No," Kendra answered, certain she would soon get used to hobbling around until the pain completely subsided in her ankle.

Shay didn't ask why, but he slumped against his car seat and kept the engine purring, kneading the bridge of his nose, with his eyes shut. "I'll be flying into New York this week," he told her quietly. "Probably Tuesday or Wednesday. I'll leave the assistant editor in charge."

"Irvin?" Kendra quivered, horrified. "But I'm—"

"Going to stay at home," Shay advised, opening his eyes and allowing Kendra to see that they were filled with concern. "That ankle needs time to heal, so it's best that you don't put any weight on it for a while."

"But I want—"

"Dammit, Kendra," Shay growled angrily, cutting off her protest. He turned his face away from her and stared out of the window, his index finger on his lower lip. "Do this one thing for me, please? Ease up on your ankle."

Kendra paused uncertainly, then reached for the door handle, teary-eyed and wounded by his outburst, upset that he was flying to New York. But at its first click, Shay turned and his hand reached out and took her arm.

His eyes looked tormented as they met hers across the leather seat. "I'll call you," he told her quietly.

He sounded pained and apprehensive, and Kendra knew that she wanted everything to be all right for them. As if the power were within her, teary-eyed and moody as she was, suspicion and fear about what had caused her accident still lurking in her mind, she found herself instinctively leaning across the seat and placing her lips lightly against his cheek. "Have a safe journey," she whispered tightly.

As she made to move away, Shay's grip on her arm tightened and he gently impelled her into his arms. They both sought restitution there, he kissing her as if she were truly escaping him, she surging to meet his silent redress with an elemental need to settle the conflict between them, though both knew it could not be settled this way.

His mouth was smooth and demanding, his tongue shameless as he attempted to offer her something beyond frustration and anguish. It felt good. It relieved. But Kendra knew the tension was still there the moment she left the car and watched as her father greeted her at the door. . . .

"Three pounds and seventy-three pence in change," a heavy voice intruded.

Kendra lurched, as if coming awake from a dream. "Oh . . . thank you."

Carefully taking the silver and copper-colored coins from the shop attendant, she placed them in her purse and turned on her heel, deciding that she would retreat from the cold weather and go home. The dial face on her watch read 4:00 P.M., and as she'd promised to cook for her father that night—a little "thank you" gesture for having looked after her in the three weeks she'd stayed at home—she made her way toward the nearest underground station, to take a tube train back up to St. John's Wood.

Resolving that her thoughts would ebb on the train before she changed at Baker Street, Kendra boarded the Circle Line tube and took a seat closest to the door in a prudent attempt to avoid being swamped by Friday night commuters when it was time to disembark. But as she began to train her thoughts while placing her handbag atop her lap and her shopping bag on the floor between her feet, a familiar voice jerked her to attention and she raised her head to find a casually dressed man approaching her.

"Trevor," she gasped, genuinely pleased to see him. "How are you?"

He took the seat beside her. "I'm fine. You?"

"Had better days."

His eyebrows rose. "That's not the spirit of a woman getting married. And it certainly isn't the Kendra Davenport I know," he added firmly.

"That bad?" Kendra grimaced. "I sound like I'm sinking?"

"Sunk."

Kendra ejected a single, mirthless huff of laughter. "You were always good at putting up with me." She smiled. "Warts and all. I'm just sorry about what happened at the *Nubian Chronicle*. It amazes me you didn't sue for unfair dismissal."

"Forget it." Trevor waved the issue aside. "Truth is, I was ready to move on, anyway. But I suppose you knew I sold the computer virus story?"

"I guessed."

"Well, I'm with Choice FM now—the radio station? They made me a job offer I couldn't pass up."

"That's great," Kendra professed, pleased that he'd found a settlement and aware that the Birmingham and South-London based music station would give him enough experience to mobilize in the future. "You like it there?"

"Just what I'm looking for," Trevor affirmed, smiling.

"That's really great."

"So," Trevor probed curiously, "what's it like hobnobbing with the American media set? Is it anything like the political elite?"

"Let's just say that I feel more comfortable," Kendra admitted softly.

"I hear you. Some politicians are simply untrustworthy, aren't they?" Trevor began, crossing his jean clad legs and folding his arms against them as though positioning himself to launch a discussion. "Just look at that McKane incident two weeks ago."

"Oh, yeah," Kendra recalled, entering the conversation to deflect her mind from the subject of Shay. "The cash for questions scandal, right?"

"Don't they ever feel obligated to the public?"

"I'm sure most do," Kendra declared, remembering clearly when the national media had reported on how members of large corporations illegally lobbied M.P.s with lucrative cash incentives to put questions forward in the House of Commons for debate.

"And there was that Caulderdale thing," Trevor continued, unaware that nearby passengers—each slicing amused glances of interest in his direction, their lips twitching in agreement with his running commentary—were silently eavesdropping on his conversation. "Can you imagine an M.P. having to resign over fraud allegations?"

A cackle of laughter suddenly erupted as one passenger found it hard to contain his amusement on hearing Trevor's perturbed tone of amazement.

Kendra smiled, too. "Scandalous, isn't it?"

"Makes you wonder whether this country is going to the dogs, the things that go on in Parliament," Trevor bleated. "I heard that the guy you were dating . . . Selwyn Owens . . . resigned from office last week." Trevor shook his head, disbelieving. "I never thought I'd see the day when a black politician resigned from office."

Kendra's mouth gaped wide open. "But . . . but, why?"

"No explanation yet," Trevor countered lightly,

clearly awed. "The House of Commons public information office is only officially confirming it. I do the news slot for the radio station and I'm dying to tell our listeners what went down. You don't know anything, do you?"

"No," Kendra wavered, annoyed that the tube should be arriving at the Baker Street station, for her connection to the Jubilee Line, just when she wanted to question Trevor further. "Look, I have to go," she told him as the train slowed, jostling her forward slightly. "But if I hear anything I'll let you know."

"Sure thing." Trevor waved as she left the train.

As the tube train doors slid shut and it went along its way, Kendra felt as though she'd submerged deeper into her unsettled mood of muzzy confusion. Why on earth would Selwyn resign? The question hovered unanswered in her troubled mind as she crossed the platform and waited for the Jubilee Line train. And as the train arrived and she embarked to take a seat, again by the door, a sense of trepidation coursed the length of her body, as Kendra wondered suddenly whether Selwyn's resignation had anything to do with her.

Ramsey Davenport's voice was loud and angry when Kendra entered her father's house. Closing the Chelsea door against the dark, cold night and enjoying the pleasing warmth which met her, she made her way through the hallway and directly into the lounge, curious to know what was going on. Two high spots of annoyance and apprehension crept into her cheeks as her eyes immediately fell on the culprit causing her father's outrage. Narrowing her eyes arrogantly, she watched as he turned and recognized her.

"So, you're back on your pretty feet?" Benjamin greeted, removing himself from his chair to toss Kendra a look of approval. His conglomerate appearance was totally in keeping with a man of his age; the starched and pressed white shirt, the grey suit, fitting like a tailor's cut, the tie, neatly placed so that every part of him reflected money and power.

Undaunted, Kendra shot a disdainful glance in his direction, then turned to her father. "What is he doing here?"

"We're discussing the old days," Benjamin chose to answer, an evasive tone deliberately pitched in each word. "Isn't that right, Rammy?"

To her father's credit, Ramsey Davenport reacted with poise, in spite of the fact that his face was dark with rage. "It's nothing for you to worry about," he assured quickly. When Kendra remained silent, he amended for Benjamin Brentwood's benefit, "We were just agreeing that I should call Reverend Marshall Leonard, whom I know very well." He gritted his teeth and turned to Benjamin. "I'll go and call him now."

"I'll arrange to book the Hilton Hotel," Benjamin challenged angrily as he watched Ramsey Davenport swiftly leave the room. Taking a puff from his cigar, he glared ruefully at Kendra. "You miss my boy?" he demanded harshly.

The question came so unexpectedly that Kendra was forced to instant sarcasm. "As much as I expect he misses me."

"Ah. . . ." Benjamin took two strides toward her. "With eyes like those . . . who are you trying to fool?"

Kendra's shoulders shook a little at his cool perception. Nervous, she turned her back to him, deposited her shopping bag by the sofa, then carefully began to take off her woolen coat. Benjamin came up behind her and helped her out of it, but as Kendra turned and held it in her hand, wondering whether she should politely thank him for his assistance, she could tell that he could see her barefaced vulnerability. "I have normal human emotions when it comes to matters of the heart," she admitted candidly. "Something I can hardly imagine you would understand."

A faraway glint crossed Benjamin's eyes and his body froze at the derision. "Do you know what it's like, Girl, to feel reborn?" he bellowed, a note of mystery evident in his voice. "It's like looking on the magical unfolding of a sunrise in Jamaica." His dark eyes bore directly into hers. "I knew a girl once who had that sunrise in her eyes."

Kendra felt positively queasy. What was he saying? That he'd once loved somebody? Never. Not Benjamin Brentwood—this man without a shred of conscience present in his sixty-three-year-old features. Wordlessly, she shook her head, seeming to have lost him for a moment. It was confusing that there should be a piece of the puzzle of Benjamin Brentwood she hadn't known was missing.

"Pops?" At a simple knock at the door Joel popped his head into the room. "Oh," he sighed on seeing Kendra. "I didn't know you were in here. Your father sent me in." He looked at Benjamin. "Are you ready?"

"Me coming," Benjamin confirmed through curls of smoke. Cigar poised, his free hand landed lightly on Kendra's shoulder. "A cloud came over my sunrise, and I never did see it again," he told her hazily. "So don't let anyone steal yours, Girl. You look for it every morning."

"Pops," Joel pleaded, impatient.

"Okay, J B." Placing the cigar back into his mouth, he murmured, "My boy called you yet?"

"Twice, my father says, but I was out both times," Kendra told him weakly, her senses still jarred at discovering just how complex a character this man truly was. The discovery showed a side she knew was seldom seen.

"Ah . . . he'll be back in time for you two to get wed," Benjamin assured, his cigar tipped precariously in his mouth as he regally left the room.

Kendra glared after him and heard the exchange of voices as he met up with her father in the hallway. Then there was the slamming of the door and her father's feet as he noisily made his way back into the room.

"That . . . man," he breathed, walking over to the wine cabinet, a certain intensity glazed in his brown eyes. Something in him struggled for supremacy. "I don't care what he wants. I'm telling you, Kendra. You are going to have a wedding that's socially acceptable."

Kendra sighed wearily. She couldn't handle another round of confrontation right now, not while the testing of her true feelings for Shay had arrived, as she knew it would, along with a nagging headache and memories of weeks gone by that were still painfully fresh. "Daddy." She rubbed her temples. "You and Benjamin sort it out, okay? I'm going to cook up dinner."

"Dinner?" Ramsey inquired. "I'm not going to be here for dinner. I'm meeting Reverend Leonard in an hour. I'll fill you in on the details later."

"But . . ." came Kendra's muffled reply. "I thought . . . never mind. Where's Arlisa?"

"Avoiding me," Ramsey declared, prying the top off a bottle of cognac. Pouring the smooth, brown liquid into a half measure glass, he bridged it against his lips, then added, "I think it's time we found that girl a job at the *Nubian Chronicle*. Nothing too demanding. Something . . . simple."

"I know just the position," Kendra said as she considered just how jumbled her life had become because of Arlisa's haphazard indiscretions. Had it not been for her she wouldn't be losing so much sleep, pining over a man who didn't love her. That was a fate she wouldn't wish on anyone.

Thinking that she might actually be losing her sharp edge, she tried to pull herself together, but couldn't. Shay Brentwood had reduced her to a kind of whimpering, pining female, and she didn't like that one bit. It was an uncomfortable feeling, not being in control of her emotions, but Shay Brentwood had chiseled away at her hardened exterior to find the soft core within, and it was a hard lesson indeed that she would have to simply accept that he possessed the power to do that.

The sound of the telephone was suddenly filtered into Kendra's troubled mind. As she was the one closest to it she nodded to her father in acknowledgment that she would answer it, then reached out to a table at the back of the sofa and picked up the receiver. "Kendra Davenport," she muttered dubiously, placing her coat down to sink into a seat.

"Hi, it's Shay," came the sullen reply.

Kendra's eyes widened instantly, her dismal thoughts vanishing momentarily. "Hi."

"How are you?" he inquired, his voice so concisely clear that Kendra could hardly believe he was calling from New York.

"I'm fine . . . you?"

"Working hard." Pause. "What's the weather like?"

"Cold."

"It's cold here, too," Shay answered, frustrated that he was making small talk. "What are . . ." He laughed weakly, as he and Kendra tried to say something simultaneously. "You go first."

"No, you."

"What are you doing?"

I'm missing you, Kendra thought miserably. "I was going to cook up something for Daddy, but—"

"You can cook?" It was incredible how this woman never ceased to amaze him.

"Of course I can," Kendra drawled. "And bake. And knit, too . . . well, only scarves." Kendra heard him chuckle slightly, but she was also aware of a tension in his voice. She felt it, too, in her own, spurred on by an anxious feeling in the pit of her stomach she could hardly attempt to assuage. It spoke of what Shay Brentwood was all about: a mere handshake deal in her life.

"Have you been into the office?" he asked, steering the subject.

"I was planning to go back on Monday, unless you have any objections?" When Shay remained silent, she added, "Irvin's on top of things, and Lynton wants to see me, and I also wanted to call the Borough of Brent Council to—"

"I've called them already," Shay interrupted. "They're looking into it."

"Oh." Kendra sighed, rubbing her hand across her forehead, as her headache protruded. "I heard Selwyn resigned last week. Maybe there's a connection. You think?"

"Last week, you say?"

"Yeah."

"I see." Another pause. "How's your father?"

"He's . . . bearing up," Kendra wavered, eyeing her father as he downed the half measure of cognac and proceeded to pour himself another. "Yours left ten minutes ago."

"Pops came over to your house?" Shay asked, disbelieving.

"In his element," Kendra derided smugly. "Planning this wedding by the book to satisfy his . . . social obligations."

"Mmm," Shay murmured. "That's Pops."

"Yeah." Kendra's eyes shadowed, remembering what this was all in aid of. "He makes very expensive deals."

"Kendra," Shay said, agonized and wounded. "Don't think too badly of him. He's wiser than you think."

Something in what he said lessened Kendra's misery. *The missing piece of the puzzle,* she thought, curious. What was it about Benjamin Brentwood she didn't know?

"I guess I'll see you in church, then." She swallowed, defeated.

"Sounds fine to me."

"Goodbye, Shay."

"Bye, Kendra."

Shay hung up the phone and stood with hands clutching both sides of the bath towel hanging loosely around his neck. *I miss you,* he told the phone set helplessly. There was so much he wanted to say, but talking to a telephone wouldn't have been the way to do it.

What he needed was time. Time with Kendra to explain himself, to make plans for the future, to simply be with her. And, he told himself, time to tell her what she was doing to him. As he defined that point more simply, Shay realized that he loved her.

Thirteen

It was a wedding that took place the Saturday before Christmas Eve, in a spectacular social whirl dripping with diplomats, celebrities, renowned dignitaries, media players, friends, acquaintances, and family.

Kendra couldn't believe that Benjamin Brentwood had arranged such a gathering in the mere few weeks since her agreeing to marry his son, nor could she scarcely comprehend that she was part of such a mass congregation. As the doors to her father's house swept open to admit another fresh cloudburst of guests, she began to feel somewhat detached from the ensemble, even as a cluster of accomplished, worldly people made claims on her attention as the bride.

"Beautiful dress," one woman said of the simple, white, form-fitting taffeta gown she was wearing, now slightly creamy with age since it had been her mother's. It was now freshly adorned with rosettes and French Alençon lace and edged in Belgian embroidery, decorated with iridescent Austrian crystals and pearls.

"Lovely day for it," another mouthed easily of the weather. It had been cold and frosty, but the sky had remained clear, mercifully allowing the morning winter sun to shine through.

"They're forecasting snow tonight, though," one

woman added dismally. "Today may be the last we see of decent weather until the spring."

They might have been speaking Afrikaan for all Kendra knew, for her mind simply wasn't paying any attention to anything that was being said. Her eyes had wandered across the lavish spread of thirty-five pink and blue decorated tables situated in the main reception room, hoping that she could see Shay from across the chattering, laughing clutter of humanity.

Then, from the corner of her eye, she caught a glimpse of him. He was deep in conversation with an elderly man, and her heart did a somersault, knowing that he was by far the most attractive man in the room. He was dressed in a morning suit, his jawline freshly shaven and his hair specially trimmed for the occasion. His manner was extremely relaxed, as though he had accepted the destiny of their fate, she decided, unflinching.

But could *she* accept it? Kendra wondered. In her mind's eye, she had pictured an uneventful, unceremonious wedding that would simply complete the technicalities of her deal with Shay. Instead, concessions had been wrung out of her from every angle. Her father, being a religious man, insisting on a church wedding with his good friend the Reverend Marshall Leonard officiating. Then Benjamin Brentwood, being a social participator, demanded that there should be a wedding party afterward.

Looking around, she realized now that he had excelled himself. With her eyes veiled in cool informality, she watched him and her father parade around the room, exhibiting pompous, flagrant profiles as they moved with grandiose gestures among the guests, as though each had pulled off the deal of the century.

At least her father was happy, she consoled herself, knowing that he would now safely receive the deed to this wonderful house that had been her home for twenty years. Now her home would be with Shay, she thought, shifting her eyes back to where she'd last seen him. Her heart sank when she saw that he was no longer where he'd been.

She was about to sweep the room in search of him again, thinking on how she'd missed him miserably in the weeks he'd been in New York, when a voice from behind her said softly, "Champagne, Mrs. Brentwood?"

Kendra spun and caught herself up short as she felt herself fall into the deep, penetrating gaze of a pair of dusky brown eyes. Smiling weakly, she took the glass that was offered her, knowing that throughout the afternoon she would probably be downing several more, and wondering whether she would find solace from the champagne's sedating effect after the weeks of sleepless self debate that had given her much fatigue. "Will it help me sleep?" she inquired, taking a long sip of the vintage Dom Perignon.

Shay raised an eyebrow. "No, but it will make staying awake a lot more fun," he answered wryly.

Kendra realized that he had that same penetrating look in his eyes, the one she'd seen when the reverend had said, *"Wilt thou have this woman to thy wedded wife, to live together after God's ordinance in the holy estate of matrimony? Wilt thou love her, comfort her, honor, and keep her, in sickness and in health, and, forsaking all others, keep thee only unto her, so long as ye both shall live?"*

It puzzled her why he'd looked at her that way, but now, as she digested the flicker of sensual awareness in his face, she realized with mounting trepidation that Shay's interpretation of that vow meant that he should make love to her, not be *in love* with her. Swallowing her champagne nervously, she couldn't stop her mind going into overdrive as to what he had in store for her that night, and though her heart warmed to the very wicked idea that he'd probably planned a very long night, her head conjured up worrying reminders of an agreement borne out of necessity and greed.

Pushing that recollection to the front of her mind, she said, "In that case, I'd better get myself drunk."

Shay gripped her wrist, his brows knitting together disturbingly. "What's that supposed to mean?" he demanded, his voice low and inconspicuous.

"What do you think?" Kendra sighed wearily. "Look around you. All this for a newspaper. Not even an investigative report can describe how on earth I got wrapped up in it all. Just how did your father arrange to get all these people here, anyway?" She looked around the room, pained. "And how did he talk my father into using this house? It's almost ironic, considering that but for this he would have lost it. I thought your father had booked the Hilton Hotel."

"Your father wanted the reception here," Shay interrupted coldly. "Pops got a phone call about it four nights ago and had to send telegrams to all those flying in. The catering firm had everything arranged, so they just scheduled it all for here while we were at the church. So you see, Pops isn't always the manipulator you think."

"But why would my father do that?"

"I don't know," Shay began, bemused, his gaze deepening as he looked down into her face. "I guess he must have thought that his pretty daughter, looking so damned sexy in her mother's wedding dress, deserved the best."

"That's right," Ramsey Davenport interceded, kissing Kendra on her cheek as he came up from behind her, startling the rush of desire that had trickled through her body as Shay kept his eyes trained on her. "You look after my child, y'hear me?" his heavy voice warned

Shay, though Ramsey kept his smile transfixed. "Because there's only Arlisa me have left, and this house."

Kendra heard the pain in his voice and felt that same sense of loss. Losing her mother, the newspaper, and now one daughter to his enemy must have been terribly trying on her father, she acknowledged worriedly. In that moment she suddenly understood why he'd wanted her wedding party there, in his home. It served as a bold, theatrical, ostentatious flaunting of family pride, of boasting the successful raising of a daughter, and it portrayed shameless arrogance by showing the world that she'd been taken into greater wealth. It was unlike her father to reveal any sense of self-glorification in giving her the wedding he'd promised her, but she was more than aware of his motives, and the knowledge brought tears to her eyes.

"I love you, Daddy," she cried stupidly, hugging him tightly. "And I'll always be here. I promise."

Ramsey composed himself quickly, gently pushing Kendra away from his lithe chest and smiling weakly. "I know." He nodded.

Shay restrained the old man's hand. "I'm going to give your daughter everything she wants," he told Ramsey sternly. "Everything."

"You do that," Ramsey threatened quietly, taking the glasses from their hands. "I'll get you both more champagne."

As he left, Kendra's eyes glazed over tearfully. "You see," she murmured, sadness seeping into her body. "This marriage is about money and property, ownership, and . . . handshake deals. I saw Rhona's face when your father announced it over breakfast. I could tell that she knew that I was being used like she had been."

Shay took hold of Kendra's shoulders then, roughly pulled her toward him. "If Rhona's feeling insecure, that's her problem." He chortled harshly. "J B's given her everything, and she can at any time make whatever she wants out of that marriage, just like you can out of ours. But what she does has nothing to do with us. I wanted you and I got you, and . . ."

Something in his voice, in his eyes, held her as Shay's voice deepened. There was a silence as his words died in his throat, as he stared into her face, and suddenly Kendra felt something shift inside her, something powerful and yet frightening.

Shay's grip slackened. "We need to talk," he finished, his soft fingers rubbing absently down her arms in a lazy caress. "Tonight," he whispered, "when we're alone."

Kendra found herself nodding numbly, believing somehow that Shay would make everything all right. It was uncanny that she should even think that of him when she recollected that he had instigated most of what had happened to her. Yet, as she looked into his face the uncertainty passed, and all she could see was a man full of sincerity and truthfulness. Trapped, she was hardly aware of him pulling her to him, that he, too, was ensnared by the same level of honesty which she exuded.

Suddenly, his lips were upon hers, shaping her mouth in deep, meaningful motions. It was nothing like the kiss he'd given her in church. That had been a simple, bashful, brush across her lips, as though he had been uncomfortable that a church full of eyes were upon them, and her heart had plummeted to the depths of despair at the almost impersonal nature of it. Now, a feeling of pure pleasure shot through Kendra and communicated itself to every niche in her body. She heard herself moan as she took delight in its warmth, her mind spinning as it absorbed Shay's low groan in response. She sensed the urgency in him pulsating with a current that touched her heart, demanding a response that she dearly wanted to give but felt unwilling to.

She knew it to be the uncertainty that was creeping its way back; the weeks of being afraid since the car accident, of hearing his secret conversation with Rugg Brown, of not knowing the truth about what had happened to her office or what was going on at the *Nubian Chronicle*.

In the weeks leading up to their wedding she'd noted a change there. Irvin seemed protective and accommodating of her every wish, and Leola informed her that Shay was the one responsible for the new procedures in sorting through the office mail. He'd truly taken over, her mind divulged even as she deliciously accepted the tongue driven into her mouth. Now, after the wedding party his father would get her shares and she would again be reminded of the dreadful quandary she was in.

It was enough to cause her to pull away, her body marked with every impression of the man she loved, her limbs shaking with betrayal of how much he'd affected her. She was breathing uneasily, but deliberately tried to slow the expansion of her chest to disguise the emotion, for she still felt caught up in a heated magic that felt eternally wonderful and yet so frightening. She knew Shay to be mindful of what he was doing to her the minute his hand began to make caressing motions down her spine.

Shay's thoughts were as chaotic and restless as her own. He wanted to express in words how he felt in his heart, how he'd agonized when her car had crashed, unable to sleep until he knew that she was all right, and how much he wanted her to find that special place in his life. Tonight, he would tell her. But for now, he had to wait.

"I promise, we'll work it out," he whispered softly, his hand brushing aside a wisp of hair which fringed her forehead beneath the crown of flowers sewn into her veil. "But right now, Baby, let's get this day over with, okay?" He dipped his head and placed a brief, compromising kiss against her cheek, but as he did so something inside him warmed to the feel of her and piercing stabs of desire shot throughout Kendra's entire nervous system as she felt herself being pulled toward him once more.

"Do you have room for me?" a cultured American voice suddenly intruded lightly.

Kendra turned her head to find herself facing Clara, a woman of fabulous origin in a peach suit and pastel green accessories, her wardrobe aptly displaying that she was invariably a woman of taste. Incredible to think that this woman was old enough to be her mother, Kendra thought as Shay released her to embrace the woman he'd known all his life.

She was taller than Kendra had imagined on first meeting her, more so now that her regal height was extended by two inch heels and her mass of brown hair, swept up by a professional stylist's knot of excellence. Her image instantly put Kendra in mind of Lena Horne. Refined and mature, she decided, and much more than Shay had described her to be, from the glowing, unblemished, olive complexion and the slim waist camouflaging any proof that she'd borne two sons to the innumerable diamond jewels which sparkled with every movement of her hands, her head, or the tilting of her neck.

"I have *two* daughters now." She smiled genuinely, releasing Shay to embrace Kendra. "You must have Shay bring you over to New York to stay with me sometime soon," she added.

"I'd like that," Kendra returned warmly. She liked Clara. Even though they'd met only briefly across a breakfast table, she'd discovered her to be an educated woman, well-versed in Afrocentric art and African mythology, and it had been mesmerizing just to hear her talk. She'd noticed, too, that while Benjamin was quietly puffing away at his Havana cigar Clara seemed to treat him and her sons with an almost noble difference. She couldn't define what had struck her first, the way Clara trained her attention directly on them or the way she listened intently to whatever they'd said. Perhaps it was the measure of admiration reflected in her eyes.

She'd noted it in Rhona, too, a reverence of duty that had held her curiously spellbound. It was a dose of wisdom she'd taken away with her when Shay finally drove her home, believing it might give her some clues about how she would be expected to behave once she'd become part of the Brentwood family.

During the next few hours they zigzagged through the crush, earmarked people for later conversations, and listened with humor to bawdy speeches. They cut through the five-foot wedding cake Benjamin had ordered and danced intimately to music. And throughout it all, Kendra kept her manner relaxed. With Shay by her side the entire time, she felt it an obligation to do so, but Kendra also knew that she was feeling a little unsettled from the overwhelming number of compliments, presents, and showers of congratulations that were being displayed to them.

She was getting her fifth glass of champagne when Arlisa cornered her at the specially erected bar, a happy, infatuated smile spread across her face as she wrapped her hand possessively over the arm of an elegant looking man.

"Kendra, I want you to meet Prince Emeka Obeng-Amoo," Arlisa purred like a stray cat having found fresh cream. "Prince Emeka, this is my sister Kendra, the bride."

"Nice to meet you," Kendra intoned, chuckling as he took her hand and brushed a soft, sovereign kiss against the back of it.

"He doesn't speak English," Arlisa crooned. "Well, maybe a little," she amended, her voice a whisper. "He's a real African prince, you know. His nickname is Twenty K, homage to his having blown twenty thousand dollars in one night at the casinos."

Kendra didn't dare inquire what had became of Raymond. Instead, she teased, "I wonder what *you've* been nicknamed?"

Arlisa flinched, but her guilt disappeared quickly. "Look who's here," she drawled cheekily as a familiar couple swept by them engrossed in an intense argument. "Serve Ms. Thang right," she said gladly, "stealing my man. She must be mad to think that she could ever tame Jerome."

"Who invited them?" Kendra pounced in amazement.

"You know how it is," Arlisa proclaimed. "Parties, weddings especially. They always attract gatecrashers—definitely the wrong breed of people. Oh, and there's Milton Fraser," she gossiped. "Did you know he got engaged two weeks ago, as a birthday present to himself?"

"Really?" Kendra laughed.

"Yeah," Arlisa chuckled. "Well, a man who works as hard as he does has no right to come home to an empty bed. He's going to have a huge engagement party on New Year's Eve to celebrate . . . oh, and now he's talking to Shay."

Kendra looked over to observe them and watched as they disappeared discreetly to one of the other rooms.

"I wonder what they're up to," Arlisa added suspiciously. "Shay is his father's son, after all. He got you and Daddy's newspaper, and—"

"And, let's not forget how," Kendra rebutted. "Excuse me, Prince Emeka. Sissy."

Knowing that she was spying again, Kendra marched

through the new wave of arrivals, past the voices vying for her attention, and was about to come to within yards of where Shay stood in a corner conspiring with Milton Fraser when a warm, clammy hand took hold of her arm. "Yo, Sista. Where's the brotha at?"

Kendra turned irritably to find herself the center of a group of aggressive looking young men, all attired in modern, street-wise apparel and sporting gold teeth and motif hats, all towering above her, caging her in like lions about to pounce on their prey.

"I'm not your sister," she corrected.

"How was heaven when you left it?" another croaked.

She ignored him. "Who do you want?" she demanded.

"We're looking for the main man," one of them interjected.

"Your husband," another added, "the groom?"

Kendra was curious. "Who are . . . where are?" She hardly knew what to ask, but they were perceptive enough and gave her answers quickly.

"We flew in from the states," they began in rapid fire. *"We're Shay Brentwood's basketball team—he sponsors us.* He gave us kids somewhere to go practice jump shots, and he came over to the States to invite us personally to his wedding. *Paid for our tickets, too.* One day, we hope to pay him back by playing the NBA. *That'll be real cool."*

Kendra brought a shallow smile to her face instantly, reminding herself that she had to remain cordial and hospitable. "Thank you for coming. It's nice to meet you all," she greeted tersely. "Shay's over there."

She pointed with her finger, but realized that she was indicating a spot where Shay was no longer present. "Oh," she gasped. "He *was* there. I'll go and find him. Help yourselves to champagne . . . food . . . whatever."

Bemused, she found herself back among her guests, sidling through a mass of conversations, knowing that she'd spoken to everyone of consequence and finding herself just wanting to leave, to get away. She headed for the sun den, reaching it just as Aunt Celi took possession of her wandering attentions.

"Me cannot believe it," she began loudly, her heavy accented Caribbean lingo exposing her as having come from that part of the world. "As God in heaven, I never know my sister's daughter would one day marry Benjamin Brentwood's son. He did love your mother, you know."

"Who loved my mother?" Kendra queried uncomprehending. What on earth was Aunt Celi talking about? Her father had insisted that she come to the wedding and had paid the airfare to get her there. The two things Kendra remembered about Aunt Celi were her aptitude for gossip and her tolerance for Jamaican rum punch.

"You never know Benjamin Brentwood did love your mother?" she said wildly. Taking in Kendra's blank expression, she added, "He never forgive Ramsey. Nineteen fifty-six," she ranted. "That was the year that evil man take himself to America and leave your father owing all that money for his newspaper."

Some of what Aunt Celi was saying was now beginning to filter its way into Kendra's troubled mind. "Wait a minute." Her eyes narrowed. She was suddenly nervous with disbelief. "Aunt Celi, are you telling me that Benjamin Brentwood was in love with my mother? That he deliberately took revenge by leaving my father with his debt because my mother never loved him?"

"True." Aunt Celi nodded, ejecting a burp, and then

decided to feed it with a shot of the rum punch from her glass.

Kendra's eyes narrowed further. She was clearly shocked. "Did my mother have an affair with him?" she demanded to know.

"Well, they did court a few times," Aunt Celi began, as though embarrassed, "but your mother was a very young girl, and Benjamin, well, he was a young man. Your grandmother—my mother—she think he was a little old, but Benjamin's papa Amos Brentwood, he did want them to get married."

"Why didn't they?" Kendra asked drily, her mind still buoyed in amazement.

"Merle meet your father," Aunt Celi clarified as though it was obvious. "And she leave Benjamin for him. Benjamin get so mad he take himself to America and leave Ramsey to pay off all that money to the bank for the newspaper. Your father pay it, though, because they were partners, and then he and my sister come here to England. By that time, Amos Brentwood is bragging to my mother how Benjamin get married to a lovely American girl and a have himself a second son."

"Shay," Kendra realized.

"So my mother tell Amos that Merle and Ramsey marry and set up the newspaper in England."

And Benjamin just had to come after her father to further his revenge, Kendra thought, feeling shaken by what she'd just been told. That meant Benjamin had studied her father's progress for all those years, not to regain his newspaper as she'd suspected, but to hit back at her father. Ramsey Davenport had been the cloud which came over his sunrise, she suddenly realized.

"I sorry me never come to the funeral," Aunt Celi babbled on, oblivious to what was going on in Kendra's head. "Your mother was a good sister. I just find it so hard to believe that God destined you for that man's son." Aunt Celi shook her head, uttering one impassive word: "Life!"

Kendra was about to pull her into the sun den to grill her intensely about other revelations, deciding that she would not tell her aunt about the feud over that very newspaper which was responsible for everything, when her eyes caught sight of someone. He was standing nonchalantly at the door which led into the library, his expression grim as he raised his glass in an ironic salute, his gaze filled with loathing. Kendra instantly felt the hatred boring into her, even with the distance between them.

Her blood ran cold and she was terrified, but she adopted a fixed, calm expression as she excused herself from her aunt and walked steadfastly toward Selwyn Owens. "I thought it was you," she said nervously as she came up within inches of him. "What are you doing here?"

"Do I detect some discourtesy?" he snapped coldly.

"No," Kendra retorted, willing herself to remain unruffled by his tone, even adding a shallow smile to her face in spite of the way he was looking at her. "I'm just surprised to see you here."

"I guess I cannot hope to marry you now," he jabbed furiously, taking a huge swallow of champagne from his flute glass.

Kendra began to grow alarmed. "I guess not," she agreed, before adding sensibly, "Selwyn, I think you should leave."

"Not until I tell you what you've done to me," he blazed, though he kept his voice reasonably controlled at a pitch that attracted no attention. "Do you really think you can get away with treating me the way you have? Leading me on like that, making me believe we had a future but never really giving me anything, not even a taste of that alluring body of yours."

Kendra swallowed, finding his air of insouciance totally intimidating. "Selwyn, I'm sorry. I didn't—"

"Didn't care?" Selwyn finished.

"Maybe . . ." Kendra's voice trailed away, aware that what she had left unsaid was tantamount to an admission. Her heart began to beat madly as she scanned the room in search of Shay, and she began gasping and twisting her hands together when she saw no sign of him anywhere. She began to feel fearful, knowing Selwyn to be fully aware of its imprint on her face. He'd become a hateful man, she told herself with caution, and he'd obviously come there to make her feel bad, perhaps even to cause trouble.

"What's the matter, Kendra?" he boomed, adding a profanity she would not care to repeat. "Looking for the man you always told me was your enemy, the one who's obviously taken you to bed before I could? You made an ass out of me. It's hilarious to think that you're now a Brentwood, after everything you told me."

Kendra felt agonized by what he was saying, and her heart twisted gravely. She knew she'd wronged him, and yet she was also very aware that she was deeply in love, too. "Selwyn, please. I would like you to leave," she pleaded as her stomach turned over.

Selwyn glared at her, unmoving. "Maybe I should make you suffer by announcing your sister's embezzlement practices to everyone here," he countered wickedly. "That should provide you with enough legal repercussions to remember me by. But I think I'll let you stew for a while."

Kendra's eyes widened in panic. "You wouldn't."

"Who knows what I wouldn't do?" Selwyn bragged, his lips pursed harshly. "I'm an M.P., remember?"

"I heard you resigned," Kendra told him bleakly.

Selwyn's face hardened. "Sir William Hendon—that imbecile thought I—"

"Kendra!" Rugg Brown interceded, causing Kendra's emotions to spring from her chest and out of her mouth in hurried, small gasps for air. "Are you all right?" he said with concern.

"Yes," she insisted, though inwardly she was not.

He looked at Selwyn, finding some dislike of the man and so pulled her away, out of earshot. "I have to go, and I can't find Shay," he said warmly. "Can you tell him I've shredded the contract as he requested, and that my invoice is in the post?" His smile widened. "You're a lucky girl, Kendra, getting to keep all your shares without your father losing this house. I guess Shay knows what he's doing. I wish you both the best of happiness."

Kendra stared at him, too blinded by shock to even answer as she watched him leave, his staggering news dropping like a bombshell on her already frazzled nerves. *Deceived.* That was the first word which loomed before her. *Tricked* and *betrayed* came close behind. The last ten minutes had certainly been a revelation in one way or another, but even with Selwyn looking across at her as he was, mad loathing spread into every part of his face, compared in no way to the crafty, sleight-of-hand hoax of a marriage she suddenly felt she'd been tricked into. Why? Her mind churned, baffled and discontented. Why would Shay marry her, knowing full well he never intended to take her shares or evict her father in the first place?

The panic that spread like a fever across her body took hold when a thought instantly sprang to mind, a thought which terrified the life out of her. Maybe, if something were to happen to her . . . he would inherit. No! a voice screamed painfully. She was confused. She couldn't think. Things were looking jangled. Her mind was tormented. Nothing was making sense.

And then, as though providence had intended to leave fingerprints, after all, Shay came up behind her. She knew it to be him the instant she smelled the tangy spice of his expensive aftershave, and from the way his arms slipped familiarly around her waist. "Are you ready to change now?" he whispered, feeling her tense beneath his fingers. Pulling away, he looked at her immediately. "What is it?"

"Selwyn's here," she murmured, too fearful to tell him of the most pressing detail which troubled her.

"Where?"

"He was standing right there," Kendra taunted, realizing now that he had disappeared. It was hard to keep track of anyone with so many people. Even Shay had eluded her several times.

"Damn," he muttered harshly. "Milt overheard some guy at his nightclub talking about Selwyn coming here tonight. You stay there." Within seconds, he was gone, leaving her thunderstruck.

She stood dazed, feeling fear take a strong grip on her heart, and she felt herself heaving for breath, knowing that she needed to find some place of solace away from the throng, where she could think and analyze her situation.

She would go to her bedroom, she decided, and hastily made her way there, knowing it to be the only private place to which she could escape. But as she made her way up the stairway, pulling the hem of her wedding dress up under her, a warm, clammy hand restrained her arm on the handrail, and Kendra turned her head to find that she was looking down into Benjamin Brentwood's triumphant face.

"So, Pretty Legs," he bellowed easily, his mouth

ejecting curls of smoke as he spoke. "I'm your pops now."

Kendra felt her body stir wildly, spurred by something akin to hatred as she looked into his devious, calculating eyes and suddenly something erupted within her which spoke of the pain, despair, and damned, frustrated suspicion which tormented her. "You could never be like my father to me," she spat out violently. "That's why my mother fell deeply in love with him, and never with you."

She saw him stiffen and he removed his hand from her arm as though she'd scorched him with an hot iron poker. "Where you hear that, Girl?" he demanded quietly, his eyes holding hers with an intensity that shook her.

"Aunt Celi told me everything," Kendra admitted with hostility, tipping her head defiantly to tell him that she'd believed it all. "You must know how surprised I was to learn how you deliberately took revenge on my father for taking my mother away from you. Your feud—it was never over a newspaper at all, was it?" Stupidly, tears sprang to her eyes and her voice croaked, but she fought them down, determined, and managed to offer Benjamin a patronizing glare that spoke of her aversion for him.

"Is that why I've been given my shares back? Because they didn't mean anything to you in the first place? Maybe you can tell me why Shay married me. Is that all part of this revenge, too?" She swallowed. "He doesn't love me. Love is something you never taught him. I only wish . . ." She paused, deciding not to torment herself by pursuing that topic. "I'm so glad my mother knew you for what you are, because she found real love in my father, something she would never have found in you, not really."

She knew herself to be crying the moment she took

one last, hateful look at Benjamin Brentwood. She ran up the stairs and into her bedroom, closing the door to shut out the truth, though she knew it to be still evident in her mind as she closed her eyes to stop the tears.

A sob echoed uncannily across the room. Kendra knew it was not hers the instant the sound vibrated, and she opened her eyes quickly to find Rhona sitting on her bed, her tawny, cherry-shaped face reflecting the same lines of despair as her own.

Cynicism caused her to say, "Two Brentwood women crying. And what's the matter with you?"

Rhona's hazel eyes were swimming with tears as she raised her head. She was a pretty woman, Kendra realized as she stepped over the seemingly thousands of boxes of presents strewn around the floor to sit down beside her. There wasn't much difference in age between them; Rhona was older, yet there was a fetching innocence about her, a quiet reserve of character that bordered on discretion. It made Kendra wonder why on earth Joel Brentwood didn't feel himself blessed, even lucky, that Senator Layton hadn't given him an uglier, nastier daughter.

That same discretion was there in Rhona's voice, too, as she spoke mildly in hardly audible tones. "I'm pregnant."

Kendra snorted. "So Benjamin Brentwood is getting his dynasty, after all."

Rhona looked confused. "What?"

"Nothing," Kendra relented smoothly, rubbing the tearstains from her own cheeks. "So," she added lightly, "why is it such a terrible thing? It gives dear Pops another opportunity to puff at an Havana cigar."

Rhona chucked then. "He's like a chimney, isn't he?" She paused. "I don't know how to tell J B. I thought Shay would help me, but he couldn't be bothered to even meet me at Sammy's restaurant a few weeks ago for us to talk."

"Oh . . . I think that was my fault," Kendra admitted suddenly as a flash of memory crept into her mind of a time when she and Shay had danced the night away. He was waiting for Rhona. She sighed with relief, thankful for the knowledge, but it gave her little comfort. "He took me to the Millenium Two thousand club that night."

"Do you love him?" The question dropped from Rhona's lips so unexpectedly that Kendra felt almost startled. Then, as though Rhona realized that she'd overstepped her boundaries, she uttered, "I shouldn't have asked you that, not on your wedding day. I'm sorry. I just hope you knew what you were doing when you married Shay, because in my experience he and Joel are both ruled totally by their father, and he's a man who never feels guilty about anything he does."

Kendra held the other woman's hand in a bond of friendship, and of something more that they both understood implicitly. "We love them," she said simply and then, thinking about Arlisa's peculiar wisdom, she added, "Who knows? Maybe that is all any woman should ask. But tell Joel about the baby. You won't be able to hide it forever."

"I know," Rhona agreed. "Anyway," she sniveled, pulling herself together sufficiently and forcing a shallow smile to her face. "Is your ankle okay, now? I've been meaning to ask you about it."

"It's fine," Kendra assured, disliking the change in conversation, for it served only to remind her of the accident she'd suffered.

"You were very lucky Shay got you out of the car," Rhona said weakly. "When I think of what. . . ."

There was a sudden, harsh knock at the door, and Kendra gazed annoyed as Benjamin Brentwood marched in without waiting for an invitation. He looked at Rhona. "I want to talk to Kendra," he jabbed sternly. "Go find your husband."

As Rhona reluctantly left, he looked at Kendra with the rage of a man who hated disobedience. "I know you think I'm arrogant," he began, dejected, "but that doesn't bother me. My son does, and if there was ever a woman alive on this earth I would want for that boy, it would be you." He walked toward her, undeterred by her angry expression. "You're full of spirit, Girl, and I like that. You're not a prissy little thing like what J B's got. But don't take it out on my boy for something that happened long before you were born."

"Why not?" Kendra demanded, angrily.

The dark rage in his eyes intensified. "Me and your father were best friends once, and yes, a woman—your momma—come between us. I love your mother very much when she was a girl, but your father steal her from me like a thief in the night, and I never forget it. Y'hear?" He hesitated and then Kendra noted his rage subsiding somewhat, but it didn't dissuade him from making an impassioned threat. "I don't want my sons to know, Kendra, or Clara. Y'hear me?"

It was the first time he'd ever referred to her by name, and as he placed his hands on her shoulders Kendra felt them weighted with more that just the secret he expected her to share. "Why don't you want your sons to know?" She wavered. When he didn't answer, comprehension set in. "You led them to believe that you were feuding with my father over a newspaper, didn't you? And you're afraid that if they knew the truth you would lose their respect."

"Pride is an ugly thing, Girl." Benjamin swallowed, melancholy, puffing at his cigar. "Because of it, I lost a very good friend. I don't want to lose my sons."

"Does my father know about you being in love with—?"

"No," Benjamin interrupted blankly. "He never did know why I left him owing all that money, and I don't want you to tell him, either." He paused to puff again at his cigar. "I never did stop love your mother," he said solemnly. "I even come to her funeral, you know."

"You were there?" Kendra rasped.

"After you all gone," Benjamin admitted, his eyes glazing over. "I looked at her grave, and I thought how things could have been, and then I remember how your papa changed all that."

"And that's why you decided to get your lawyers together and launch a bid to recover rights in a newspaper you'd relinquished years ago," Kendra surmised bitterly. "You waited until Momma died, when my father was hurting so much—"

"He stole everything I ever wanted," Benjamin blazed.

"He stole nothing," Kendra railed. "My mother had a choice, and she chose him. And you still have Clara."

"Clara," Benjamin repeated hazily. "Yes, she's a good woman. She give me two sons." His focus shifted abruptly and his gaze intensified. "And my son Shay loves you, Girl."

"No he doesn't," Kendra chimed in, too pained to hear him say it.

"Don't tell me that he doesn't," Benjamin blazed. "I know. And I want you to love *him,* dammit."

"You can't command me to love," Kendra challenged harshly, pulling off her veil and throwing it on her bed. "Command *him.* He's the one who got me married, who tricked me and . . ." She thought about her car accident and closed her eyes briefly. When she opened them, her body shook when she realized that Shay was in the room.

"What's going on?" he inquired, looking at her and then at his father.

"Your father was just leaving."

Benjamin looked at her murderously. "Remember what me say?"

She nodded, knowing that she would keep his secret, however painful it would be for her. And when he left, she looked at Shay. He came over to her, his hands dug into his pockets, his expression guarded as he looked into her face. His eyes narrowed. "You were arguing?"

"I was telling him what Rugg Brown told me," Kendra prevaricated wisely as she swallowed the hardened lump in her throat. "I'm told the contract has been shredded and the bill is in the post. Maybe I can be told also what further terms of our agreement are to be amended without my knowledge."

Shay grimaced. "I was going to—"

"I don't want to hear it," Kendra screamed tearfully. "No amount of excuses can change what has happened to me today." She breathed shakily, looking at her wedding ring, even stupidly admiring the delicate gold band in her sadness. "The sanctity of marriage," she murmured anxiously. "You don't even know what the words mean. So let me tell you what the new terms of our agreement are." Her voice was crisp and businesslike now, devoid of emotion. "I sit at the dinner table, I accompany you to social engagements, and we work, as partners, at the *Nubian Chronicle.* I do not jump through your father's hoops, or get told what to do, and I do not share your bed."

Shay glared at her, his dusky eyes rolling menacingly before his voice shook the room. "Can you be suggesting that you don't want your husband to make love to you, Mrs. Brentwood?" He bristled furiously. Slipping his hands around her waist and pulling her toward him, he murmured against her ear, "If it were not for the number of people running around this house, I'd take you right now and show you just how ridiculous that particular clause is."

He crushed her to his rigid frame, and Kendra was made deliciously aware of just how true that was, because her limbs had begun to instantly react to a need that had erupted within her, a need so powerful that she uttered a lustful gasp from the sheer force of it.

The whirling, hazy effect it had on her was amazing, taking her back to when they'd desirously consumed each other with their bodies, offering and sharing everything. His lovemaking had been exciting, surreal, wondrous, and she desperately wanted to experience again what they'd meant to each other that night, even as some suspicious inner thought took shame in her craving for it.

Through the layers of lace that made up her wedding dress she could feel Shay's hardened muscles, his hardened thighs, and something more which spoke eloquently of how much he had a need for her, too. And as he abruptly released her arm and looked into her face, she could see it there; a telling sign that touched all her nerve endings and marked her soul, which he stoically, quickly, closed off to her as his gaze turned cold.

"Get dressed," he said. "We have a plane to catch. I've decided that I'm spending Christmas with my family in New York, and as my wife you're coming with me. We're all leaving in a couple of hours." He marched toward the door, then added, "Our wedding night may be spent on a plane, but don't worry, Baby. This conversation isn't over with."

He slammed the door and Kendra stared at it, too awed to think how she would react when he chose to bring that subject up again.

Fourteen

Kendra closed her eyes and leaned into the plush, leather-coated seat as the plane cruised at a steady thirty thousand feet against the backdrop of a night sky. The purr of the private jet was beginning to have its disorientating effect on her, and she relaxed her muscles, aware that her body desperately longed for sleep.

It had been a tiresome day, first having been married, then the wedding party, and then the sudden, untimely rush to pack a small suitcase of clothes, toiletries and underwear; and then Shay hurried her to his house to collect the necessary items he required for the transatlantic journey.

She had just enough time to kiss her father, hug her sister, and leave brief instructions by telephone with Irvin at the newspaper that they would be back in time for the New Year's issue before she'd been ushered into the private plane, which stood diligently on the tarmac at London's Heathrow Airport, awaiting their arrival.

Still disbelieving that she was actually on her way to New York, she opened her eyes and stole a tired look around the pleasant interior of the small plane. Tucked beneath the warmth of a checkered blanket, Benjamin Brentwood was scanning several sheets of paper while puffing away absently at his smoldering cigar. Rhona and J B were huddled in their seats sleeping away the toils of the day, and Clara was busy kicking off her shoes though the rest of her was busy shuffling around in her seat as if she were finding it difficult to get comfortable.

Cautiously, Kendra's gaze fell on the man in the seat beside her. Shay's profile was outlined vaguely against the dim lights above his head, and Kendra found herself absorbing the almost intimidating coolness about the way he kept his eyes straight ahead, on an invisible dot it seemed, an indication that he was deep in thought on some subject unknown to her. She told herself that she would get through this journey as long as she didn't react to his calculated silence, to the same quietness of character which had remained consistent since the moment they'd left her father's house.

What a sorry state of affairs. She grimaced, feeling exhausted and miserable. Sighing, she closed her eyes again and the dusk of the night, the purr of the engines, and the ethereal whirl of the supreme hush around her demanded that she sleep.

Time passed, and then Kendra awoke to the sound of turbulence beneath her seat. Startled, she looked about her. Everyone was asleep, unperturbed by the vibration which had unsettled her, but when she looked at Shay, assuming that he, too, would be asleep, her heart skipped madly to discover that his dusky gaze was trained instead on her.

His features had softened, and his eyes were warm, inviting, coaxing her to stay awake for him. Kendra didn't know what to make of it. She was only certain of how she felt at his attention; electrified, heady, even crazy. She wanted him to look at her like that forever, but he seemed embarrassed suddenly because she'd caught him staring, and to her disappointment his eyes became serious, losing the very warmth she'd found so enlivening.

"We've entered a snowstorm," he told her quietly.

"Is that bad?" She panicked, knowing nothing of these things.

"It doesn't look like a heavy storm," Shay declared calmly. "And, Phillip and Ronald are good pilots. They know what they're doing."

Feeling that she should say something, anything, to sustain the momentum now that they were actually talking, she queried, "Did your basketball team find you at the wedding party today?"

Shay looked at her, uncomprehending, for a while, then raised an eyebrow in acknowledgment. "Yeah, they found me."

"I was wondering," Kendra continued curiously. "I know what you told me, about living out your basketball dreams by having your own team, but why did you feel it was an option to invest in teen kids, without any guarantees? I mean, are they any good?"

The faintest of crinkles touched the corners of Shay's eyes. "Helping people less fortunate than yourself isn't an option, it's a responsibility," he began candidly. "They're all good kids, and so far they've been reeling in those trophies."

"Yes, but is that reason enough to get involved?" Kendra pressed.

Shay's eyes narrowed. "Who's going to look after the brother man if those of us who can make a change don't?" It was a question he left hovering in the silence around her as he unbuckled his seat belt and rose to his feet. "I'm going to see how Phillip and Ronald are holding up."

As he left, Kendra pondered Shay's strong sense of duty. It did not surprise her. Much of what he'd told her about himself displayed him to be a man in touch with his own personal notions about his obligation to others. She'd instinctively known this about him the moment she'd seen him standing motionless beneath a streak of lightning on the night their paths had crossed for the first time.

It was the telling sign built into the hardened lines of his face—which was reflected in the depth of his dusky brown eyes and was revealed in his demeanor—that spoke to her. She'd identified it as a sense of self-empowerment, but now she knew that his purpose was not to shape his destiny down the same, narrow alleyway of deceit and revenge his father had traveled, but rather to shape and contribute to the lives of others. And as she thought of how her own life was caught up in the tangles of his invisible web, she felt herself begin to panic.

So many things had happened that desperately needed explanations. Since she'd met Shay there had been the computer virus, the car crash, Shay's impeccable control over what was going on at the *Nubian Chronicle,* the fact that he was returning her shares, her father receiving the deed to his house, her marriage, and the revelation of a family secret. Did Shay really know about it, or was Benjamin really frightened that she would tell him? Everything was a mass of confusion to her, and with the addition of Selwyn's behavior, which somewhat surprised her, she wondered why she'd not yet reached cuckoo land and made a homestead there.

Huddling in her seat, she decided to clear her mind entirely. As long as she was on this plane, with the snowstorm outside and the sound of soft pellets banging faintly against the Plexiglas, she would not tempt fate by thinking of anything further that related to the dysfunction and shortcomings in her life. And with that resolution firmly implanted in the front of her mind, Kendra slept.

For what seemed like an eternity she slept in

snatches, once half waking to the voice of Benjamin Brentwood demanding coffee, another time twisting in her chair to find Shay next to her again, his eyes closed but intuition telling her that he was not asleep. There was a time, too, when she'd felt him reposition the blanket over her, and for some silly reason her mind dazedly took her back to the night he'd shown her the joys of being a woman.

Then at last she was wide awake, and there was no sound but the shuffling of feet and Clara announcing that she should put on her coat. Kendra looked through the window and realized that they had touched down. They had arrived in New York, and her first thought was of how she'd missed the breathtaking skyline she'd read so much about. Her watch said 9:04 A.M., but she knew that it was much earlier because it was still dark and deadly cold.

"Don't put your suitcase down," Shay advised as they disembarked and strode slowly across the snowy tarmac toward a car parked ahead. "JFK has the best thieves in the world, even at this unearthly hour."

It was a limousine, Kendra realized, startled, as they came up against the long stretch vehicle that immediately embraced and sheltered them all from the blistering cold weather. Even in England, Kendra had never felt it to be so cold. As the car surged forward she told herself that New York was five hours behind her watch, so that meant it was just after 4:00 A.M. eastern time.

In contrast to the plane, the ride did not take very long. Though tired and perhaps suffering a little jet lag from her flight, Kendra couldn't help but feel a new wave of excitement as she wondered what lay beyond the limousine doors when it finally pulled up in front of a large, vintage Colonial building in Chappaqua, Westchester County. Her hand stiffly held Shay's as he helped her out of the car, and that was when she gasped for breath; her mink-colored eyes were staring at a grandiose, turn of the century mansion house.

"Come on," Shay urged, gently placing a hand on her shoulder. Shallow steps led to the solid oak front door, where a polished, brass knocker caught the morning dusk light. Kendra realized that the house must be one of the icons in the vicinity, because they'd come down a tree-lined street and had passed similar, though darkly shadowed, houses in their progress.

"Nice neighborhood," she uttered in awe.

"Yeah," Shay agreed. "You've got your uptown folks, your law and order bunch, senior citizens, kids, animal lovers, basketball fans—"

"I get the picture." Kendra nodded warmly.

A minute passed before she was standing in a dimly lit foyer. The house was warm, and Clara was being greeted by two of the domestic staff who were already taking her orders to take their things upstairs. She was struck by the staircase as it loomed majestically in front of her like something out of a classic, North Carolina melodrama, but as Clara turned on yet another set of lights she was held spellbound by the gigantic, life-size portrait at the top of the stairs of a man whose eyes peered almost regally down at everyone below it. It bore an exact resemblance to none other than Benjamin Brentwood.

Kendra winced at the painter's accuracy in depicting the cold harshness she herself had witnessed in the man. And the manner in which it was hung—staring, watching, contemplating—reminded her of an earlier epoch, of Victorian times, when an artist's work almost always took pride of place in the home of its subject.

She felt like offering a mock salute as she followed Shay past it to one of the bedrooms. Then, as she heard the door close behind her, she realized that for the first time since they'd been married she and Shay were alone.

Shay deposited his suitcase on the bed and a briefcase on the floor, then looked at her with a faint, softening smile in his eyes. "Bathroom's over there." He indicated a door behind her before he began to unbutton his jacket.

Kendra swallowed. Despite everything she'd said about not sharing his bed, she knew that the impact of him, standing there, looking at her the way he was, was having an overwhelming effect on her. Even now the arrogant masculinity of the man roused an answering feminine response in her body, tired as she was, and she suspected that any time now he would remind her that she was his wife and exactly what that obligation entailed.

But she was surprised. Shay told her simply, "You'd better sleep off your jet lag. Ma will have you on your toes before long, showing you the sights."

Kendra glared at him. She hadn't expected this. She'd expected a clash of words, an argument, maybe, and then . . . reconciliation. Wonderful reconciliation. Suddenly she felt disappointed, and the letdown made her awkward, even clumsy, as she placed her case on the bed and found that she'd somehow managed to get the lock stuck.

Annoying tears of frustration sprang to her eyes. Why did she desperately want him to make love to her after all that had happened? She should never let him near her again, never allow him to touch her, her mind warned sensibly, because he was dangerous. He'd never intended to take her shares, had never intended to evict her father from his house, and he'd tricked her into marriage. What else was he doing that she didn't know about?

"What's wrong with your case?" Shay inquired, pulling a jumper over his head as he spoke.

Kendra winced. "The lock's stuck."

"I'll deal with it in the morning," Shay told her, walking briskly over to a set of drawers from which he extracted a white shirt. "You can wear this." He tossed it lightly toward her, then added suggestively, "like before."

Kendra instantly felt cold. Before. That was when she'd been involved in the car accident, when she'd regained consciousness to find herself wearing one of Shay's shirts in his bed. And exactly what damage had been caused to her car to warrant it junk, ready for the scrap heap, when she herself was not hurt dramatically? According to Lynton, who was glad to see her upon her return to the *Nubian Chronicle*, Churchill Brokers had confirmed their receipt of the police accident report and were handling her insurance claim. Resentment that an accident would never have happened at all had it not been for Rugg Brown's papers rose up inside her.

Without quite knowing it, she chided, "You're a fool, Shay Brentwood, if you think that anything could ever be like before."

Shay stood silent, not moving, just looking at her with his expression slanted as though he hadn't expected her defiant outburst. Then, with a dangerously low voice and his eyes dark and irritable, he muttered, "Okay, Kendra. Let's have it so I can get me some shut-eye."

Kendra swallowed her breath. She felt her heart thump heavily against her rib cage as she looked at Shay's resigned expression. She didn't want them to fight, not really, but she couldn't ignore what was going on, that some conspiracy was being plotted against her. And with that one thought at the front of her mind, she said, "I want to know what else you have got in store for me. What other surprises am I to expect?"

Shay threw an annoyed look across the room. "First surprise, I'm gonna kill Rugg Brown."

Kendra grimaced. "He was only following your orders."

"Mr. Loose Mouth was told not to say anything to you," Shay drawled, striding slowly toward her. "Look, your mother wanted you to have those shares as a wedding gift, so they're yours."

"Just like that?" Kendra chided truculently. "And that was reason enough to trick me into marriage, was it? Into something you obviously don't believe in."

"Look, Kendra," Shay began, his manner verging on annoyance as he placed consoling hands on her shoulders. He didn't know how to begin to tell her the truth, because right now he felt unsure she would believe him. "I wasn't going to sit back and watch Owens have you."

Kendra's eyes widened. "You decided you were better for me than Selwyn?" she returned scathingly, disbelieving that she was actually hearing the low note of triumph in his voice.

Shay looked down into her troubled face, knowing that was not what he intended to say. He tried to rephrase. "I wasn't going to wait for you to agree to marry him. What do you think I pay lawyers for? Delbert figured there must be a will left by your mother and discovered she had shares in the newspaper. You were desperate to keep the *Chronicle*."

Kendra felt blessedly numb. Was she really hearing this? That Shay could exercise so much control over her life without her collaboration, consent, or knowledge? She wouldn't have minded if he'd loved her, if he had been conditioned to act because he would've considered his life empty without her. Instead, he had been more interested in getting what he wanted. Wasn't that what he'd once told her? *When I was a child and I saw something I wanted, I always doubled my efforts to get it, but I never cheated and I never played dirty.*

It was all coming back to her now. And what made her feel worse was knowing that there had been nothing she could've done to stop him. He *had* cheated, and he'd played dirty. Selwyn was testament to that. Poor Selwyn. He'd been right all along.

Thinking only of him and with tears in her eyes, she studied Shay's satisfied expression, knowing that he really had no understanding of what he'd done. How could he? Like Arlisa had said, he was his father's son. "Selwyn's such a good man," she defended remorsefully. "And I've been a pushover, because I never believed a word he told me about you."

Shay's face hardened and Kendra noted that his eyes had glazed over like coffee beans. He released her harshly and dug his hands into his pockets. "You want to know about Selwyn Owens?" His voice held a harsh sting which got her attention instantly. "The guy's a psychopath, okay? The police have been investigating him ever since your car accident. They believe that the company who stripped down your office was hired by him. The proprietor's recollection of the man who'd paid them and took away your things fits Owens's description. They also suspect he might have had something to do with the London Borough of Brent Council canceling their advertising with the *Chronicle,* because he can command influence there. And I wouldn't put it past him that he was the one responsible for the computer virus."

Kendra studied the seriousness in his face, but her mind was in total denial of anything Shay was saying. "You're unbelievable," she ranted harshly. "You just never stop, do you? You'll be telling me next that he was the one who tampered with the brakes of my car."

When Shay stood silent, shock etched into his face, she ranted on. "Oh yes, I overheard you," she boomed knowingly. "Just like I overheard you talking with Rugg Brown about my shares. And all the time your father never even wanted them." She was so filled with fury that she found herself about to tell Shay why. But then she remembered her secret with Benjamin Brentwood. "Well, now that I've got them back and my father has the deed to his house, the only thing I require from you is a replacement of my car, or were you lying about that having gone to the scrap heap?"

Shay's face twisted with fiery contempt. "You can't have your car back, Kendra, because it's a burnt-out shell, okay? The thing exploded about two minutes after I got you out," he barked, his voice trembling so violently that it left a quaking echo in the room. "And another thing," he added in a tone that called for Kendra's specific attention, his hands snapping open his briefcase, from which he removed a bundle of envelopes. "Before you go singing any more praises about Mr. M.P., he's been sending you letters. Lots of them." He thrust the bundle into Kendra's hand. "The man's got a bad case of heroine worship gone awry. That's why I brought you here. I was getting worried about what he would do next, but the police couldn't touch him without his having physically harmed you."

Kendra inhaled a slow, ragged breath as her eyes fell on the envelopes in her hand. She felt her body shake, felt anxiety rise up in her as she knew herself to be frightened, because Shay was now making sense. Her office—Selwyn had innumerable opportunities to copy her keys, and, knowing of the unscrupulous behavior by M.P.s of late, he could feasibly have called in favors at the Borough of Brent Council. But to try to kill her?

Peering into one of the nine opened envelopes she'd been given was all it took for her to realize that she had made a dreadful mistake. She recognized Selwyn's handwriting immediately. The long, curling strokes made by his blue-tipped pen were similar to those in the notes he'd often sent her at the office. The letter was ugly, nasty, and made awful references to seeking revenge. It ended with the simple word Me at the bottom, but it was evidently penned by Selwyn.

"Oh my God," she moaned, stunned with shock as she collapsed onto the bed, appalled by the sudden rush of weak tears flooding her eyes and clogging her throat. It didn't seem possible. She'd always thought Selwyn to be the epitome of goodness and civility.

"One of them had a dead spider in it," Shay told her quietly. "Leola felt you had enough problems with the staff already, and decided to come to me. I told her not to say anything to you, but the police know about these, too."

Instantly squeamish, Kendra threw the entire bundle onto the floor, ejecting a terrified moan as she did so. Shay was immediately by her side, holding her close, comforting her, as her eyes suddenly released guilty tears. She was choked with a mixture of pain, of embarrassment, humiliation, and guilt that a man Shay had known her to trust so explicitly could turn so violently against her. It couldn't be happening to her, she wept. Not to her. What on earth had she done to Selwyn to deserve it?

"You should have told me," she blurted out angrily.

"You deserved to know. I'm sorry," Shay said, his solemn voice bouncing against her hair. "I'm sorry I didn't tell you sooner." She heard the torture in his every word and her mind spun in all directions of frantic fear, heightened by the sheer resonance of it.

It was some time before Shay finally let her go, his gaze worried and tired as he planted a brief kiss on her trembling lips. "Let's get some sleep," he whispered, urging her toward the middle of the bed.

Kendra meekly pulled herself up to join him as he leaned against the bedpost, feeling the gentle urging from Shay's strong, encouraging hand that she snuggle next to his warm, muscular chest. She felt deep comfort lying next to him, but her limbs were still shaking with trepidation, knowing that Shay had saved her life. And she couldn't help agonizing about what she was going to do. "Shay?" she whispered in her weakened voice as she looked up into his sleepy face, feeling herself about ready to dissolve into another tearful tailspin. "What I said about Selwyn, I didn't know—"

Shay placed a finger over her mouth, looking deeply into her eyes as he spoke. "Still think you got the wrong guy now?"

Kendra shook her head. "No."

"Good. 'Cause we're in this together."

Kendra awoke to the full glare of day some time in the afternoon to find herself alone in Shay's bed. Her arms and legs felt stiffened by the long sleep, and she still felt disorientated, knowing that the full effects of her jet lag hadn't worn off.

She looked around the room fretfully, wondering where Shay was as her mind began to reassemble everything that had happened to her. But as her eyes came into focus her thoughts became curiously occupied with studying the contemporary props around her; the collection of books by authors such as C.L.R. James, Bobby Seale, Stokely Carmichael, and Chester Himes all stood to attention like soldiers on a shelf, reminding her that Shay had told her he liked to read. The stylish, Afrocentric graphics on the wall, an obvious input of Clara's, a small, mini deck CD stereo, monitors, TV and video recorder neatly encased in dark furniture, and a desk littered with papers and small basketball merchandise in the shapes of a pencil sharpener, a paperweight, and a letter opener all added character typical of the modern American age.

With probing interest, she went over to the wardrobe and found her eyes falling on expensive suits, trainers, jeans, windbreakers, boots; all the apparel for whatever image Shay chose to project.

There was one item in the room which struck her as indubitably being the property of Shay. It attracted her attention the moment she'd closed the wardrobe, and it was sitting on a small table near the window. It was the scale model of a building, and at first impression she took it to be a childhood toy, custom-made with the art of a growing boy.

But as she began to scrutinize the structure, she realized that it was as complex and convoluted as the wedding cake she'd recently cut into. It was no toy. It was a vision of the future, and a notation at the bottom read, Brentwood Productions, Inc.

She kept staring at it as she changed out of her clothes and located her suitcase. The lock was already opened, an indication that Shay had somehow managed to unlatch it for her, and the image of the model stayed there in her mind as she plucked out the clothes she required—a pair of red slacks, white shirt and black jacket- before seeking the haven of the bathroom where a long shower served to revitalize her completely.

She was dressed, her face made up, and was in the process of styling her auburn hair when a brief knock sounded on the door. Rhona popped her head through. "Feeling better?" She smiled upon entering.

Kendra nodded, then asked, "Have you told Joel yet?"

"I've decided to announce it tomorrow, on Christmas Day," Rhona returned warmly. "What do you think?"

"Wonderful," Kendra agreed. Turning her head to the model, she probed, "Do you know about this?"

"Shay's idea," Rhona said, looking at the miniature building. "Pops is against it, though. He believes Brentwood Cable Television, a division of Brentwood Communications Group, Inc., should continue to buy regular productions, but Shay has the long-term objectives of financing young black talent to produce exclusively for BCT. He and Joel have this thing about those who control the imagery control how people are seen."

Kendra smiled wryly. "Seems I still have a lot to learn about Shay Brentwood," she told Rhona. "Where is he, downstairs?"

"The Brentwood men have all gone into their Manhattan office today," Rhona declared with a cynical chuckle. "I thought, how about we girls go Christmas shopping? Clara and I can show you the sights." She lowered her voice to a whisper. "And when Clara isn't looking, maybe I can pick up some baby things to surprise everybody."

Kendra laughed. "You're on." Following Rhona out of the room, she asked quickly, "How many months pregnant are you, anyway?"

"Four."

"You're four months pregnant without Benjamin Brentwood knowing?" Kendra teased with pretended wide-eyed amazement.

"Isn't it bliss?" Rhona laughed.

"Absolutely," Kendra agreed.

"You look like your momma, you know that?" Benjamin Brentwood told Kendra absently, a little misty-eyed, as he faced her from the head of the dinner table.

Nobody else heard him, and Kendra wondered if this was his way of goading her, or perhaps being a little intimidating. She couldn't quite decide. Yet, somehow, the odd way she felt about knowing that he had once loved her mother made her in some way understand why he was saying it.

He'd lived so much in the past, she thought. In fact, it'd haunted him in very much the same way a distant, unpleasant childhood memory could intrude upon the tranquility of an adult, she thought. And he must have been but a young man at the time—hardly, she suspected, equipped with the faculties to understand true love.

She would take his remark on face value, she decided sensibly, and make nothing of it. That way, she could keep his secret intact within her guise of innocent coyness without showing any signs of self-betrayal. And so she uttered a bashful, "Thank you," in reply and turned her head to study the four other people at the table.

Benjamin acknowledged it with hazy eyes, but did not stray from the subject. Sober in demeanor and attire, his sharp business suit and silk tie in keeping with the corporate giant that he was, he appraised Kendra, steadfast and determined, then caught her attention by adding, "You're so much like her. She had this credible sense of justice, like you."

Kendra returned her gaze. "She also had the good sense to teach me about forgiveness," she relented, knowing that his kind of justice had long since been against her father.

Benjamin chuckled softly. "Ah . . . you have your mother's strength, Girl. You're much stronger than you think." He then launched himself back into the conversation with his sons, mulling over the events of the day while Clara hung on to his every word with parted lips.

Kendra sat passively and listened, wondering

whether she or Rhona or Clara would be asked about their day. They'd shopped for presents all afternoon. She'd never seen such commercialization of the Christmas season as New York offered.

Despite the cold, she'd enjoyed herself thoroughly, taking in Macys, late lunch at The World Trade Center, then going back to Bloomingdale's for more shopping. They'd come home to find the house alive with noise and laughter, discovering Benjamin had invited his most senior media junkies over for pre-Christmas drinks. She'd changed clothes, dressing in the only evening gown she'd thought to pack—an off-the-shoulder, jade taffeta and lace dress—emerald earrings, and jade patent leather shoes.

It had been riveting listening to the foibles and fickleness of the media business, and a little daunting having to parry the congregation's inquisitive comments and American phraseology that boggled her mind. But Shay was by her side the entire time, his hand around her waist, interpreting the jargon and weaving her in and out of the clusters of people making polite introductions.

Yet even among the harmony, the laughter, and the chattering, her mind traveled back to England, back to the problems which still lay there. As the thought stuck, she'd felt less and less like drinking champagne with people who were, after all, strangers, and more and more like being alone to get her bearings.

Correctly detecting her mood as always, Shay had steered her to another part of the house, to a room where it was silent and only the distant sounds of voices could be heard against the low sound of bells that twinkled mischievously from an enormous Christmas tree sited there.

"Don't shut me out, Kendra," he told her, his soft, dulcet tones stroking feathery brushes of consolation against her skin. "I don't want you to think about him. He's not worth it."

"I know," she protested, "but—"

"No buts," Shay had warned gently against her lips, pulling her so close that she'd been mentally alert to every part of him, to her skin tingling deliciously because of the feel of him, her senses aware of a sexual chemistry at its most potent. "Think of this." He'd taken her lips, languorously, seductively, and so sweetly that she still felt it now.

She could still feel the clean smell of his breath inside her mouth as it'd been then, remembering the tongue that had softly pulsated in it, forcing her to welcome every amorous demand without hesitation. He tasted so good, she thought dreamily, her mind still spinning with the erotic deliberation that had made her forget everything but the necessity of ensuring that such pleasure never stopped.

But it had stopped, when reality struck, reminding them that they would be missed, that there was yet an evening to get through. And as the last guests had rushed away to be with their families, Benjamin had deemed that they should sit down to a late dinner of turkey and stuffing, rice and peas, baked yams and turnips, served with all the finery of a banquet.

Suddenly, she heard the clock in the foyer strike midnight, and her eyes settled on the man across from her who was very much still part of her mind, her mouth smiling sweetly at him as she now thought of the engraved solid brass pen she'd bought him, aptly inscribed TO HANDSHAKE DEALS on its black lacquered surface.

"Merry Christmas," Benjamin announced loudly, a turkey leg in his cigar hand and a glass in the other. As everyone reached for their glasses, Kendra was surprised to hear his voice become unusually emotional.

"There's only one thing a man can really ask of God in life," he began, "and that's for family. I raised a good family. I'm proud of my sons and their mother." Turning to Kendra and Rhona, he added, "And I know I'm going to be proud of you girls, too. Then, raising his glass in salute, he said, "To family."

Kendra nudged Rhona, who quickly interjected, "And to the newest addition. I'm having a baby."

"What!" The whole room dissolved into giddy laughter of unexpected delight.

"I'm going to have me a son," Joel shouted disbelievingly. Everyone was caught up in the sudden whirl of surprise so that when a small, inarticulate little sound of choking shot through the room it went unheard, smothered and squashed by the pervading excitement. Overshadowed by the rush of voices deeply engrossed in congratulating Rhona, Benjamin's anxious face went unnoticed by his family until he inadvertently knocked over a sherry glass and his body doubled over in pain.

Kendra was the first to look. "Pops?"

"Turkey bone," Benjamin strained. "Stuck . . . hospital."

"Everybody?" she gasped, her voice so sharp that the room fell silent. Kendra had never felt her stomach muscles turn so anxiously as when she watched, almost in disbelief, the instant, frantic motions of Shay and Joel perceptively gripping their father by the arms and shifting his tall frame quickly, nervously, into the foyer. Benjamin was still on his feet, but he was crippled by pain and he was gasping erratically, as though short of breath.

"J B, let's get him to Lenox Hill," Shay was ordering.

"I'll drive," Joel returned hurriedly.

"I'm coming," Clara breathed.

A backward glance was lacking as they shot out

through the door, swiftly leaving her and Rhona trembling and stunned.

Three hours crawled by, minutes dragged on endlessly, and on the surface nothing had changed. As though by tacit consent, Kendra and Rhona were still at the table, clamoring for some measure of inward control, though Kendra knew herself to be much more together than Rhona. They'd heard nothing. It was as if time had stood still, and she was about to ponder whether she should believe the old adage that no news was good news when she heard the door in the foyer bang open and footsteps.

Kendra shivered, tensed and shaking, as Shay entered the room first, forlorn, followed by a solemn Joel, his arm around Clara's drooping shoulders. She shot out of her chair, Shay's face telling her more than any words could, though it was Joel's savage, bitter monotone that verbalized them.

"Pops is dead."

Rooted in a frozen pose of shock, she stood mortified by the ripple of doom which ran through the room, her body seized by a peculiar sort of paralysis as Joel explained, "A turkey bone punctured—"

She was not allowed to hear Joel finish. As her ears caught Clara's haggard scream Shay had caught her wrist and marched her out of the room. He hung on with a viselike grip as he took the stairs two at a time, but Kendra, bemused, lingered in the shock she was suffering.

As the bedroom door slammed shut behind her and Shay released her abruptly, she slowly became aware of the contorted look of rage in his eyes. Politeness forbade her to say anything of it, so she muttered a low, benevolent, "I'm sorry," hoping the words gave some measure of comfort.

But Shay's eyebrows furrowed. "You knew, didn't you?" he accused brusquely.

"Knew what?" Kendra wavered, unable to hide the frisson of fear she felt beneath Shay's freezing scrutiny of her.

"Don't play me, Kendra," Shay spat out angrily. "Pops told me. Before he died he ranted on and on about your mother, about how he once loved her."

Kendra gasped. "He swore me to—"

"Keep it a secret," Shay finished. "Well, Pops didn't want to go down without making his last confession. Your momma must have been a pretty piece of work, twisting him up the way she did, hurting him by marrying your father."

Kendra's whole body trembled with fright. She couldn't possibly be hearing this on top of everything else. That the man she loved more than life itself could be fraying her nerves and wearing her down with such false accusations. She felt afraid. Benjamin Brentwood had entrapped his fury and jealousy inside a time warp, had kept it alive for over thirty years through a feud over his founding a newspaper, and now, it seemed, he was successful in having spurred it forward to the present day.

Anger and damnation of it all suddenly shook her. Feeling pride rear up in her to the point where it was beyond the warnings of caution, she railed, "I don't care what you think about me. I don't even care if you never love me," she lied, whimpering, "but I care what you think about my mother, and she had nothing to do with it. Your father had the whole lot to do with it. I always thought him incapable of loving anyone or anything. Then I discovered that he'd loved my mother when she was maybe a slip of a girl, I don't know. But she fell in love with Daddy, and Benjamin had no right to take revenge for that on my father, without having the guts to tell him why."

Shay stood back, as though hit by a full megaton force. "Ramsey never knew?"

"No. Daddy always thought his feud with Benjamin was because of the *Nubian Chronicle.*"

Shay's face seemed to turn cane pale. "How did you find out?"

"Aunt Celi, after we were married," Kendra said mildly. It'd taken an old woman traveling halfway across the world from the Caribbean to help her piece the puzzle together. "Benjamin simply confirmed it, and made me promise never to tell anyone." She paused. "I take it Joel and Clara know?"

"He didn't tell them," Shay declared. His eyes clouded as he remembered his father weakly whispering that he wanted to talk to him alone. "Only me." He looked at her point blank. "That's why you and Pops were arguing?"

She nodded.

A recognition of something crossed his subdued profile. "That's why he didn't bat an eyelash when I told him I wanted you to keep your shares." He sighed absently. "I thought I knew Pops."

"Shay, don't hate him," Kendra pleaded. "Please."

The moment she spoke the words Shay's body stiffened and he stood staring at her with such dark, forbidden, agonized tension in his eyes that Kendra could have wept for him as well as herself.

"I don't hate him." One step was all it took to pull Kendra into his arms. She willingly leaned against his heaving chest and listened intently as he forced out painful words in understanding of his father. "Love is a word people put to work when they want to use somebody, he told me once," Shay began helplessly, almost shamefully. "But I misunderstood him. My Pops found love, and I never knew it. He must've loved Ma in some way, too."

"Yes," Kendra agreed, closing her eyes and feeling Shay's torment as he crushed her tangible body against him as though his very life depended on it. She was fearful, frightened of what this new discovery about his father would mean to him. Perhaps this would be the best time to tell him something concrete and sustaining which he could hold on to. Something trusting and truthful that would serve to heal his open wound, she thought.

At first she couldn't think of anything to say. Then, knowing how much she loved him and knowing how much she'd wanted him to know that, she looked up into his chiseled face. With a hollow numbness in her voice which seemed almost unreal, she whispered, "Shay, I love you. I'm in love with you. Do you believe me?"

His dusky gaze penetrated hers, sensing the revealing depth in it, and then Kendra saw tears there. Without words, this was the communication she'd always wanted; the lowering of the barriers, the dismantling of his hardened exterior which had once led him to tell her that he was not given to outward shows of emotion. And though she longed to hear him say the same words, knowing he would not, she nevertheless felt a warm stirring inside as she let hope grow into a certainty that he loved her, too. A hope that grew the moment she felt his hand rubbing gently across her cheek as if he were truly cherishing her.

"Show me, Kendra," he whispered hoarsely against her lips. "Show me."

With every muscle taut and straining, he took her lips and accepted freely what she offered. Kendra melted into him, knowing Shay was caught up in something he could no longer control. On impulse, she began to remove the clothes which strapped his heavy limbs, kissing him throughout, taking delight as inch by inch, his caramel body became naked beneath her arousing fingers.

He kissed her, too, with an abandon that was new, almost shyly helping her shed the worldly impediments covering her trembling limbs. She dimmed the lights and gently coaxed him onto the bed, deciding that she would give him everything she could feel, show him something that would reach the very deepest part of him, that would reveal to him the true meaning of her love.

Their last lovemaking had taught her something of his touch zones, where flesh was rigid and where it was soft and tender. Where pleasure might be pushed almost beyond endurance. To her, Shay was like a free-spirited, black stallion in a fresh, dewy meadow, his glistening, velvety skin alive beneath her touch, the sheen of his bronzed, caramel flesh shining in the dim bedroom lights.

She sensed his impatience, heavy-laden with despair, as he began to trace the fullness of her ebony breasts, his eyes revealing his disbelief of her complete surrender to him, and in that moment she knew that she would be the strength that he needed. She would make him forget himself, forget the present, forget the past, and think only of what love could do.

Her eager tongue defined his body, committed it to memory, shaped his tormented profile into one of longing and need until his breathing became panting like a wild animal's as he swept her up into his arms. He kissed her like he'd never kissed her before, joyfully, tenderly, demandingly, like a magnificent stallion tasting new pastures.

And they rolled together, reminiscent of two innocent horses playing in that fresh meadow, fingers tangled, bodies joined, pulse beat against pulse, sweat mingled with tears until she could no longer tell which body parts were hers and which were his.

Yearning to give him what he wanted, she adapted herself and felt him invade the portals of her soul, consuming every niche of their passion and bonding them together for all time. Later, when she gave a breathless cry of supreme fulfillment and had coaxed him to the pinnacle of shuddering ecstasy, she stroked his sweating head against her midriff, feeling his body quake in tearful mourning over the loss of his father. She would love him, she told herself with glazed eyes. Just as Benjamin Brentwood had commanded her, she would love him with all her heart.

Fifteen

"Hog, dog, or frog?" Arlisa whispered rudely into Kendra's ear as they both placed bloodred roses on the white coffin that rested on its webbing above an open grave. "That's what they should put on his headstone after what he did to Daddy."

"Sissy," Kendra said murderously, her voice low and strained as she out-glared her sister. "If I hear you come out with anything like that again, I'll slap you with my bare hand. You should have respect for the dead."

"Well," Arlisa drawled shamelessly, though thoroughly shaken by the anger she saw reflected in Kendra's face. "I resent being here, in New York, on New Year's Eve, too. And Daddy's been hateful, stopping my allowance and forcing me to come here. Now I'm going to miss Milton Fraser's big bash in London."

Kendra cast her eyes upward in frustration, deciding that the best thing to do would be to ignore her sister entirely. It was admirable of her father to decide to come all the way from England, and as she looked over at him standing forlornly alone as though his mind had taken him back to a time in Jamaica where he'd shared a boyhood friendship with Benjamin Brentwood, she sighed with a half smile, knowing how proud she was to have him as a father.

Quickly, she turned on her heel and hurried back to

where Shay was standing. He was framed beneath an enormous, black umbrella which had sheltered them both from the mushy, feather-like crystals of snow falling overhead, dressed impeccably in a thick, dark sable-colored suit and a long, black leather overcoat to protect him from the harsh elements, though his eyes were shielded by densely dark tortoiseshell glasses.

It was mercilessly cold, but she felt some semblance of warmth as he took her hand and squeezed it tightly with his trembling fingers. "I always thought him indestructible," he told her quietly, his tone wavering.

"In many ways, he was," Kendra answered weakly. "I don't think he'll be forgotten in a hurry."

And as quickly as she'd said those words, a rangy man strutted over from among the vast crowd, his voice loud and boisterous against the freezing cold air. "I'm sure glad I knew your father," he began proudly in a Texan drawl. "He never had fairy dust in his eyes. Was a real mammajammer who knew how to kick this media real good, and we had a blast, him and I. I sure am gonna miss him."

"He was a hell of a deal maker to hook up with," another intruded. "Knew the slings and arrows of the business, all right. Played hard when it came to the bottom line, but always gave you the score. Y'all be proud of him now, y'hear?"

Just as quickly, many more followed, voicing similar opinions and shaking Shay and Joel's hands, their eyes betraying dollar signs, knowing who they would be doing business with in the future. Kendra felt some awe of the man as she listened to the oratory, doubting almost that they could really be referring to Benjamin Brentwood. In all the time she'd come up against him, he'd displayed only callousness and tyranny.

Yet, he had achieved honor and respect that morning. Clara cried copiously during the ceremony, dressed elegantly and looking *soigné* in her expensive, black fur which fit her snugly, her heavy, black veil and black gloves a trifle ostentatious even against the single string of white pearls ornamenting her wrist. Reverend Beresford Tooney had kept to a simple service, which was what Clara had wanted.

A commemorative "Amazing Grace" had been sung by the congregation of the church filled to almost overflowing capacity with visitors, and she'd listened as the mayor of New York delivered his eulogy, a message she knew described the man eloquently. "Benjamin Eli Brentwood died," said the mayor, "with a life-held commitment to the Great Black Hope, and retaining the spirit, energy and enterprise that American dreams are made of."

Pulling her navy blue overcoat over the simple, collarless, black dress she was wearing, she turned to face Shay with an understanding of what he was going through. "Do you want to stay a while?" she whispered up at him, recalling what she'd done at her mother's funeral.

"No." Shay grimaced, his eyes shifting to watch the mourners file out of the burial ground across the thin sea of snow to their limousines, Rolls Royces, and black Mercedes-Benzes. "Let's go."

The foyer of the house was pulsing with people when they finally arrived there, where further communal outpourings of affection and respect were plentiful. Kendra found it hard to keep a smile on her face because she was mindful of how the condolences might be affecting Shay.

The last few days had been trying for everybody. None of them had had any real awareness of the passing of time. The Christmas presents had gone unopened, the phone calls from the press went unanswered. When people had arrived at the house questioning the TV news bulletins, it had been left to the domestic staff to tell them what had happened. It was the sheer unexpectedness of it all which had made it the more awful. But she'd been there for Shay, listening, digesting, understanding his need to talk.

And in the middle of the night, she often awoke to find him sitting in the chair which faced the bedroom window, staring at the starlit sky as if he were hoping to find something there that nobody else could. She succeeded in coaxing him back to bed, made him forget the torment which troubled him. But last night had been different. She had detected a barrier between them, and that worried her. Finding him awake as usual, she had wanted to reach out to him but he'd stared down at her naked, ebony flesh, whispering a simple, "Go back to sleep, Kendra. I'm all right," and placed a tentative hand against the back of her shoulder.

It was one of her touch points, and she'd felt a tremor of excitement rush up inside her, but lovemaking was not what Shay had needed then. Peace of mind was. And since the day his father had died, she'd never been able to give him that.

Yet all morning he'd kept her by his side, kept her hand in his, and she'd felt needed. *He needed her.* Deep down, she told herself that he loved her, and her need to hear the words spring from his lips made her heart ache more than anything. Would she ever hear them?

She looked into Shay's brooding face. He had removed his dark glasses and she wanted to see a telling sign that would give her hope, give her faith that she could make him love her, but Shay's dusky eyes were gazing admiringly at the majestic portrait at the top of the stairs. So, it seemed, was everybody else.

"Do you know what Pops last words were, about your father?" he asked her, briefly glancing at Kendra to see that he had her attention before his eyes traveled back to the painting. "He said, *'Tell Rammy me sorry.'* "

Kendra was stunned. "Those exact words?" She asked in amazement.

"Direct quote," Shay answered. "I told your father this morning."

He took her hand, clasping his fingers around them as Kendra's mind spun. She was hardly aware that she'd reached for a glass of champagne from the passing waiter, nor of Joel climbing to midpoint on the stairway in readiness to make a speech to the assembly below. All her mind told her was what it must have cost Benjamin Brentwood to apologize.

"He's a man who never feels guilty about anything he does." That was what Rhona had told her. Now she was to learn that Benjamin had died easing his conscience, and the thought touched her, infiltrating her mind with such vitality that she almost missed Joel's emotional toast to the man who had controlled so many things.

"To the Godfather of Black media," Joel bellowed loudly against her ears. He had joined everyone in the foyer who'd raised their champagne flutes in a salute of honor to the man in the giant portrait looking down at them; the boss, the *Serussa,* the legend who would live on in his sons.

She couldn't help but raise her own flute, not out of any sudden respect or admiration but in simple acknowledgment that she was thankful he'd found it in his heart to forgive. She was aware of the firm pressure of Shay's strong hand against hers as he watched her tilt the glass, and as Kendra looked into her husband's warm, dusky brown eyes, seeing the deep, desirous pool of emotion within them, she knew that she would keep her hope alive, because now she no longer nursed any resentment toward Benjamin Brentwood. That meant she was truly free to shower everything in her enchanted heart on the man she loved.

Two days later Kendra found herself back in England, back at her desk at the *Nubian Chronicle*. Life felt difficult, and she was staring dazedly out of the large, double floor-to-ceiling windows behind her desk, absorbing the wind and rain battering furiously against each other in the first of the winter storms. The late afternoon sky was grey, just like the color of her mood, as she reminded herself that Shay was still in New York.

She'd flown back to England with Arlisa and her father on a first-class Concorde ticket to oversee a commemorative edition of the *Chronicle* to honor Benjamin Brentwood, but she would rather have stayed in New York. It was only at Shay's insistence that she'd left there at all.

"I have got to take care of business here," he'd told her at JFK, holding her shoulders and looking into her face as though he'd needed to make sure that she understood. "J B and I need some time and space, okay?"

"Your mother," she'd protested. "She needs—"

"Rhona's there." She was overridden instantly, and she'd felt shunned, rejected in every sense of the word.

She'd wanted to cry. *Ask me to stay and I'll stay,* she'd pleaded inwardly. She would have begged him, too, if her mind had not been alert to the fact that there were things that really needed to be sorted out. An empire, with its newest drivers at the wheel intent on accelerating the company engine to top gear, needed reassembling. She knew it would take time to oil all the inner nuts and bolts with the new premium required to run the Brentwood media machine at a fresh, optimum pace, and so she'd accepted leaving.

"These are the keys to the house in London," he'd

said firmly. "Move your things in, everything. And this is the key to the Maserati. Use it until I get back, okay?"

"How long will you be?" Already, she'd felt desperate, again that whimpering, pining female missing her sharp edge.

"I don't know." It'd been an honest answer under the circumstances, and she could tell that the question irritated him. Yet, as he planted a brief parting kiss against her lips she'd sensed something; a tremor in his arms as he'd held her, the lingering motion of his mouth as he savored the taste of her, the soft pained sigh of his breath as he let her go. And she could've sworn he was going to tell her something as she saw a sweeping, agonized look in his eyes before the abrupt announcement of her flight intruded.

Then, within seconds, he was gone.

Now as she looked at the dial face of her watch and saw the time approaching five minutes to five, she decided that she'd go home and unpack. Maybe relax in a hot bath and then pamper herself for total revitalization. But just as she began to move from her desk to get her coat, go home, and do exactly that, there was a brief knock at her door and Leola entered with a shallow smile on her face, her expression one of complete exhaustion.

Having to catch up with the workload after the Christmas break was always tiring, Kendra thought, particularly when pressed with editorial deadlines and a moody, irritable editor adding to one's troubles. "Come in," she invited wearily.

"I'm just getting ready to go home now," Leola explained curtly. "I just wondered if you needed anything before I leave."

I need Shay, Kendra's mind pleaded. "No, thank you," she answered.

Leola acknowledged the dismissal, but as she turned

to leave Kendra delayed her departure. "Leola, wait." Raising herself from her chair, Kendra walked steadily toward her secretary and touched the girl's elbow. "I haven't taken the opportunity to thank you for taking Selwyn's notes to Shay . . . Mr. Brentwood. He told me what you did, and I thought that was very considerate of you."

Leola's green eyes displayed her acceptance of Kendra's sincerity. "I didn't know what else to do," she admitted. "You were going through so much . . . with the merger and your wedding . . . the staff asking questions, and the computers going down."

"Yes," Kendra agreed, unable to believe that she had gone through all that. "Anyway, you did the right thing. Mr. Brentwood has informed the police. Have . . . have there been any more notes?"

"No," Leola responded in relief, shaking her head and shivering. "He sent one with a bug in it, and that was it. Mr. Brentwood wasn't there at the time, so Irvin called the courier company and told them we would not be accepting any more deliveries."

Dear Irvin. Kendra sighed. *No wonder he'd been so protective.* "Well, as I said, thank you." Then, quickly moving on, her limbs eager for that bath she'd dreamed of, she asked, "Have you typed up Arlisa's job description for that vacant position we have in the mail room?"

"Oh yes, Mrs. Brentwood."

"Now that Daddy's stopped her allowance, I think it's time she was some place where I can keep an eye on her."

"But the mail room?" Leola said, stunned that the former proprietor's daughter should be down there, among common citizenry.

Kendra reached for her coat. "Believe me, it's for her own good. Besides," she added, wrapping herself in the heavy cashmere, "she can take charge of the new mail room procedures."

"Okay," Leola exclaimed. "I'll make sure her job description leaves tonight."

"By express delivery," Kendra ordered. The younger woman braced her hand on the doorknob. "And Leola, less of the Mrs. Brentwood, okay? As much as I love to hear it, I'd like you to call me Kendra."

Leola beamed at her new command. "Good night . . . Kendra."

"Good night Leola."

Three hours later Kendra pinned up her auburn tresses, removed the makeup from her oval, ebony face, then rummaged through the bags and cases strewn all over the main bedroom floor at Shay's London house in search of her favorite rosemary-scented bath salts to fill the steaming hot water in the bathroom Jacuzzi.

After the long soak, when she had the house all to herself after the last of the domestic staff had gone home, she went downstairs into the reception room and began to open the first of the huge hoard of wedding presents which her father had arranged to have sent over that morning.

Clad in a pair of silky, violet pajamas and propped on her knees, she opened one after the other, aghast as wonderful, expensive gift items were revealed to her exuberant gaze. As reels of paper began to litter the room in a rainbow of vibrant colors, she began to relax and allowed a sense of well-being to enter her mind.

She was hardly aware of the doorbell until it rang again. It alerted her, as her mind had been deep in thought over the present she'd not yet given Shay. Her mood had mellowed somewhat, and she felt enlivened as she got to her feet and placed all the wedding cards which had lain stacked against her lap on the soft carpeting.

Heading for the door, she released the catch and then swung it open. A heavy gush of wind rushed in and then her body froze. Selwyn stood there. Horrified for one second, she glared at him, then attempted to push the door shut, but Selwyn used his foot to wedge the door and inched his way into the lobby. Then his strong hands slammed the door with a deathly thud.

Kendra had the oppressive feeling that she was a prisoner the moment she looked into his menacing, cold eyes. There didn't seem to be a shred of human conscience there, and that terrified her. His clothes were damp, from the mild sleet, she suspected, and he appeared ruffled, uncomposed, as if he'd ferociously battled the wind outside with a sword and dagger before he'd brought himself to her door.

She felt the chandeliers above her tremor as if in warning that she should run. She should get away, hide. Selwyn was not himself, and she turned her head frantically, wondering where she should go. But she had not moved quickly enough. Selwyn caught her wrist and pulled her toward his rigid, cold body, nuzzling his face into her neck, invigorated by the sweet smell of her body.

"I'm going to have you," he muttered, his tone distinctly nasty against her neck.

No!" Kendra cried loudly, shifting her body in panicked attempts to break free. Her groan was uttered with such heartfelt disgust that the big, harsh hands which held her loosened their grip instantly, and Selwyn glared down at her.

His thick eyebrows shot up. His mouth—a thin slash in the rugged, bearded jaw—tightened, and then his lips curled into a sneer. "Stop playing games with me." He bit out the words icily. "I know you married Shay Brentwood for his money, because there was just no other way you could get your hands on it, was there?

But I never thought you were stupid enough to come on to him the way you came on to me."

Kendra heard the words, but they made no sense. "That's not true," she said, floundering helplessly.

"Liar," Selwyn barked.

Kendra could feel the violence seething in him, but willed herself to remain calm. "What do you want?" she rapped out irritably.

Selwyn made a noise of extreme exasperation. "You," he snarled.

She trembled. "Listen, you have to leave," she implored. "Shay will be here at any moment and—"

"Wrong," Selwyn jabbed in interruption. "He's in New York. I heard the old iron stick collapsed and died. What a doggone shame."

"Get out," Kendra spat.

Selwyn eyed her superciliously. Then he laughed, a huge, hysterical, metallic laugh. "I'm not hearing this," he mouthed arrogantly "Don't tell me you'd fostered feelings for Benjamin Brentwood before he died?"

"I don't have to explain anything to you," Kendra railed angrily.

"For your sake I hope you do," Selwyn warned. "You see, I'm really confused. I've never been good at metaphors or code breaking." He marched past her into the house. "So, was it all for this?" he chided, allowing his menacing eyes to roam around. "The money, the glamor, the lifestyle? Tell me. I want to know."

"I can't," Kendra protested, too fearful to give him the true answer.

"Can't, or won't?" Selwyn yelled demandingly, his voice spitting out in anger. "Can't, or won't?"

"I fell in love with Shay!" Kendra screeched, the ill-chosen words falling helplessly from her lips before she had time to consider their implication.

The lobby fell silent and for a long dreadful moment

Selwyn stared at her, his eyes wide with alarm. "You hussy," he seethed, heading straight for her.

Kendra screamed and made for the darkened lounge, instantly diving under a chair, like a horrified mole diving into its burrow. She knew Selwyn had followed her the moment a shadow loomed against the open doorway, where the light from the lobby strayed into the room.

"I know you're in here," Selwyn tormented as Kendra heard his faint footsteps sink into the deep, pile, melon carpet. This was the room where she and Shay had discovered each other for the first time, and now it seemed it would be the room where she would meet her doom, she thought as she crawled helpless under the chair to the other side. Her heart was racing as she scrambled on her knees, too panicked to even think of strategies for getting out of her situation.

This wasn't the same man she'd known for ten months; the sensible, conscientious, Minister of Parliament who'd seemed focused and organized and knew what he was doing. He'd changed, drastically. This was a jealous, unforgiving maniac who'd tried to kill her, and she was terrified.

Suddenly, Kendra felt hands against her ankles, pulling them and tugging harshly until she began to kick her legs violently at her unseen terrorizer. She hurriedly crawled to her feet and headed for the door, but suddenly steely arms were around her.

Kendra lashed out with every bit of strength she could muster, goaded beyond all thought of caution as to the consequences of her actions. She connected with Selwyn's sneering, ugly face, a deep scratch from her nails causing skin to rip on the upper part of his cheek.

Seeing her opportunity to escape, she hurried to the lobby and yanked the door open, running out blindly into the night and into the face of a relentless wind which had gathered enough speed to take her breath away. Her bare feet took her to the back of the house, the wet, cold gravel beneath her soles causing her to shiver and contract with such pain that she felt unsure she would be able to make it across the rear patio to the greenhouse within easy reach from where she stood.

The wind driving at her face caused her to stumble as she cut the short distance through the stony walkway and into the greenhouse. Closing the glass door, she scrambled to the hard rock floor, afraid to breathe as she saw the shadow of a tall body move slowly against the glass panes outside, saw peering, glittering hateful eyes peer through each one in search of her.

Then the door shot open with such brutish force that the raging wind which invaded caused pots of plants to fall crashing to the floor and a scream to erupt from Kendra's throat. Within seconds, she felt her wrist caught within a deadlock grip and her body being dragged upward until she was on her feet, facing Selwyn's unforgiving, malicious face.

Enraged, he caught her in a steely grip and twisted her arms behind her back, pinning her to his rigid body. Tears sprang to her eyes as Kendra felt him press his bearded cheek against hers, his voice harsh as he whispered, "If I can't have you, nobody else will."

Her heart plummeted downward toward the pit of her stomach. This time Shay was not there to protect her, and she was mindful that she would have to deal with Selwyn entirely alone. She was petrified. For an instant her fear became sharpened by the knowledge of Selwyn's attempts at trying to harm her. He was deadly serious, she realized suddenly, amazed that his hands were actually grabbing her as she uttered words in blatant, anxious accusation.

"Don't you think you've done enough?" she shrieked tearfully. "You could've killed me when you tampered with my car brakes. Shay saved my life."

She felt Selwyn shrink from her, his possessive grip loosening slightly. "You can't prove anything," he admitted bluntly, though she heard the momentary surprise in his voice. "Nobody knows I had access to your boat."

"Boat?" Kendra wavered. "What boat?"

"Your car," Selwyn snapped. "Or that I copied the keys to the *Nubian Chronicle* office."

"You rigged the computers," she hissed knowingly. "And stole my things."

"Circumstantial evidence," Selwyn taunted.

"And all those letters." Her teeth clattered.

"Unsigned." He sneered nastily. "I can argue it wasn't me. I didn't do it, I wasn't there. You can't prove anything."

"What about—"

"The Borough of Brent Council?" Selwyn finished. "Your sister gave me an idea or two about forging signatures."

Kendra shivered, anxiety filling every part of her body. This was the man she'd once thought respected everything in life; a man she'd once been contented with because she'd thought him to be almost as honorable as her father. Never in her wildest dreams could she have thought that Selwyn could be so violent and vengeful. Something had pushed him over the edge. Surely it could not have been only that she'd turned down his advances, rejected his proposal of marriage, and had never returned his love. Had that caused such a drastic turnabout of his character? He wanted her punished. He wanted revenge, and he was telling her so harshly. "I'll never forgive you, Keisha," he threatened against her ear. "I'm never going to let you leave me."

Keisha? Now Kendra felt totally confused. Was she losing her sanity, or was Selwyn confusing her with somebody else? Closing her eyes, she felt weakened with cold blisters and her body trembled from frostbite, but she forced herself to remember who she was. She was Kendra, not someone called Keisha. *Kendra Brentwood,* she told herself, and as she did so an image of Shay sprang into her tormented mind.

His perfect features loomed up in front of her—the caramel profile, the square jawline, his raven black hair and those dusky brown eyes she'd always found lustfully inviting. He seemed so real in her head that for a second she believed him to actually be there. Then, as though magic had struck, she thought she heard his voice.

"This must rank as unfinished business," he cursed loudly in his American accent above the thundering wind.

She would not have believed it possible had she not felt the clawlike fingers around her arms release her suddenly. As her body reacted to the chill of another fresh outburst of wind, she was certain that someone else had entered the greenhouse. Instinct told her that it was Shay, but she was too paralyzed with cold to move her feet.

In the dark she could sense that Selwyn had bolted to the far end of the greenhouse, and she could see the shadowy outline of Shay's body moving toward him. He was within reaching distance, seemingly about ready to pounce on her tormenter, when there was a horrendous cracking sound from outside and a sudden, ferocious, gusting wind tore at a tree situated behind the greenhouse. For one horrific second, Kendra saw the dark, dancing shape of branches against the glass roof. Then she heard Shay yell, "Look out!" before the slim trunk of the nearest tree snapped. There was the hideous noise of shattering glass as it showered over Selwyn and the back end of the greenhouse before the top part of the tree came crashing in entirely, bringing with it more splintering glass and foliage.

Selwyn was thrown to the ground instantly, struck

by the tree's branches, and Kendra felt her heart rush up into her mouth as she wondered whether Shay had been struck, too. Panicked beyond measure, she inched her shivering body two steps, then screamed Shay's name as an agonizing cramp-like pain, spurred on by cold, crippled her body entirely. The wind was howling like a banshee through the gaping hole in the ceiling, and she wondered whether Shay had heard her or whether he was even conscious at all.

She was so exhausted and so cold, that she just wanted to fall where she stood. To drift into some tropical paradise where it was warm and sunny, where her limbs would no longer be as freezing as they were now.

Her mind began to slip into that fantasy, and somewhere in her head there was a bubbling, crazy hysteria as strong arms swept her up frantically and a voice whispered over and over again, "Baby, I love you. I love you." There was the heady smell of a familiar aftershave, the feel of kisses being placed against her neck. She didn't so much as sway into those protective arms as crumble into them, suddenly weightless. . . .

The first thing Kendra registered when she awoke was the silence. There was no wind, and where she'd once been numbed with icy pain now felt warm and soft again.

Daylight stabbed at her eyes as she struggled to remember how she'd gotten into Shay's bed. Then, as her thoughts began to clear, she remembered that it was now *their* bed she was in, and that there had been a terrible accident and Selwyn had been hurt. But what had happened to Shay?

She sat up instantly, suppressing her anxiety somewhat but unable to stop the shocked sigh of anguish escaping her lips as her eyes immediately zoomed in on the forlorn sleeping body slumped heavily in a chair by the bed. Shay stirred, opened his heavy lids slightly, and then they were staring at each other.

Tears immediately sprang to Kendra's eyes. He was still in one piece, not a scratch, not a bruise, not a graze, evident on his caramel face. She ached to touch him, to be certain that he was there and not still in New York, as she'd imagined. Something in her sleep had told her that she'd dreamt up her rescuer, that the savior of her nightmarish ordeal had not been real and that Selwyn was still there; lurking, waiting, anticipating another pouncing attack. Yet, even as the thought had come into her hallucinating mind, a sixth sense told her she had known all along that Shay had come for her. He was destined for her, she even thought absurdly as she looked into his troubled face. "You're all right," she whimpered in dazed disbelief. "I thought—"

"Sssh . . ." Shay whispered.

"Oh, Shay," Kendra crumbled as memories flooded into her mind to haunt her. "He was trying to kill me. I didn't know what—"

"I know," he intruded, stopping her from recalling too much of that dreadful night. He rose out of the chair and sat by her on the bed, but Kendra realized that his eyes were clouded and a nerve flickered in his jaw as he held her hand, rubbing against it absently. "I should never have sent you back here alone," he began in a cracked whisper, riddled with guilt and blame. "I knew he was psycho and still I sent you back. He could've damned well killed you, and it would've been my fault."

Kendra felt confused. "Your fault?"

Shay rubbed his forehead as though irritated. "I just had to have you, didn't I?" he rasped grimly. "And I didn't care about anything else."

Kendra shook her head, feeling suddenly troubled. "Shay—"

"Kendra, hear me out." She was overridden firmly. "I was jealous. Owens had enough feelings for you that he proposed marriage, feelings I didn't understand or know about." His face creased with self-condemnation. "I wasn't in love with you when I thought about how I was going to take you away from that jackass," he admitted angrily. "I just told myself I wasn't going down without a fight, and I had plenty of game plays to do it, too. The *Nubian Chronicle,* your mother's will...."

Kendra stared at him, breathing raggedly, several different emotions chasing through her innards as the tiny seed of hope she'd kept harnessed within her heart evaporated into thin air. She'd been right. As much as she'd hated telling herself that she was probably the biggest challenge in Shay's life, here she was, listening to the man admit it for himself.

Her mouth trembled and she felt weak, but somehow she felt arrogant enough to keep her gaze fixed, to stare into those dusky brown eyes that had adored and enchanted her in the name of seduction. "Don't forget the wedding," she added painfully.

Shay eyed her uncertainly. "I haven't forgotten about that," he said in truth. "I think that's what sent Mister M.P. over the edge." He dragged in a deep breath. "The police were here—a Detective Inspector Sullivan. He's coming back later for you to make a statement."

Kendra panicked. "Is Selwyn—?"

"No. He has a nasty bump on his head and a few cuts," Shay explained. "And get this, the rookies had him on file. Six years ago, he stalked his wife after she left him and filed for a divorce."

"Stalked her?" Kendra gasped.

Shay nodded. "Then she died in some freak boating accident with her lover, and he must've either kept it all in or blamed himself, I don't know."

"He kept calling me Keisha," Kendra remembered suddenly. "But I thought her name was Katherine?"

"Katherine, Keisha, they're probably the same to him," Shay declared quietly. "Detective Inspector Sullivan told me that there was a notation in their files that Selwyn was displaying a mild degree of mental aberration caused by depression after his wife died, and it was advised that he seek counseling."

"Are you telling me that Selwyn is mentally ill?"

"They think it's neurosis," Shay clarified. "Apparently, a ... Sir William Hendon was interviewed by Sullivan when he was looking into my complaint about Owens. Hendon told the police he suspected Owens was suffering from a maladjustment of character. Selwyn was stressed and overworked, provoked by you leaving him, was still adapting to a new career, all just the sort of things that trigger a neurotic personality. And his wife's boating accident is obviously something he hasn't gotten over. That's probably the traceable origin of his illness."

"It was no accident," Kendra whispered, recalling a part of her horrible ordeal. "Neurosis or not, I think he caused that, somehow. He did it."

"Yeah?" Shay answered, disbelieving.

"He did it," Kendra insisted.

"Well, whether he did or he didn't," Shay said, relaxing, "that's Scotland Yard's problem."

"Where is he now ... in custody?" Kendra hesitated.

"No. He's been taken to hospital," Shay told her sympathetically. "He's probably going to need psychotherapy."

Kendra put her hand to her mouth. "I can't believe I'm taking all this in," she said. "I must've looked like this Katherine ... Keisha, or sounded like her." She sighed. "Selwyn never once gave away that he was emotionally unstable, or maybe he did and I didn't recognize the signs. He always seemed so . . . together."

"He was probably on tranquilizers. I don't know." Shay explained. "That's how most neurotics treat their acute phases of panic, or phobias. He wouldn't have wanted you to know that about him because he wanted you. And, that's something I can understand." Shay curled her fragile fingers into his. "If someone tried to take you, I'd—"

"You'd what, Shay?" Kendra extracted her hand from his warm grip, instantly recalling everything he'd just said. "Rustle in more lawyers?"

Shay stared at her, taking in her pained face and tormented eyes, the familiar limpness of her pillow-ruffled hair, the way her mink-colored, almond shaped eyes darkened like black pearls, and he knew now more than anything how much he wanted to share with her.

He grinned as though he found the prospect funny. "I'd *make* them understand that you're my lady and save myself the fee, for once."

It was Kendra's turn to stare, stunned because there was something so different about Shay now that she was unable to put it into words. Yet ignorance as to what was going on spurred her to ask, "What are you saying?" She didn't dare believe that she could put hope back into her heart again.

Shay took her hand again. "I'm saying I never made love to a woman the way I made love to you. That somewhere between plotting how I was going to get you and having you I realized that you were the one girl I didn't want to hurt." He scowled at himself. "Since Pops died there's been something else sort of lurking over my shoulder. I think that I may either have been too confused or too traumatized to believe what you'd said or whether you meant it, but I made a mistake in not telling you something."

This is it, Kendra agonized. Shay was going to tell her that he'd acted irrationally, that he'd won his little challenge but had never really wanted a woman in his life. She couldn't even begin to think back to why he'd tricked her into marriage in the first place, because so many things had gone through her mind that she felt unable to make sense of it all. The one thing she did know, though, was that she couldn't bear to hear him reject her.

But he was going to, she thought as he stared down into her eyes with so much self-directed irony that she caught her breath. Her mouth trembled as her eyes begged him, *Don't do this to me.* In fact, she was so terrified of hearing what he had to tell her that she decided to speak first. "You don't have to say it," she mumbled, tears springing to her eyes as the words stuck in her throat like a boiled sweet refusing to go down. "I know you made a mistake."

"Yeah," Shay admitted absently. "But I'm going to tell you anyway, because I don't think you heard me last night. I should've told you a long time ago that I'd fallen in love with you. I should've told you after the car accident, because I think that's when I knew, but like an idiot I wait until something else happens to you. I kept telling you over and over again last night, but you were freezing. You were so cold. I don't think you heard me."

"Oh my . . . goodness," Kendra mumbled shakily, feeling herself wanting to burst, cry, yell with joy. *I did hear you,* she recollected muddily. *How could I forget, having wanted to hear it for so long?*

"What is it?" Shay panicked.

Kendra searched the depths of his sincere eyes. "I thought—"

"That I would be like Pops," he surmised. "I don't think I ever was. The night you bravely came up against my father beneath that thunderstorm, something about you hit me then. And if my ideas about falling in love hadn't been so warped, I would've recognized what you'd done to me."

Kendra opened her mouth, closed it, then said with some ambiguity, "Are you sure?"

"What do mean, am I sure?" Shay answered, teasingly offensive. "Of course I'm sure." He laughed, sweeping her up into his embracing arms and hugging her with such affection that a wave of tenderness suffused Kendra's entire body. "I'm not interested in giving fifty percent of myself," Shay told her sincerely. "You're going to get a hundred and one percent of me, and more if that's possible, because without you I'm not complete."

Kendra's lips parted to accept him and he obliged her, kissing her ardently, drawing her to his warm, steely chest until Kendra could sense a man's urgency growing in him as his mouth devoured hers completely. Then, releasing her with a low groan, he looked into her loving face. "Do you think Irvin would want a pay raise if we ask him again to run the paper while we're away?" he whispered, caressing her cheek like a delicate rose petal.

"He's been there long enough," Kendra answered, capturing his adoring gaze, imagining Shay to be a powerful Pharaoh, her own private Akenaton. "Why?"

"I want to get away for a while, just the two of us," Shay told her warmly. "That's why I took the next plane out and followed you. I don't need time and space with J B to get it together now that Pops is gone. He's got Rhona and I *need you*. So let's get away, have a honeymoon or something. I'll rent a villa on Fisher Island just off Miami's Biscayne Bay."

Kendra smiled happily. "I'd like that."

Sixteen

Kendra raised her head above the cool, clear water of a clean pool and looked around the small, private hideaway Shay had rented on Fisher Island off the Florida coast.

Palm trees loomed up against the villa in front of her, empty wooden deck chairs soaked in the mid-afternoon sun, and birds chirped happily above her head as they flew in patterns across a flawless, turquoise sky. There was a sense of serenity and tranquility about such a place, she thought, allowing the warm water to creep up her neck and soothe the muscles there. It was peaceful and relaxing, and she was sharing it with the perfect partner.

She looked across at Shay, seated against a reclined wooden chair. His dusky brown eyes were partially hidden behind half-closed lids, their long lashes creating needle-like shadows as he basked in the glare of sun. He looked too comfortable, she thought mischievously, pulling herself from the water and padding quietly toward him on wet feet. Then, expelling a shriek of laughter, Kendra shook her wet hair over his dry body, watching as his eyes shot open and narrowed on her feisty expression.

Dressed only in his swimming trunks, Shay's caramel-hued body became showered with droplets of water, but he grinned luridly at Kendra's barefaced candor and jumped to his feet to shake himself down. "Hey," he chuckled, catching hold of her in one fell swoop. "So you want to play, do you?"

Sweeping Kendra off her feet and ignoring her delicious squeals of protest, Shay marched to the edge of the pool and jumped in. The water felt wonderful and refreshing, offering the languid sense of freedom both needed after the long air flight and the weeks of anguish they'd shared.

"I'll race you to the edge," Shay challenged, splashing water against Kendra's skin.

"You're on," Kendra accepted, launching quickly into a steady breaststroke.

"That's not fair." Shay chuckled, realizing she'd started without him. Pouncing into the water, he attempted to catch up with her, putting weight into every movement as he swam, certain that he would reach the edge first. But Kendra was climbing up the steps when he got there, giggling as she stepped onto the marbled ground, a triumphant smile on her lips.

"I won," she crooned, relaxed and happy.

"Cheat," Shay teased, content that he was responsible for putting the smile there.

He followed her out of the water and they took seats on the heated chairs, reaching for towels laid on the floor beside them.

"It's lovely here," Kendra breathed, blotting the water out of her relaxed hair before lowering herself back into the chair and allowing her mink-colored eyes to sweep across the clear, blue sky, enchanted and fascinated. "I can't believe we're going to be here for two whole weeks."

Shay reached out and gently held her hand. "I know," he agreed, complacent, feeling the same buzz of satisfaction. "Let's sit here and enjoy it for a while."

Kendra curled her fingers in his and allowed herself to adore the thrill and starry-eyed bliss of being with Shay. They sat there for a full half hour, holding hands, rubbing thumbs, caressing fingers, and partook of the peace to their hearts' content, accepting the unspoken sensual foreplay until a deeper yearning fueled an impatience neither could ignore.

As Shay led and Kendra followed, they entered through large French doors which overlooked the pool into the elaborate bedroom suite, furnished and styled for people such as they were: honeymooners.

As Shay's lips sought hers Kendra felt her trembling limbs sink into the plain white, cotton-covered mattress, her own lips laxly claiming Shay's, slowly pulsating at first, then becoming more insistent as the gradual intrusion of his tongue built up an ardor she couldn't resist. He took his time and she marveled at her impatience, using her own fingers in kind as they roamed across shoulders, backs, buttocks, and breasts, a deeper yearning to remove the wet swimming pieces from their quivering limbs becoming stronger at each stroke and motion. Then Shay tore his mouth away, panting and breathless as he remembered something.

"I have a present for you," he murmured, jumping from the bed.

Kendra sat up and stared at him, her own lungs short of breath. "What?"

"In my travel bag," Shay murmured, rummaging through the luggage situated close by on the bedroom floor. Finding what he wanted, he returned to the bed, his swimming trunks bearing ample evidence of how much Kendra had aroused him. "It was a Christmas present," he began, handing over a black velvet box. "There's an inscription inside."

Kendra bent down on her knees and opened the gift Shay had offered her. Inside, bedded on purple silk, was the most delightful diamond ring she'd ever seen. "Oh . . . it's so beautiful," she gasped, pulling it from the box and turning it over to find the tiny engraved inscription hidden inside the gold band, beneath the stone. It read: "TO HANDSHAKE DEALS."

She chuckled softly. "You're not going to believe this." Handing Shay the box but holding on to the ring, Kendra shuffled off the bed and located her handbag, from which she extracted her present to Shay.

"What's this?" He smiled, as his hand took hold of the long, thin, silver box she offered him.

"Look inside," Kendra urged.

Shay placed his own box to Kendra on the bedside cabinet, then began to slowly peel away the metallic silver wrapping paper until his eyes met the royal blue colored box beneath it. Opening it, he saw the solid brass pen laid against white satin. "This is nice," he said, removing it carefully from the box. Rolling it between his fingers, he read the inscription against the black lacquered surface. "To handshake deals," he read, swallowing in disbelief "This is—"

"Incredible," Kendra finished. "I think so, too. So much for me trying to stop the hand of providence." Their eyes locked, and somehow both knew that the choice had never been theirs at all, not since that fateful day when they'd met beneath a torrent of thunder and lightning.

"I love you," Shay said proudly, taking the ring from her hand and placing it against her wedding band.

"I love you, too," Kendra returned, admiring its accurate fit.

A hot, weakening kiss met her and Kendra melted into it, feeling Shay release the catch of her bikini bra as he lowered her to the bed. His tongue teased the corner of her mouth as he removed it, and she teased him back, enjoying the way his eyes sparkled at hers, telling her he'd truly found his virtuous woman. *I'll never get enough of your dusky brown eyes,* she thought. *Not until I live to be eighty.*

I'll never get enough of your curled-lip smile, Shay mused wickedly, pulling her bikini pants from beneath her. Tapping her stomach gently, he whispered, "I want to put some babies in here."

Kendra whispered in acceptance. "I hope they all look like you, because I was an ugly duckling."

"But you grew up to be a beautiful swan," Shay whispered as their lips met again, in a series of brief, plucking kisses, at the end of which Kendra boldly removed the wet swimming trunks from beneath Shay's trembling limbs. And as they reacquainted themselves with the bed, eradicating the narrow space between their hips, she felt his hand shift to the nape of her neck, tickling the soft spot there until she shuddered in excitement, his mouth all the time nibbling and teasing her lips until she instinctively gave him what he wanted.

Her warm hand slid down the angles of his neck, across his shoulders, caressingly down his back, and teasingly across his hips, down until she reached the pinnacle of his arousal. There, her fingertips skimmed across the bare surface, at times squeezing against the juncture until she felt him weightless against her.

"I love the way you touch me." His voice quivered, the tip of his tongue wetting the skin behind her ear, his hand trailing down her bare arm, not quite touching her nipple as he passed, across her midriff, and to a place he knew would make Kendra just as weightless. She was adrift in ecstasy when his touch caused her head to loll slightly to one side and back, awed knowing that this man would always be able to command her body to his will, time and time again

Her mouth opened, hot and wet, and his tongue delved with ripe demand for response. She gave it wholeheartedly, savoring the moisture, her breathing becoming labored as her emotions swelled. He followed her lead and allowed her to slip her tongue between his lips, answering her quest to taste his ardor. "Mmm. . . ." Kendra moaned over and over.

Against the soft hollow beneath her hips, his urgency was transmitted by the thrust of his pelvis, which she acknowledged by moving rhythmically against him. Unsure that she could endure the agony of welcoming him, she bit his chin and used her tongue to lick it, feeling his body shudder at her primitive nature, knowing he understood what she needed.

Then his palms were on her breasts, moving from left to right, shifting back and forth before he gently twisted the nipples between forefinger and thumb. Currents of fire swept through Kendra's body from her lips to between her legs, to a place he returned to coax her to his demand. "Shay . . . please," she gasped hoarsely, arching her back against him.

"Not yet," he whispered, his palms replaced by his tempting tongue, circling, provoking, riding along her nipples with such intimate slowness that Kendra felt she would most surely die of pleasure.

A deep groan vibrated in his throat as she gripped him harder and allowed her hand to take on a rhythm that was in tune with his thrusting hips. He followed her example, while continuing to brush provocative ministrations against her nipples with his lips, his own craving impatient and nearly beyond his limit.

Shay lifted his head and looked into Kendra's yearning face. Their gazes caressed and spoke of their need for one another. Instantly, she braced herself on both elbows, her mink-colored eyes holding his dusky brown ones, and almost wept with delight as he plunged into her.

Kendra's fingers gripped the cotton sheet and

twisted. And twisted. Until the sun laid down its sleepy head, they reached and collapsed time and time again. Finally, as Shay slept, lethargic and limp, Kendra sat with her head against the bedpost, sipping water to moisten her throat from the rasping cries Shay had forced out of her.

Calm and happy, she gazed dazedly at the setting sun as it invaded through the open French doors into the villa, casting its burnished shadows of yellow and gold, orange and lilac, across her naked, ebony skin. The pool rippled quietly as an easterly breeze swept by, and the palm trees whispered soft endearments to one another, shaking their leaves and rustling their branches, and so lending an air of enchantment to the approaching night.

Shay was oblivious to it all, but Kendra was to see how the setting sun emphasized the warm, caramel-brown of his satin smooth skin and the soft spots of sheen that spoke of how his body had worked that evening. He looked adorable, she thought, putting down her glass of water so she could stroke her fingers down his back. She took delight when he stirred, and instantly pulled her beneath him.

Dropping his head, Shay placed a kiss against her lips. "Mmm . . ." he murmured softly.

"Mmm . . ." Kendra echoed into his mouth. "Shall we order something to eat?"

"You're hungry?"

"Very."

Shay grinned at her devilishly. "I'll ring for a menu."

"Well, do it now, partner," Kendra urged quickly, knowing that they could easily forget the late supper.

His head rose and he backed away a little, but only enough so that they could look at each other. "Partner?" Shay drawled, with that lazy, intimate smile she knew affected her so profoundly. "Do you realize that as you're my partner in the *Nubian Chronicle,* we'll have to spend an inordinate amount of time together?"

"Really?" Kendra returned, devilishly sweet, stealing a kiss against his chin. "What did you have in mind?"

"Nights. Long nights," Shay declared. "Breakfast, lunch, and dinner. And long vacations . . . to get away from the kids. Any problem with that?"

"No problem." Kendra grinned.

"Do you also realize," Shay added cheekily, inching her closer to him and running a finger down the line between her bare breasts. "That you haven't told me how much I now score on the Kendra scale."

Kendra chuckled as she snuggled under him. "Ten," she whispered as he lowered his mouth to take her lips once more. "And then some."

4 FREE
ARABESQUE
Contemporary
Romances
are reserved
for you!

(worth almost $20.00)

see details inside...

ZEBRA HOME SUBSCRIPTION SERVICE, INC.
120 BRIGHTON ROAD
P.O. BOX 5214
CLIFTON, NEW JERSEY 07015-5214

AFFIX
STAMP
HERE

WE HAVE 4 FREE BOOKS FOR YOU!

(If the certificate is missing below, write to: Zebra Home Subscription Service, Inc., 120 Brighton Road, P.O. Box 5214, Clifton, New Jersey 07015-5214)

FREE BOOK CERTIFICATE

Yes! Please send me 4 *Arabesque* Contemporary Romances without cost or obligation, billing me just $1 to help cover postage and handling. I understand that each month, I will be able to preview 4 brand-new *Arabesque* Contemporary Romances FREE for 10 days. Then, if I decide to keep them, I will pay the money-saving preferred subscriber's price of just $16.00 for all 4...that's a savings of almost $4 off the publisher's price with a $1.50 charge for shipping and handling. I may return any shipment within 10 days and owe nothing, and I may cancel this subscription at any time. My 4 FREE books will be mine to keep in any case.

Name _____

Address _____ Apt. _____

City _____ State _____ Zip _____

Telephone ( ) _____

Signature _____
(If under 18, parent or guardian must sign.)

AP0598

Terms and prices subject to change. Orders subject to acceptance by Zebra Home Subscription Service, Inc. . Zebra Home Subscription Service, Inc. reserves the right to reject or cancel any subscription.

Get 4 FREE Arabesque Contemporary Romances Delivered to Your Doorstep and Join the Only New Book Club That Delivers These Bestselling African American Romances Directly to You Each Month!

No Obligation!

LOOK INSIDE FOR DETAILS ON HOW TO GET YOUR FREE GIFT.....

(worth almost $20.00!)

WE INVITE YOU TO JOIN THE ONLY BOOK CLUB THAT DELIVERS HEARTFELT ROMANCE FEATURING AFRICAN AMERICAN HEROES AND HEROINES IN STORIES THAT ARE RICH IN PASSION AND CULTURAL SPICE...

And Your First 4 Books Are FREE!

Arabesque is the newest contemporary romance line offered by Pinnacle Books. Arabesque has been so successful that our readers have asked us about direct home delivery. We responded to your requests. You can start receiving four bestselling Arabesque novels a month delivered right to your door. Subscribe now and you'll get:

- 4 FREE Arabesque romances as our introductory gift—a value of almost $20! (pay only $1 to help cover postage & handling)
- 4 BRAND-NEW Arabesque romances delivered to your doorstep each month thereafter (usually arriving before they're available in bookstores!)
- 20% off each title—a savings of almost $4.00 each month
- Just $1.50 for shipping and handling
- A FREE monthly newsletter, *Zebra/Pinnacle Romance News* that features author profiles, book previews and more
- No risks or obligations...in other words, you can cancel whenever you wish with no questions asked

So subscribe to Arabesque today and see why these books are winning awards and readers' hearts.

After you've enjoyed our FREE gift of 4 Arabesques, you'll begin to receive monthly shipments of the newest Arabesque titles. Each shipment will be yours to examine for 10 days. If you decide to keep the books, you'll pay the preferred subscriber's price of just $4.00 per title. That's $16 for all 4 books with a nominal charge of $1.50 for shipping and handling. And if you want us to stop sending books, just say the word...it's that simple.

See why reviewers are raving about ARABESQUE and order your FREE books today!